Recipe For Love

Patti closed the door behind Tegan, then turned to look at J.T., who was studiously applying paint to the wall in front of him.

"I'm really sorry you had to find out this way," she began.

J.T. shook his head as he turned to look at her.

"Why? There's no reason for you to tell me about your private life, is there?"

He looked seriously at her.

Patti nodded, "Yes, there is. I do remember enough from my birthday to know there's unfinished business between us. I feel ridiculous talking about it like this, but you already know how I feel about you, right?"

J.T. regarded her, his light blue eyes intent on her face. "Do I? I thought I did; but now, with your ex in your house again, I guess anything I might have been planning is going to have to be postponed indefinitely."

Patti looked miserably at him. "You're not going to leave town on me, are you? I mean, before we get a chance to find out what we'd be like together?"

J.T. carefully put his paintbrush down and walked over to stand in front of Patti. He was so tall, when she was wearing flats she didn't even come to his shoulders. She looked up expectantly at him and he put one finger under her chin and lifted her face up to look at him. Slowly he bent his face down and his lips lightly brushed hers. One kiss, another kiss, another…then with a groan, Patti melted against him and wound her arms up and around him, pressing herself against his hardness and feeling the danger and excitement of trying to control a man so much bigger than herself.

J.T. groaned too, and used one large hand to fondle her butt, pressing himself into her, so she could feel the length of the hardness she had been imagining for months. He moved his other hand up and down her curves; now holding a breast, now rubbing her hip, then he wound his fingers into her hair and used the two contact points of lips and groin to make her feel his desire. He moved his head slightly. His lips kissed along her face to her ear then to her neck. His tongue licked a trail along the curve of her face to her chin, then he kissed her once more. Reluctantly he moved away from her and smiled at the expectant look on her face.

"Nope," he said simply, then he turned to go back to his paintbrush.

Other Works From The Pen Of

Fiona McGier

<u>**Never Too Old For The Game of Love**</u>, April 2009. Almost 40, Tegan is a divorced mother of 2, convinced that she has no time for romance. Alexander is 42, divorced, and enjoys playing the field. They have nothing in common...except love

Wings

RECIPE FOR LOVE

by

Fiona McGier

A Wings ePress, Inc.

Encore L'Amour Romance Novel

Wings ePress, Inc.

Edited by: Christie Kraemer
Copy Edited by: Jeanne Smith
Senior Editor: Christie Kraemer
Executive Editor: Marilyn Kapp
Cover Artist: Richard Stroud

Wings ePress Books
http://www.wings-press.com

Copyright © 2009 by Fiona Gierzynski
ISBN 978-1-59705-958-9

Published In the United States Of America

August 2009

Wings ePress Inc.
403 Wallace Court
Richmond, KY 40475

Dedication

To Mom, for teaching me to read before I started school, beginning my life-long love affair with words. And to Paul, my real-life love affair; yes, honey, you are my muse.

One

Patti Johnson cursed softly under her breath as she carefully picked her way through all of the unattached appliances and huge boxes crowded into the small space that was in the process of becoming a kitchen. She was planning on using the kitchen to make all of the food offered by her catering service. She threw herself onto the only chair that did not have stuff piled on it, tossed her cell phone onto the tiny, visible counter space and started to rant her anger at the offending object.

"What the hell was I thinking? How on earth am I supposed to get this place ready when the contractors keep canceling on me? It's not like I can hook up the appliances myself. I can't even move them around! And this kitchen is supposed to be done in time for me to cook for over a hundred people in two months?"

She glared around the room, taking in the fact that while all of the appliances had been delivered, none of them were in the proper place, and none of them were usable yet. The counters had been installed, but the tops were covered with lumber and drywall that still had to be put up. The chairs had paint cans and boxes of nails on them, and the cabinets were in boxes piled up along the back wall. In short, there was a whole lot of potential, but nothing visible suggested this was going to be a serviceable kitchen space in the near future. At least not until the recalcitrant contractors could be made to honor their commitments and actually appear to do the work for which she had hired them.

Patti returned to her rant.

"And you promised there would only be about fifty people—tops!"

She mimicked her best friend and business partner.

"Oh, Patti, don't sweat. There won't be that many people at the wedding. Just a few close friends and some of Alex's relatives who live close by. No big deal, girl."

"That's what you told me when you asked me to be your maid of honor, too. I told you I was afraid I wouldn't be able to do both on the same day, and you told me it would be a piece of cake. You lied!"

Patti quietly stared at the cell phone before she reached over to pick it up and hit re-dial. She waited until she heard the phone answered, took a deep breath and began to speak.

"Hello?" Said Tegan O'Neill.

"Hey, it's me again. I was thinking about it after you dropped that bombshell on me about a hundred guests, maybe more. I mean, I knew Alex and Edgar had a big family, but I thought they were mostly in Mexico."

"I thought so, too," answered Tegan. "But most of the addresses I got from Juanita are in California or Texas. I guess so many of the Reyes folks have been sneaking their way across the border for so many years; there are more of them up here than are down there anymore. Who knew?"

Trying to control her agitation, Patti continued. "Well, it's just that it's kind of stressful to think about having to cook for so many people...most of whom are from Mexico, so they will already be critical of an Italian woman making Mexican food. Then to have to worry about all the stuff I will have to do to be your maid of honor, too? I mean, come on, honey. Can't I just do one or the other? Not both?"

There was a silence, the same kind of break in sound as when a child falls down, and while he thinks about just *how* hurt he is, the parents wait for the inevitable wail, that will let them know by the loudness level just how bad he feels. Patti waited and held the phone away from her ear, just in case.

"W*hat*?" shrieked Tegan. "This is going to be the most stressful day of my overly-stressful life, and you are saying you won't be there to support me? Aren't you my best friend? After all we have been through together? How could you even think of doing this to me?" She stopped to take a breath.

Patti jumped quickly into the conversation, "Honey, I know you are getting more pregnant every day. Don't get so upset...it's not good for the baby, you know. But I'm under a lot of stress here, and I..."

Tegan had caught her breath and was back for another salvo.

"*You* are under a lot of stress? *You*? What about *me*? Are you the one who is pregnant again at forty? Are you the one who is getting married again, trying to make sure your kids don't feel neglected while they get to know the new man in your life? Are you the one who had to sit and sign your name a gazillion times last week to sell your old house after you signed it a gazillion times two months ago when we bought this house, then had to move all of our stuff into it? Are you the one who has to find a wedding dress that will be flattering at my steadily advancing stage of pregnancy? My stomach is threatening to expand so much I will have to shop in the pup-tent department of a sports store! *I'll just stick my arms through the screen windows, thank-you. I'll put a belt around the whole thing and use the rain fly as my veil.* Yeah, *that* will go over big with the guests."

Tegan stopped to take a breath, but before Patti could get a word out, she yelled, "And you say *you* are stressed? You don't know the meaning of the word!" She panted heavily into the phone.

Patti tried to reason with her best friend; even though it was becoming obvious it wasn't going to do any good.

"But Tegan, you are going to need me to be there for you as your maid of honor. Can't we just hire someone else to do the catering?"

Tegan abruptly changed gears and sniffled audibly, "No chili *rellenos* a la Patti? No delicious morsels of spicy goodness only *you* can make? When I've been bragging to everyone on the invitations about the indescribable delicacies we will be serving to all, as we party all night, celebrating the second and *last* wedding either Alex or I will have?"

Tegan sniffed again, saying sadly, "I guess we *could* serve the usual beef-chicken-pasta stuff *everyone* else

4

does…or maybe pizzas all around. Hey, it's not like I'll be wearing white or anything that would be stained if I get sloppy tomato-based food all over it or anything."

Patti knew when she was beaten.

"Okay, okay. I'll cook for you."

Tegan spoke brightly, "You will? Really?"

Patti sighed, "But you will have to get Alex to help me light a fire under these contractor guys. I'm sitting in what is going to be the kitchen of my place, but the only indication it will be a kitchen is the huge boxes in the middle of the floor that say 'refrigerator' and 'oven.' Nothing has been hooked up, and I can't get the rest of the space fixed up until that happens."

"I thought it was supposed to happen last week," Tegan said.

"It was, but the guys never showed up," said Patti.

"Give me the number," said Tegan. "You know that's what I do best, girl. Parties by Pat-Teg would *never* be the resounding success it is if *you* set everything up and I did the cooking. So you let me make some calls, and I'll get those contractors out there if I have to drag them by the hair myself. All you are supposed to be worrying about is what you are going to serve, and how much of each of the ingredients you will need to feed the hungry horde that is going to appear."

Patti sighed.

Tegan sounded apologetic. "Hey, I've been falling down on my game, haven't I? I'm sorry. It's just that moving in with Alex was such a big deal, such a change in my life that I'm still reeling from it. And being pregnant is taking a toll on my energy level. It's a whole lot harder being forty and pregnant than it was when I was younger having Katie and Kevin."

"I know," Patti responded. "But I miss seeing you all of the time. And even when we do get together, it's usually just to work a party. We don't get much time to talk anymore, and we can't blow off steam getting drunk since you are not the only one in your body these days. Even I draw the line at getting an unborn baby drunk,, besides, what does the little tike have to be stressed about?"

"Maybe he's thinking, *hmm, Mom's not exercising like she should be, so her heart is not as efficient. And she's feeding me all of this adrenaline, making me feel jumpy and anxious.* Ya think?" Tegan giggled.

"Yeah. *Sometimes Mom's heartbeat starts speeding up a lot, and there's this voice I hear all of the time telling me he's my Dad, only it's not talking to me. Then there's this enormous snake that keeps poking at me when I'm trying to sleep. What's with that?"*

Now both Patti and Tegan were laughing.

"Okay," Patti finally spoke. "If you promise to help me with getting the contractors here so my kitchen is done in time for me to do some practice cooking before the wedding, then I will agree to do both duties on your wedding day."

"No matter how many guests we end up having?" asked Tegan.

Patti sighed. "Aren't you limited by how many you can fit in your house? I mean, I know it's a lot bigger than your old one, but still…"

"No, Alex and I have been talking it over, since the guest list keeps on growing. We are going to rent some tents… one for over a temporary dance floor and one for over a sitting area," Tegan said. "We figure the food will be set up on the back porch, and people can sit there or in the house or out in the yard. Remember, Alex and Edgar tore down the fence between our yards, so we now have double the space… people could just walk to the back of our yard, through Edgar and Juanita's yard, and go into their house if they want another place to sit. Most of the relatives are going to be from their side of the family anyway."

"So, did you decide if the actual ceremony is going to be in a church yet?"

Tegan spat out. "No. It's not. The priest Alex wanted to use started going on and on about how since Alex's first marriage had been annulled by his ex-wife, he was able to get married in a church, but since I wasn't married in a Catholic church, mine didn't count. I started to yell at him that my kids weren't bastards! I *was* legally married in a real church with God invited and everything. Alex figured he needed to get me out of there before I hit a man of God, so we left. He talked to his parents about it, and it turns out one of his uncles on his mom's side is a priest. He lives down in Texas, but he was planning on coming up for the wedding anyway. Alex called him and his uncle said he would be glad to do the honors for our wedding. We are going to have the ceremony up by the back porch under the tent that will have all of the chairs. Even if it rains, we will be able to fit everyone in who wants to see the actual wedding vows."

"I see," said Patti thinking it over. "So I will have gotten most of the food already set up on the back porch before the ceremony?"

"Uh-huh," Tegan agreed. "If you need help getting the food here, Edgar is Alex's best man. Both he and Juanita keep asking us to let them do more to help. Maybe they can help you deliver and set everything up."

"Maybe," Patti said. "Let me give it some thought. You said about a hundred people. When are you going to have a final number?"

"Probably not for at least another month. I just sent out the invitations today. Based on that, if everyone comes it will be about a hundred people. But Alex's mom keeps remembering other people we should invite. I keep telling him to tell her no more, but she's such a sweet old lady, I find it hard to tell her no to her face." She giggled. "And I think Alex is afraid of her."

"Makes sense," Patti sniffed.

"What does?" Tegan asked.

"Well, he was raised by a strong woman... now he's marrying another one. The best thing he can do is placate both of you. The worst thing that could happen is you two butting heads. He'd be stuck in the middle and have no way out."

"You're not insinuating Alex is afraid of *me*, are you?" Tegan asked ominously.

Patti laughed. "No. But maybe he should be. Remember, I've watched you in action when you get going. And that was without pregnancy hormones giving you an extra edge. Don't you dare get angry with me! This is me, Patti Johnson, your best friend you are talking to. I know you better than you know yourself. Let's just agree you are strong, since I need your strength and your organizational skills to help poor little me get my place in shape in time for me to be able to cook for your wedding."

Tegan sniffed haughtily. "What would you do without me?"

Patti laughed again. "I sure wouldn't be able to run a business by myself, that's for sure. If Alex hadn't offered me such a huge chunk of change to open my own restaurant and catering place, I wouldn't be in this predicament at all."

"But he needed to do something with the money he made from selling the original artwork he had all over his condo. My kids won't be going to college any sooner than yours will, so there's plenty of time for you to start making so much profit you can pay him back in no time."

"I was just lucky this place was available. Close enough for me to ride my bike to and on a busy street with lots of foot traffic. Rosa has already drawn up a bunch of plans for me to look at for how to set up the restaurant area in the front of the store. She says this is good practice for her since she plans to go to college to become an interior designer."

"Let's just get your kitchen up and running first, okay?" Tegan said. "Give me those numbers and I'll get on making some calls. I'm feeling just stressed enough that yelling at some contractors is going to be a fun form of stress relief."

"You are totally weird, you know that?" Patti laughed. "But that's why I love you so much."

She gave Tegan the phone numbers and hung up. She looked around again, with an expectant feeling replacing the depression she had been in earlier.

"If anyone can get this place done in time, you can, Tegan," she chuckled.

She took one final look around, locked the back door and rode her bike home.

Two

Tegan made the phone calls, and miraculously the contractors not only rushed out to do the work that week, but were apologetic about why they had not done so the previous week.

"In fact," giggled Patti to Tegan on the phone the day the appliances all got hooked up, "I thought they were going to bow on their way out the door. What the hell did you say to them, anyway?"

Tegan just chuckled evilly. "Let's just say I made it clear to them just how much in their best interests it was for them to honor their commitments, and leave it at that, shall we?"

"Any further news on the guest list?" Patti asked.

"Nope," Tegan answered. "Just that Alex's mom keeps on thinking of more relatives to invite. I swear, we are going to have the entire village in Mexico they came from along with a mariachi band."

Patti sighed. "Well, I have always wondered what it would be like to have to cook for a large crowd. I guess I'm going to find out."

"Uh-huh," Tegan replied. "Now I'm heading out the door, and you'd better be on time to meet us at the bridal store I told you about. Katie is insisting she's not going to wear *some ugly piece of crap* for my wedding day, even if I beg her to. I told her since she's the junior bridesmaid, her dress needs to coordinate with yours, since you're the maid of honor. She ran upstairs and slammed her door, insisting she'd rather go with Alex and Kevin, pick out a tuxedo and just be an usher, like Kevin. I have to go up there and drag her out and stuff her into the car, but I'm still planning on being there by one-thirty."

Patti sighed again. "Okay. I forgot that was today. I'll be out the door in a couple of minutes and I'll see you there. I'll drag Chelsea along, too. Maybe we can find her something to wear, also, and kill another bird with that stone. I'll tip her off in the car on the way there that if I give her a significant sign of some sort, known only to us two, she is to help us convince Katie the dress she is trying on is perfect and not *some ugly piece of crap*."

"Thanks, you really are a sweetie," Tegan said. "See you soon."

Patti smiled at her phone after she hung up.

"Boy, am I ever glad it's *you*, not *me*, having to go through all of this. Of course, I don't have a big gorgeous hunk of man in my bed, so there's that."

She sighed, then headed out of her home office to yell, "Chelsea! Get yourself ready right now. We have to go shopping for *some ugly pieces of crap* to wear for Tegan's wedding!" She chuckled as she grabbed her purse.

Three

Two weeks later, after spending the better part of a Saturday morning cooking in her new kitchen, Patti frantically dialed Tegan's number and waited for her friend to answer.

"Hello?" a low masculine voice said.

"Alex?" Patti tried to modulate her voice. "Is Tegan there? I really need to talk to her right now."

"She's still asleep," Alex answered. "She…uh…got to bed really late last night."

Patti snorted, "To bed, or to sleep? You animal! She's a pregnant woman! You have got to let her get her rest, you know."

Alex smiled so broadly it was almost audible. "I'm aware of that. Why do you think she's still asleep at this late hour of the morning?"

"Because she's a lazy slug who likes to sleep away half the day? And you're the enabler who is letting her do it?" Patti teased.

"Guilty as charged," Alex responded. "But what are you calling about? Is it anything I can help you with? Or can I take a message for you?"

Patti sighed heavily.

"Well, it's just that I've spent the whole morning making some of the tapas I plan to serve at the wedding, and I was timing the whole thing to see how long it takes to make twenty-five of everything. Believe me, with the time it took, making a hundred or more of everything is going to take days. And then the food won't be fresh for the wedding day. I have no idea how I'm going to be able to do this *and* be the calming influence Tegan is going to need so much on her wedding day."

"I see your dilemma," Alex answered. "And thank you for everything you do to calm her down. I love her so much, yet I'm still learning how to react when she flies off the handle as she has been doing more and more frequently lately. I'm not sure if it's her hormones since I have never lived with a pregnant woman before; or if this is just the way she responds to the extreme stress of planning a huge event like our wedding is turning out to be. But every time she talks to you, or sees you, she is much easier to live with."

Patti chuckled, "You are going to have to learn other ways to calm her down besides distracting her with energetic sex, *señor*. Pretty soon, that will be nigh on to impossible, what with how huge she will get. After the baby is born, you will have to wait the requisite six weeks or so before you can resume that sort of thing."

It was Alex's turn to sigh heavily.

"So I have been told. Edgar rubs his hands together with glee every time I complain about her behavior. I really think he is enjoying hearing about my pain."

He changed gears.

"But what can we do about your problem?" he mused. "How do they handle large crowds in banquet halls or big restaurants?"

"They have more than one chef, that's for sure," Patti answered.

"That's it, then," Alex replied. "You need to hire someone to help you do the cooking. Not only will this extra set of hands come in handy for our wedding day, but once your restaurant opens, you will not be able to do all of the cooking yourself once the place takes off, as I'm am positive it will."

"I don't know…" Patti began, but Alex cut her off.

"After all, Tegan won't be able to help you much after December, because she will be busy with our baby. You two will still be able to run Parties by Pat-Teg together, since she can do most of the planning of events from her home office, on the phone and the computer. But running a restaurant *and* a catering business is too much for you to do by yourself."

"But I'm not making any money yet," Patti said anxiously. "I don't have anything to pay another person with. I wasn't planning on taking any salary for myself even, much less taking any money out of what little profit I might make in the start to pay someone else."

"Do you need me to put more money into the account I set up for you to draw against?" Alex asked.

"I can't ask you to do that," Patti said quickly. "You are marrying my best friend, not me. Besides, every time I think of how much of your money I have already used, I get sick to my stomach, worrying about how I will ever pay you back."

"Patti," Alex began gently as if he were lecturing a child. "Listen to me while I tell you the two reasons you are not to feel like that. First, the whole point of investing your money is to make more of it. When I bought all the original art pieces I had in my condo, it was with the idea I would make more money when I sold them, which I did. I consider investing in your restaurant, ultimately in your cooking skills, to be a worthwhile use of my money. I fully expect to realize a profit once you have been in business long enough for the clientele to materialize. So don't worry about the money aspect."

"I guess," Patti said uncertainly.

"And secondly," Alex said even more gently, "You and Tegan come from small families, so you are not as well-schooled as I am in supporting *your own*. What I mean is you are even closer to Tegan than her sister, so I consider you *my* sister as well. There is no favor you could ask of me that I would refuse to consider if I was capable of doing it for you. I have already committed to supporting you as you start up your business. A few dollars more, here and there, are not really an issue for me. Please remember that, and do not feel guilty at all."

Patti sighed.

"Boy, oh boy, not for the first time am I jealous as all hell you are marrying her, not me! You are really a good man, you know that?"

Alex chuckled warmly.

"And you are a good woman. Remember, I told you last year that as soon as I get a wedding ring on Tegan's hand, I will turn my full attention to finding a man good enough for you? Just be patient, Patti. There are other good men in the world. We are everywhere, but we aren't always easy to pick out of a crowd. You never can tell when *the arrogant bastard*, as my *cariña* so eloquently described me once, is going to turn out to be the man of your dreams."

"Okay, if you say so," Patti said, sounding less than convinced.

Alex smiled into the phone again.

"You go ahead and put an ad in the paper looking for a part-time chef to help you do your cooking duties. Do it soon, since you will probably need some time to train this person to make your foods. If you find someone in the next week or so, you will have about a month to do some sharing of recipes."

"I will," Patti answered. "And thanks, Alex. Usually I'm the one who does the calming down whenever I call Tegan. This time, you calmed *me* down."

"Glad to be of service," he answered. He confided, "Besides, Tegan is not the only one who has been bragging to all of my relatives about the gourmet foods they will get to have at our wedding. My mother is already complaining about how enthused I am about your cooking."

"Oh, great," Patti moaned. "No pressure or anything, huh?"

Alex chuckled again. "Bye, Patti. Run that ad and everything will work out. Just let me know if you need any more money."

"Okay, bye," Patti said.

She looked out the window for a while, as she absently picked at the tapas she had made. Then she packed all of the food into some of her catering containers and headed home. Once she got there, she went on-line and found the website for the local paper. She put together an ad to run for a few days, looking for an experienced cook to work part-time for her catering service.

Four

"So, how are the interviews going?" Tegan asked her best friend when she gave herself a break from wedding planning. "You are having them all come in today, right?"

Patti sighed heavily, "Yes, but the two that came in this morning just weren't experienced enough to be able to help me much. One was a single mom who hasn't done much cooking, but asked me 'How hard can that be?' and the other had only worked at a burger joint before. Other than burgers and fries, she didn't know how to make much. Neither had ever cooked in the quantities I will need them to handle for the restaurant, never mind the catering business."

"Are there any more coming in?" Tegan asked sympathetically.

"Yeah, there's two more coming later in the afternoon. One more woman, who says she's from a big family, so she can handle the volume, and the other is a man who said he had lots of experience cooking in all kinds of situations."

"A man?" Tegan sounded surprised. "Are you really considering a man for the position of assistant cook?"

Patti giggled, saying, "Why not? I've 'considered' men for *lots* of positions in my day!"

Tegan laughed, "Yeah, you bad girl; but as a cook? Would a guy would be able to take orders from you and work together in such close quarters, without thinking he was working for a 'bossy bitch'?"

Patti sighed again, "Well, if a certain best friend and partner of mine was *not* getting married in such a hurry, though God only knows *why*, since the 'bun in her oven' isn't due until December, for crying out loud, then I wouldn't have to find someone to help me so quickly! Or if I could be released from my vow to be your maid of honor?"

Tegan whined, "*No!* You *have* to be there for me. You are partly responsible, after all, for the situation I'm in. If you hadn't invited Alex to my fortieth birthday party, then he wouldn't have had unprotected sex with me while I was too drunk to object, all night long. I wouldn't be pregnant and we could plan to get married sometime next year. But *no*, you *had* to invite him, and now look what we have to deal with! Since it's partly *your* fault, you *have* to be my maid of honor. There's no way around it."

Patti laughed. "I'll admit to setting you up by inviting him. But no one held you down and made you have unprotected sex for hours."

Tegan snorted, "Well, I'm not really sure, since I don't remember much, but I'll bet *he* probably held me down, at least for part of the time."

"Fine, blame me! But once this wedding of yours is over, we are even-steven, okay?"

"Deal," Tegan agreed quickly. "Besides, no one does Mexican food like you, and since Alexander's whole family is going to be there, including some cousins, I want you to blow their socks off with your cooking. I want his mom to be begging you for the recipes. I want his dad offering to leave her for you, if only you'll cook for him!"

They both giggled now, at the mental image that created.

"I'm hoping he likes my cooking, but not *that* much. She may be old, but I wouldn't want to arm-wrestle her. She looks pretty strong for her age."

"She raised nine kids, girl. I think she'd still put in a pretty good showing. From what Alex tells me, they all gave her a lot of grief. He says strong women raise strong men. He said that to Kevin the other night, and that was how he got Kevin to go out in the yard and play soccer with him, Edgar and his boys."

"Is Kevin still worried because his dad's gay, he will be?" Patti asked.

"I'm not sure. But when I asked Alex if I should have a talk with him, he advised me to sit back and let things take their course. He said he'd let me know if he thought I needed to get involved. Quite frankly, I'm relieved, since as you know I only have a sister, and I'm not the biggest expert on male psychology!"

"Hey, girl, I'd love to keep on chatting all day, but I think I see my next applicant coming up the sidewalk. I'll call you later to let you know how it went," said Patti briskly.

"Okay. Talk to ya," Tegan said. She got back to planning where she wanted everyone who had RSVP'd to sit for the wedding ceremony.

An hour later, Patti sighed again as she contemplated the dismal prospect of either having to hire one of the unsuitable and inexperienced candidates she had interviewed, or making Tegan choose to find another caterer or another maid of honor. The most recent woman had been from a large family, yes, but a large Italian family like hers. She was well-skilled at Italian foods, but had no experience or interest in Mexican cooking. That was one of Patti's special favorites, both to eat and to cook; and Tegan was marrying a man whose parents had immigrated to Chicago from Mexico years ago… legally, he assured her. So the upcoming wedding was to have tapas and main dishes that were all influenced by the spices and seasonings which gave heat and flavor to the foods from south of the border. The woman, while an interesting prospect for other times, was not a good choice for immediate help.

Patti was staring idly out of the window when she heard, then saw, a Harley Davidson motorcycle pull up and park right in front of her storefront. Since there was still a "closed, opening soon" sign in the window, she didn't think the large, burly man who turned off the "hog," then got off and walked up to the door, was trying to be fed. With a shock, she realized the tall, muscular, bald and tattooed man with a lot of facial hair was probably her last interview of the day.

He strode up to the door, then knocked on it. When she waved weakly from the front window, he tried the door and finding it open, walked in.

"Are you the owner of this place?" he asked, in a surprisingly gentle, low voice, while he removed his mirrored sunglasses. He seemed like the kind and size of man whose voice should boom in a small, enclosed place.

"Yes," she began, "I'm Patti Johnson. And you are?"

"Jules Marks Tremenczyk, but I go by J.T."

"I would, too," she told him, smiling. "Are you here to interview for the position of cook?" Patti asked, even though it appeared to be obvious. The man had presence that seemed to fill most of the space in the room, and she was already mentally asking herself if she thought she could envision spending time with him, working side-by-side in her adequate yet rather small cooking area in the back.

"Yeah," he said, adding, "I don't have a resume, since I've done most of my cooking at places in so many different states, most bosses don't bother to call anyone. But I've done all different kinds of cooking, from tiny cafes on two-lane highways to fancy upscale places in big cities. I can give you the names of some, if you really want to check up on me."

He smiled at her. Since he had taken off his sunglasses once he entered the door, she noticed when he smiled there were "crinkle" lines around his light blue eyes, as if his face was very used to smiling. She guessed he was probably close to her age, but then, he was so tan he might have aged his skin prematurely, spending so much time exposed to the sun and wind while riding his Harley on the highway.

She realized he was still standing there, waiting for her to say something instead of studying him. Patti cleared her throat, "Have you done much Mexican-style cooking?"

He threw back his head and laughed, "Oh lord, yes! I lived in Texas off and on for about ten years, and before that I traveled around parts of Mexico spending time in Guadalajara and some smaller towns; then, for a while, I cooked for a couple of major hotels in Mexico City. I even spent some time moving around on the Baja Peninsula until I got worried my extra weight would start the San Andreas fault to shifting around too much; so for the good of everyone out there, I headed up north back to the United States."

"Why?" he asked, looking closely at her, "You don't look Mexican to me. I'd guess Italian, with those almond-shaped dark eyes of yours and that long, straight dark brown hair."

She smiled self-consciously at him. "Yes, both of my parents are Italian. My mom is second-generation, but my Dad's parents immigrated here together, once they were married. So of course, I learned from my grandmother how to cook real Italian-style, thus starting me off on a life-long weight battle that comes with excess consumption of pastas and other high-carb yet *delicioso* foods."

"Mind if I sit?" he asked her. When she shook her head, he pulled the chair opposite her out from the table, sat down and immediately leaned back, balancing on two legs just the way she always yelled at her kids not to do.

"The thing is," he drawled, "I find most women worry so much about how much they are eating, they forget it is one of the major pleasures God gave us to enjoy while we are still on earth. If you balance that with doing enough of some of the *other* pleasures, like moving your body around, then you will be able to find a balance, and that's what's right for you. Take me, for example. I'm a big man, so I have big appetites. I don't argue with the way I was made; I just enjoy what I can and give thanks for the pleasures I can enjoy. Life is a whole lot easier that way."

Patti had to force herself to focus on what he was saying because her brain had recognized he had used a plural for "appetites." She found herself looking at his hands and wondering if all the other parts of him were as large as his calloused, thick fingers.

She cleared her throat again, "Well, the only problem is I had expected to hire a woman to be my assistant cook."

He raised an eyebrow, "That's discrimination."

She smiled at him, "Yes, but I don't have any employees right now, so I'm way too small for those federal laws to apply to me. You see," she continued, "the kitchen area is big enough for now since I haven't really opened for business, but it will be close quarters once there are two cooks in there. Would that bother you?"

As he raised both of his eyebrows this time, she clarified, "I mean, you're not claustrophobic or anything like that, are you?"

When he shook his head, she asked, "And would you have a problem with doing what I say…with following orders from a woman?"

Once again, he threw back his head and laughed. "Honey, both of my parents are Roma, so some of my earliest memories involve getting ordered around by my mom, both of my grandmothers and the aunts who tried to keep themselves in practice by ordering me around; especially once I got taller than all of them!"

"Roma?" Patti asked him, "That sounds familiar, but I'm not sure from where."

He sighed, "You said your grandmother came from Italy?"

She nodded.

"Did she ever warn you about Roma? The Romani people? "

She shook her head.

"Travellers? How about Gypsies?"

Patti nodded now. "Oh, yeah. She said one of her cousins had run away to be with some gypsy bimbo, and his leaving was the cause of his grandmother's early death...at ninety-two." She made a face, adding, "I got into trouble for laughing at her, because when I was a child, I thought the idea of dying at ninety-two meant you were *ancient*, NOT dying early."

J.T. nodded, "You were right. But that kind of thinking is what we face all of the time. 'We' meaning those of us who are Roma. Do you know why we don't like being called 'gypsies'?"

She shook her head, "Is it an insult? Like to 'gyp' someone is to cheat them? And like us Italians get called 'wops' or 'dagos'?"

He nodded again, "Yes, yes and yes. Also, the term comes from the old, mistaken belief among some

Europeans that we came up into their lands from Egypt. Genetically, it has been established we are descended from ancient nomadic people who left India and headed out in all directions. We have inter-married wherever we stayed, so we don't have one 'look' to us…we can be blond and blue-eyed or dark and brunette. We have no homeland or one language, so we are outcasts and strangers no matter where we go. But moving around is in our blood…it is the one birthright we all share. That's why I've worked in so many different places. I've been moving around on my own since I became old enough to run away from home for the first time."

He smiled, "Which is really kind of a misnomer since I had no one place to call *home* to run away *from*. My parents own a big RV, and they are never in one place for very long. Cell phones are one of the greatest inventions of mankind, if you ask any of my people."

Patti cleared her throat, "Well, I've never been a prejudiced person, so I'm certainly not going to let any of my grandmother's warnings bother me. But I still don't know if you will be able to do the kinds of cooking I need. I've never hired anyone before since this is my first attempt to open a business. So I'm not sure how to find out."

He looked at her closely, "Are you planning on being here tomorrow morning? Like around ten?"

She nodded. "I have to keep working on the lists of ingredients I will need, since my best friend and partner in the catering end of the business is getting married in a little over three weeks. That's to be my first attempt at catering to a group larger than I can cook for by myself.

And I'm her maid of honor, so I'll be doing double-duty that day. She is working on getting the final RSVP's so she can give me a head count. She's marrying a Mexican guy whose entire family will be at the wedding. My chili *rellenos* and *tamales* are favorites of both of them, along with my *guacamole* and *salsa*. That's the theme we have, and that's where I'll need some help."

He looked thoughtful again, "Are you planning on serving any *sopes*, or *tortas de papas*, or possibly, flan? I can make a really good coconut flan that is an unusual twist on an old Mexican favorite; I learned how from an old woman in Guadalajara."

She looked at him in surprise, "No, I hadn't thought about any of those. Why?"

"How about if I buy some ingredients and meet you here tomorrow morning? You can do whatever you need to, and I'll make up some of my specialties. I'd do it somewhere else, but I'm staying with some friends right now, and they don't have the kitchen space I would need. That way, you can try my cooking and decide if it's a good fit with what you're doing. If you don't like it, then no harm done and you'll have to keep looking for a cook. If you do like it, then hire me and I'll be glad to add my dishes to your list. I'll share my recipes with you, if you share yours with me. That way we both get to be better cooks."

Patti smiled at him, "But you have to let me pay you for the ingredients, either way, okay?"

He shook his head, "If you don't like them, no charge. If you do, then I'll give you the receipt and you can add it to my first paycheck. Deal?

She nodded. "Deal."

He put out his hand for her to shake and she was alarmed by the tingle that ran up her spine as he engulfed her hand solemnly in his.

"Then I'll be moving along now, to let you get back to your business. See you in the morning, Ms. Johnson."

"Please, call me Patti," she said.

He smiled at her again, "Okay, Patti. Bye."

He turned and walked out of the door, strode over to his motorcycle and turned it on, revving the engine. He waved at her through the window when he noticed her watching him, and put his sunglasses on before he rode off up the street. Only then did Patti realize she had been holding her breath as she let it out in a big whoosh.

"Watch it, girl," she warned herself, "If you hire him, you'll have to keep your hands off of him, lest he bring you up on harassment charges!" She laughed as she imagined him standing next to all five-feet-four of her and trying to insist she had forced this over-six-foot mountain of a man to submit to her.

Five

Later that afternoon, Tegan called Patti with the final head count for her wedding and asked, "So, how did the rest of today's interviews go?"

Patti was preoccupied adding up the numbers Tegan had given her.

"Well, the woman was Italian, like me, but hates Mexican food. So she wasn't a good choice. But the man has lived all over the country and spent some time in Mexico and Texas; he's been a cook wherever he goes, so he's got a lot of experience in southwestern-style cooking."

"That sounds really encouraging," Tegan responded.

"Yeah, so since I didn't know how to decide if I should hire him, he offered to come back tomorrow morning and make up some of his favorite regional things, like *sopes*, and *tortas de papas*...even coconut flan. Things I have never even thought of offering, since I don't know how to make them." Then she added, "Yet."

"What about worrying if he can take orders from a woman boss? Or be comfortable working in the cramped space in your kitchen?"

"He says he is a Gypsy…excuse me, a *Roma*, and he had lots of training from his mom and all the females in his family, at following orders from women who are smaller than him. He's been moving around since he was born, so he's used to kitchens of all sizes, but spent a lot of time in ones that come in RV's. So I think he might work out okay. That is, if I like his cooking."

"Hmmm," Tegan mused, "A Gypsy, huh? Is he, perhaps, good-looking?"

Patti cleared her throat. "Why do you ask, oh nosy one?"

Tegan laughed, "Because I love you, that's why! Because we've been best buds lots longer than we've been partners. And because the first thing you asked me when Alex and I got together was 'How was he?' So inquiring minds want to know."

Patti laughed, too. "Well, he's not conventionally good-looking. What I mean is, he's a big man, tall and wide, and bald with lots of facial hair. And he's got lots of tattoos."

"Curiouser and curiouser," Tegan said. "What about the beard? Does he need to wear a hairnet over it?"

"I'm not sure how that works," Patti said. "If I decide to hire him, I'll ask him if he knows what the law says. He's been a cook and chef in lots of different states, so I think he'll be up on the laws; a whole lot more than I am."

"And?"

"And what?" Patti asked defensively.

"Do you think he's hot?" Tegan asked.

"Well, at one point I did find myself fixating on his large hands, wondering if, on the scale of things, he's proportional all over, if you know what I mean!"

They both laughed.

"Patti, it's been *way* too long for you. But you don't want him bringing you up on harassment charges. Maybe wait until he decides to move on, then seduce his big self. You know, as a 'going away' present?"

Patti smiled, "Let's wait until I try his cooking tomorrow. If I don't like it, I may just jump on him then, you know, as a kind of consolation prize."

"Whoo hoo!"

"But if I do like his cooking, he promised to trade recipes with me; and any time I can expand the list of Mexican foods I can offer, and just incidentally eat myself, then I'm a happy camper. If that means I have to keep my hands off Mr. Big, Hairy and Tattooed, then I guess I'll just have to. I've been getting by with Mr. Happy's brother for so long, I guess he and I are probably common-law by now!"

At this, they both broke up laughing. Tegan's ex-husband had given her Mr. Happy years ago, so she would stop pestering him for sex. She had not known then he was gay, and according to him, neither did he. But when she found out Patti's husband was spending his time cheating on his wife, Tegan had bought her a battery-operated man-substitute of her own, and they had decided it would be referred to as Mr. Happy's brother.

Tegan stopped laughing first, to say, "Oops, sounds like my soon-to-be-husband has returned home. I think I'll have to hang up and talk to you tomorrow after you 'audition' your biker-chef."

"Why? Does he always come home expecting your full attention?" Patti asked, only part sarcastically.

"Why yes, if you must know," Tegan replied with a giggle, "If he's not horny when he walks in the door, it doesn't take much to get him that way. Remember, he's no more used to having *it* daily than I am. We're like two kids in a candy store. And we are taking full advantage of the fact the second trimester is the easiest one...it'll be the third one soon enough. So I'm going to have to go now, okay? Talk to you tomorrow."

Patti sighed, "Okay. I'll try to swallow my jealousy yet again. You're lucky I love you so much, girl. Or I'd be over there trying to steal him from you. Not that it would be possible, since it's obvious he's head-over-heels in love with your skinny-ass self. But since I do, go ahead and enjoy him. Just don't yell so loud I hear you from my house. I really *have* to draw the line there."

"Okay," Tegan giggled again, and Patti distinctly heard Alexander's low voice in the phone, saying, "Good-night, Patti."

Patti sighed again as she hung up her phone. She went to check on her kids to be sure they were both doing their homework, as it was a school night, and threw another load of laundry in before she made dinner. Afterwards, she took her shower and fell asleep as soon as her head hit the pillow. She dreamed of large bikers fighting over her in biker bars, while she wore only a leather bustier and thong and even in her dream, she was surprised to look down at herself and see tattoos on her own skin.

Six

Jules didn't want to be seen as too eager, so he forced himself to wait until ten in the morning before he headed to the grocery store to pick up fresh produce and dairy ingredients, then made his way to his possible place of employment. He was anxious to please the woman he had met because she interested him, and he had not found himself interested in any woman for a long time. He was glad for an excuse to do some cooking again, and especially to make some of his favorites. Despite what he had told Patti, he didn't eat much when he was on the road traveling. The idea of being able to eat the lion's share of what he was going to make made him dream about food almost all night long...except for when he was dreaming about introducing Patti to the pleasures to be had riding on the back of his Harley.

About ten-thirty, he roared up to the front of Patti's Place, unloaded the ingredients he had picked up and carried them through the unlocked front door.

Patti was sitting at the same table again, with a pile of lists in front of her. She looked up and smiled at him when he walked into the room.

"Do you need some help getting that into the kitchen?" she asked.

"Nah, it's only three bags. I got it covered," he answered her.

"How about doing the cooking? Do you need any help?" she asked hopefully.

He smiled at her, "You don't like doing paperwork, do you?"

She shook her head, "No. I hate it. That's why in the party-planning business with my pal Tegan, all I do is the cooking and serving. She's the 'planner' and I'm the gourmet. But I still have to figure how much of everything to order, based on how many people are going to be eating. Then I have to guess how many of each dish people are going to want, figuring how many adults, how many kids, how many will be drinking, wanting more munchies, etc."

She made a face. "Bleah! I'd rather be in the kitchen cooking for hundreds than chained to a table with paper and a calculator!"

He carried the food bags into the back and Patti followed him.

"So, do you need any help? Like maybe finding the right pots and pans, or bowls? Or knives? Anything?"

He smiled at her, "Well, boss, you could show me around, so I can learn your way of organizing stuff. Then when I get it all cleaned up, I'll put it all back where you want it again."

Patti spent the next half hour showing J.T. where she had put all of the utensils he would need and then she perched on one of the high stools that were in the kitchen and watched as he started getting things lined up for processing.

"Don't you have a written recipe?" she finally asked, when she noticed him getting pans onto the stovetop, and starting to chop ingredients.

"Nah, I carry them in my head." He winked at her. "Lots safer that way. No one can steal my recipes and claim them as theirs."

"Are you sure I can't help?" she asked again.

He handed her a knife and said, "Why don't you mince the garlic and green chilis, then you can chop up some cilantro. I'll get the bread dough together for the *sopes*, and brown the beef for the chili."

The next two hours were spent companionably preparing food together, which both Patti and J.T. really enjoyed. Since they each had their own ways of doing things, they were interested in learning how the other had mastered things like chopping the green leaves of cilantro...Patti used a pair of kitchen scissors, while J.T. used a big carving knife. When it came time to flip the *tortas de papas*, J.T. flicked his wrist and they flew into the air, then he caught them in the pan, while Patti used the more conventional spatula method. More than once they argued about whose method was better, but they finally agreed to disagree, figuring since they both enjoyed the food, the method wasn't as important as the results.

Once all the food was ready, Patti got out a couple of serving plates and J.T. grabbed a couple Mexican beers he had brought with him from the fridge. They sat down to sample what they had made. Patti was excited about the *sopes*, which were little corn cakes meant to be topped as desired by each consumer. They were a perfect addition to the buffet table that was going to be set up on Tegan's back porch. The chili was hearty and flavored with beef, three kinds of beans, lots of tomatoes and peppers, and would be a good topping as well as being good by itself for those who might be choosing low-carb items.

"Although," as Patti said indignantly, "Eating low-carb…what's the point? Adkins, schmadkins! Food is supposed to be filling as well as tasty! Otherwise you're hungry again five minutes later, right?"

After they ate the *tortas* and the *sopes*, Patti got some coffee going and they chatted amiably about the logistics of setting up the many food items on the buffet table. They tried to figure out which ones needed warming dishes and which could be set out in insulated plates that would keep warm only for a short time.

When the coffee was ready, J.T. brought out the cups of coconut flan and Patti found bliss on the tip of her tongue.

"Oh my God, is this good!" she told J.T., while he smiled at her reaction. "I'd hire you for this recipe alone, even if I hadn't enjoyed every other mouthful of stuff you've made today. Now I have to be concerned that people will like *your* cooking way more than mine."

J.T. laughed. "But how will they know, boss? Your name is on the catering service, not mine. I'm just your assistant cook. So it will all be our little secret, okay?"

Patti smiled at him. "And you won't open a competing restaurant right across the street from me and steal all of my customers?"

He shook his head. "No, ma'am. I'm not the business-owner type. I'm more the worker-type. Easier to move on when I'm ready to go. As long as I'm in town, I'll work for you and after we cook together enough, you'll have learned all of my recipes, too. That will be my parting gift to you. Deal?"

She smiled at him again, nodding. "I won't be able to pay you what your recipes are worth, but once I start making some profit, I'll share it with you. Okay?"

He put out his hand to shake on the deal. Once again, Patti felt a tingle down her spine, as his hand engulfed hers. She had a fleeting desire to feel those rough, calloused hands on her bare skin. When she looked up at him, both of his eyebrows were raised and he looked at her speculatively, as if he was thinking along the same lines. She cleared her throat.

"We'd better get those dishes done, huh?"

"No, ma'am, not you. I'll do them. Since I'm the junior employee now, it's my responsibility to do the grunt work. So that includes the cleaning up afterwards. You take your coffee with you and go back to doing that paperwork. Just call me if you aren't sure how much of everything you'll need to mass-produce my recipes. I've made them for just two, like I did today, and I've made them for two-hundred."

"Speaking of employee status, I'm going to need your social security number, your birth date and a mailing address, I think. Oh, and I wanted to ask you, what are the regulations for beards in the cooking industry? Do you know, or do I have to go online and check?"

J.T. followed her into the next room, picked up her pen and wrote on a piece of scrap paper, then turned to her and said. "That's all you need to do payroll, I think. I'll shave the beard when I get back home today. The regulations differ from state to state, but why bother when I can just shave it off, then grow it back when I leave? No big deal," he smiled at her expression. "Really, I don't mind. I'm looking forward to the job, so it's no big deal at all."

"I won't be able to pay you much… at least for now," Patti said apologetically.

"That's fine. One of the guys I'm staying with is a bartender at a local watering hole. He told me they can always use another bouncer, so I'm already working there at night. It's easy work since I'm big. I don't usually have to do much besides stand around and scowl at people, and they pretty much do what I tell them to. Between the two jobs, I'll be doing all right. Let me get the dishes done now and maybe we can talk logistics after I'm done, okay?"

At Patti's puzzled look, he said, "When you want me to report to work, how much of my recipes can be done ahead of time, when we are going to do it as well as exactly when the wedding is so I'll be sure to ask for that day off from the other job. Also what you expect me to wear. I'll probably have to rent something, since few weddings involve servers wearing jeans and leather."

Patti was still working on ingredients lists when J.T. got done with the cleaning. He joined her at the table and added the quantities for his items, as well as helped her decide how to set up the main buffet table and the smaller side tables. They were still talking and planning when Chelsea and Jake walked in the door.

"Hey, it smells really good in here! Any left?"

Patti quickly looked at her watch, and realized she'd spent the better part of the day with her new employee.

"I'm going to pay you for your time today. No arguments... you've been a really big help."

She turned to her kids and introduced them. "Chelsea, Jake, this is J.T. He's the new assistant cook I just hired today. He's the one who made the stuff that smells so good. Since he cleaned up, he'll have to tell you if anything is left. J.T., these are my kids, Chelsea and Jake."

"Pleased to meet ya's," J.T. said. "If you'll follow me into the kitchen, I think we can find a little of everything I made to audition for the job as your mom's assistant. She's so good in the kitchen I can't wait to learn her recipes. Today, she watched me make mine."

He was still talking as he led the kids into the kitchen.

Patti's phone rang so she couldn't follow them in for another taste, but she got another reprieve from having to attend to her paperwork. Predictably, it was Tegan calling.

"So, how did the tasting go?" she asked.

"Girl, his food is divine! Wait 'til you taste his flan. Yum! And the *sopes* are going to make excellent additions to the *tapas* table. Chelsea and Jake are in the kitchen right now making yummy noises while they eat all the leftovers. I'd bring you some, but J.T. and I ate a lot, for quality assurance, of course. My kids are probably going to finish what's left. But he's going to mass produce stuff for the wedding, so there'll be plenty."

"J.T., huh? That's his name?"

"Yeah," answered Patti. "His name is really Jules Tremenczyk, so it's pretty obvious why he goes by J.T. I'll bet only his mother and grandmothers can get away with calling him Jules without him beating them up."

They both giggled.

"Well, you did say he's a big man, so you're probably right." Tegan added. "How did you two fit into the kitchen together? Was it a tight fit or was it okay?"

"He's really generous about sharing recipes, as well as space, so there was no problem. I guess all those years spent cooking in RV kitchens got him used to not spreading his stuff all over. He said since he's the assistant, he'll do the cleaning up. In fact, he did the whole kitchen once we were done eating."

"Hmm, a good cook, willing to clean up after himself... I wonder if I can talk Alex into hiring him out from under your nose to cook for me?"

"Don't you dare! Or you'll have to find yourself another maid of honor."

"No! I need you. Girl, you can't desert me now," Tegan wailed.

"Why, what now?"

"Why don't you see if you can scarf some of that flan you were talking about from under the kids' noses and come over here. Let me tell you just how hard it is to plan this wedding with no wine allowed for my nerves."

"Okay, I'll see what I can do. Okay if I bring the kids over with me?"

"Of course. Just bring some food and I'll let you all in the door."

"See you soon, partner," Patti said as she hung up the phone.

She walked into the kitchen in time to hear Jake asking, "Those are all real tattoos, aren't they?"

J.T. smiled at him. "Yeah, they are. I started getting them when I was just a little bit older than your sister. Want to see my first one?"

He rolled up his shirt, and pointed to a heart tattooed near his heart.

Jake and Chelsea looked closely at it then Chelsea said, "Born to Rom? You spelled it wrong! What a bummer, to have a tattoo with a misspelling."

J.T. shook his head, smiling, "No, honey, it's not a misspelling. It's a pun, actually. I was born to two members of the Romani people, to two Romas. One is called a Rom, so I was born to a 'Rom' man and woman, as well as born to be one myself. And of course, we are travelers, so we are also born to roam, which is pronounced the same. Understand?"

Chelsea nodded, and turned to look at Patti, saying, "Pretty cool, huh Mom?"

Patti was having difficulty breathing while she stared at J.T.s muscular, hairy, broad chest. The tattoos only served to draw her eyes from his bulging pectorals to his almost flat abdomen. Its line of dark hair drew her eyes further down to where his belt interrupted her view. She became aware Chelsea was waiting for an answer at about the time she looked up to see humor in J.T.'s eyes, as if he was reading her thoughts and finding them amusing.

She hoped her blush wasn't too noticeable and was grateful when Jake broke the silence, saying, "Hey, I just thought of something…if you had a sister named Chelsea Denise, then she'd be a C.D.Rom, right? Get it?"

Chelsea groaned, long used to bad puns coming from her brother, "What a nerd! You are such a computer-geek! Sheesh!"

But J.T. laughed, saying, "Hey, that's pretty good. I'll have to run that one by the family next time I see any of them."

On a roll now, Jake continued, "You mean, the next time you see 'a Roma'? Or do you smell them? Get it? Aroma?"

Even J.T. groaned at that one, and to save them all from more bad puns, Patti forced herself to look away from J.T.'s chest and asked, "Is there any more flan left? My mucho-pregnant partner is having major cravings and asked if there was any I could sneak over there for her."

J.T. nodded, "Sure there is. Do you want me to run it over for her?"

Patti shook her head, "No, she wants to talk to me, too. But if you want to meet her, I'm sure she'd really like that."

"How about if I follow you over on my hog, then I'll just head on home from there?"

Jake's eyes got really big. "Do you think you could give me a ride over there on your motorcycle? I've never been on one before."

J.T. turned to look at Patti, "All right with you, boss?"

She smiled at him, "I guess so. As long as you give me a ride on it someday, too. I haven't been on one since my early college days when I had a boyfriend who rode one. I've still got a scar on the back of my calf from a burn I got when I climbed off the wrong way after a long ride up to Lake George."

She collected the flan bowl from the fridge and found there was enough chili to top the few *sopes* that were left…but the *tortas* were gone. She put everything into one of her carrying boxes, loaded it into the car along with Chelsea and both children's backpacks. Then Patti locked up her front door and they all headed over to Tegan's house.

Seven

Tegan licked her spoon again then sighed with satisfaction as she looked at the nearly empty flan bowl.

"I guess I really should save a little bit for Alex, huh?" she asked Patti.

Patti was watching out the window as J.T. gave all four of their kids a chance to ride on the back of his Harley for a tour around the block. He had also let them sit on the seat, rev the engine and showed them his more interesting tattoos.

"He's really good with kids, isn't he?" Tegan asked. When Patti still didn't answer, she snapped her fingers in front of Patti's nose. "Earth to Patti, Earth to Patti, come in, please. Stop all that feverish pornographic fantasizing you're doing before you slide right off my kitchen chair!"

Patti shook her head and laughed, "I can't help it! I mean, the view of his chest when he pulled up his shirt? Phew! The room suddenly got so over-heated. I almost tore off *my* shirt as well. I wonder how he would have reacted."

Tegan smiled, "Way to keep your distance from an employee, *Boss*."

"Hey, I can dream, can't I?" Patti asked.

"As long as dreaming is all you do, at least until after my wedding. I don't want to take any chances you two will have a falling out and I won't be able to have his yummy food, in addition to yours, to blow everyone away!"

"Oh, pul-leeze. Dreaming is probably all I'll ever get to do. He's younger than us, did you know that? I had him write down his social security number, his full name, his birth date and his temporary address. Since he's staying with friends, he says he has no permanent address other than Planet Earth. And that's when I discovered he's only thirty-four. I'm going to be forty at the end of October."

"So?" asked Tegan.

Patti sighed, "Too bad. I'd have loved to lick my way from one tattoo to the next."

Tegan laughed at her, "Five years is nothing by the time you get to our age, girl. Alex is two years older than me. So what? Don't get hung up on numbers. Age is relative."

"Yeah, but Jake is five years older than me, and he seems ancient to me despite his immaturity when it comes to women."

"That's because he doesn't take care of himself. He drinks way too much, smokes too much and hangs out in bars when he's not working. All of that ages a person."

Patti sighed again, "I suppose. Uh oh, there comes your intended and the Harley is still in the driveway. I'd better get out there and introduce them before he mistakenly thinks you are having an affair with a biker and injures my new assistant cook. I'll get my kids on home for dinner.

Tegan said "Oh!" as the baby kicked her, then rubbed her belly. She smiled at Patti. "I think the baby likes flan. Okay. I'd better come out there with you."

They both walked to the driveway to find the kids had already introduced Alexander to J.T., and the two men were busy discussing the benefits of various makes of Harleys versus other kinds of motorcycles.

"Yeah, that was my fastest one, so even though it broke down a lot, it was my favorite." Alexander said as J.T. nodded, smiling, and said, "I had one of those, too. Finally had to dump it because it was too unreliable. But she sure was a speed-demon!"

They both turned when Tegan said, "I didn't know you were into motorcycles, honey."

Alexander laughed, "You never asked me about that big scar on my left arm either. That's from the time I got thrown off my bike and left most of the skin from my arm on the pavement. Luckily I was wearing a helmet, or I'd have left my brains on the street, too. That's about when I decided expensive cars were a more sensible ride for me."

J.T. nodded, "I'd love to take your Ferrari for a drive sometime. I could never afford a car like that, but I like to dream. Maybe you could take my Harley for a ride? A trade?"

"I don't think so!" said Tegan, continuing, "I was just getting to like you, J.T. Don't mess things up by encouraging my baby's daddy to risk his neck taking a joy-ride, okay? He wants a ride, I'll give him all of the joy he can handle."

Katie rolled her eyes, "Jeeze, you guys. Can't you give it a rest? I can't wait until you are on your honeymoon, so at least we'll have a week without you two making goo-goo eyes at each other and snogging and fondling in the kitchen while I'm trying to eat my dinner. Sheesh!" With that, she stomped up the driveway and into the house, slamming the door on her way in.

Alexander, who had moved over to put his arm around Tegan and kiss her, smiled at Patti, while Tegan shrugged, "Hey, we're not even newlyweds yet. She's gonna have to get used to it."

Chelsea sniffed, "Oh, she's just upset because that boy she likes was kissing someone else near her locker today. Must be hormones," she continued, knowingly winking at her mom. "Can we go soon? I'm starved."

"Out of the mouths of babes, eh?" Patti laughed. She got Jake to get off the Harley, both of her kids climbed into the car, and they waved as they drove up the street.

Tegan said, "Alex, you have *got* to try this man's food. I saved you one of the *sopes*, and just a smidgeon of flan. Patti hired him, by the way, so he's going to help cook for our wedding."

Alexander smiled at J.T., "I figured as much. It's not every day I find a biker in my driveway when I get home. I'd have been jealous, if I didn't remember you telling me about Patti having him audition his cooking for her today. As it is, I'm keeping my arm around you, to show him you are beyond a doubt off-limits to everyone except me. Right?"

J.T. laughed, "No problem, man. She's too tall and too skinny for me. I like 'em rounder, with more meat on them. I break out in hives around pregnant women anyway. I'll be getting a move on myself, since I've also got a job as a bouncer at The Party House up the road."

Tegan and Alexander exchanged a smile, "That's where Patti had my fortieth birthday party last year," Tegan said. "Alex was an unexpected guest. The rest is history." They kissed again.

J.T. cleared his throat, "I see. Well I won't be expecting to see either of you there in the near future, since you appear too busy to be going out much."

"We may have the rehearsal dinner the night before the wedding there, though," said Alexander. "To give Patti a break from all the cooking she's going to have to be doing before and after that."

"Okay, then. Be seeing you around. Nice meeting both of you."

With that, he got onto his Harley, revved the engine, then rode up the street. Kevin, who had moved onto the porch to do his homework, remarked, "I think I could even give up video games for a ride like that." He eyed Tegan significantly.

She and Alexander both laughed. "We'll talk about that when you are eighteen…maybe."

They all went into the house to see about dinner.

Eight

Patti and Tegan went into overdrive over the next two weeks. They were experienced party-planners, but even they had never undertaken an event as large and complicated as a wedding. Tegan took to complaining it would have been easier to elope, but secretly she was glad for something to think about besides her steadily enlarging abdomen. At the age when most women were heading back into the workforce, she was sticking her head back into the noose of at-home motherhood; but since she was so in love with Alexander, and he was so thrilled with every part of the pregnancy experience, she didn't have the heart to say anything to him about her misgivings.

"That's why I have to complain to you, you see," she told Patti during one of their marathon planning sessions. It had started right after the kids went to school and was still going after they had taken a break for lunch.

"Because Mr. Big, Tall and Latino doesn't realize you aren't as thrilled about a new baby as he is?" Patti asked. She was adding up ounces of champagne per person, trying to figure out how many people would be drinking beer and how many would prefer Alexander's sangria or the do-it-yourself margarita bar.

"It's not that I'm not thrilled to be having *his* baby," Tegan complained, "But he's not the one who has been through all of this before. I try to tell him about sleepless nights and nipples so sore from nursing that I'll kill him if he tries to touch them, and he just laughs at me. Then he makes love to me again until I forget what I was even complaining about."

Patti sighed, "And you are an absolute *saint* to put up with *that*, let me assure you. It's a tough job, but someone has to do it. However, if you ever get tired of it, like I told you, he's the top choice in the playgroup's fantasy-top-five. I'm sure there would be a volunteer or two willing to make the supreme sacrifice and take your place, to scream and moan from delirious pleasure with him just to give you a rest."

Tegan stuck out her tongue at Patti, and they got back to working out the details of the beverages count.

Later, after they were done, they sat back and relaxed for a few minutes before one of them had to go pick up the kids from school.

"So you two have your honeymoon all set up, right?" Patti asked.

"Uh-huh," Tegan replied, while she thoughtfully chewed a bite of one of Patti's oatmeal-pecan-chocolate chip cookies. "Alex has always wanted to go on a cruise, but he agreed with me. I'm not exactly in the right shape to be sunning myself on the sand when I'm afraid the natives might try to shove me back into the water thinking I'm trying to beach myself. So the Caribbean is out, at least until we are doing some anniversary in the future. He found out this is a really good time to book a cruise up around Alaska, to go see what's left of the glaciers in the National Parks. I can still walk around okay, for now. And since my metabolism is so high right now that I'm sweating even from just from sitting around talking to you, he agreed I'd probably be more comfortable where it's cooler, especially at night."

Patti nodded, "Good idea. John will have the kids stay with him for the week?"

Tegan nodded, "Yes, and he's looking forward to it as much as they are. I'm so glad the kids are all right with their father being gay and living with a partner."

Patti eyed her closely, "And you really are okay with it now, too?"

Tegan shrugged, "It's not like I can do anything about it, is it? No one can. Besides, if John hadn't left me for Bill, I'd never have met Alex. I'm so happy with him that anything that contributed to getting us together has to be a good thing. Or at least something I'm not going to complain about."

They sat in companionable silence for a moment before Patti asked, "Isn't one of Alex's brothers gay, too?"

"Yes," Tegan answered, "Roberto. I've only met him a couple of times, but he seems like a real sweetheart. A really nice guy, and he looks like a younger, thinner version of Alex. He idolizes his oldest brother, so he told me that since I make Alex so happy, he's thrilled we are getting married. I told him there will be other gay men at the reception...not that it matters, of course. But it must be really difficult to always feel like the only one who is different in a group of people. Kind of like being the only black or the only woman employee in a boardroom."

"Umm-hmm," said Patti, as she studied the numbers on the sheets once again, "Or being the only fat person in the room. You feel like everyone is judging you, afraid to put their hands too close to the plates of food, for fear you'll eat their hands, too."

Tegan looked at her in concern, then laughed as Patti smiled at her and said, "It's a joke, girl. A joke!"

Tegan cleared her throat importantly, then said, "Speaking of others who might call you fat... did I tell you J.T. assured Alex he wouldn't *ever* be interested in me, because I'm too tall and too skinny for him? Interesting, huh?"

Patti rolled her eyes, "Yeah, he might have said that, but I'm still his boss, he's still five years younger than me and not once has he tried to make a move of any kind. Sometimes I get the feeling he's thinking about it, but then something interferes and the moment passes. I guess I'll just have to wait and see with this one...every love affair is different, just like every recipe. No hot and spicy, wild sex to start things moving along, like you and Alex had. Some girls have all the luck."

Tegan said, "Not to change the subject too much, but speaking of large people, have you decided what to have J.T. wear to the reception?"

Patti nodded and smiled, then pulled a drawing out of her pile of papers and showed it to Tegan. "Like it? Chelsea designed it. I've already ordered it from the tee-shirt place in town. Actually, I ordered a few of them for you and me, an XXL for J.T. and a few extras for our kids, to help advertise our business."

Tegan studied the drawing, saying, "What color are the shirts?"

Patti smiled, "I *was* going to use black, figuring no food stains would ever show up on it that way. But J.T. talked me into a dark red, kind of brick red, since he said research shows people eat more when they see the color red. Since I want people to get hungry when they see us in the shirts, I had to agree with him."

Tegan pointed to the drawing, "I like the way she put a small logo on the pocket on the front with our company name on it."

"We'll put the person's name on the front pocket too, right under the logo, so we'll always know whose shirt is whose," said Patti. Then she turned the paper over, "Did you see the back of the shirt?"

Tegan laughed as she read out loud, "Don't just be lookin'! Let Pat-Teg do the cookin'!"

"And here's *your* shirt," said Patti, showing her the other drawing.

"Your parties will be slammin' when Pat-Teg does the plannin'!" Tegan made a face at Patti, "Slammin'?"

Patti smiled, "Hey, what does it matter if *we* don't understand teenager slang? Chelsea and Katie assured me that *slammin'* is a *good* thing. Who are we to argue? And to answer your question, I told J.T. as long as he wore a pair of black jeans with the shirt, he'd be dressed up enough, considering all of the cooking and cleaning he's going to be doing outside when the weather is supposed to be kind of warm. Is that okay with you?"

Tegan sighed heavily.

"What would you rather have him wear?" Patti asked, concerned.

"No, I'm not sighing because of his clothes. Black jeans will be fine. But do you realize just as soon as Kevin stops being an annoying teenager and goes away to college, this younger one now playing soccer with my belly button, will be gearing up for *his* teenage years? At that point, I'll be almost 50? What the hell is wrong with me that I'm doing this again?"

Patti smiled at her best friend, "You are head-over-heels in love with the baby's daddy, remember? And might I add, the baby's daddy is so hot, that half of our playgroup would arm-wrestle you for the chance to have him, even just for one night, if they thought they had a chance at all. Instead, all we get is the paltry few details you are willing to share with us about his love-making skills. So stop with the complaining, already. You are positively glowing with happiness. We are almost done planning the best wedding of the year, which will be yours. After that, you will have Alex in your bed for the rest of your lives. And he adores you."

Tegan smiled at Patti. "Yeah, you're right. He's the best I've *ever* had in bed. I guess if I have to tie myself down with one man for the rest of my life, it's a really good choice to pick the one who makes me scream and moan every time. I just hope he sticks to his promise to only want one more baby with me. He's offered to get himself fixed after the second one. I told him they'll be *in there* anyway, since my babies are always c-sections, so I'll get my tubes tied. Then we can have all of the unprotected sex we want…hopefully we'll get a few years out of it, before I go through my menopause. I'd hate to go through all that trouble only to find out it was unnecessary."

Patti laughed. "Did I ever tell you that you are a pessimist by nature?"

Tegan laughed, too. "Yeah, frequently. You're right, too. That's why I need you as my best friend. So, old buddy, old pal. Are we just about done here? The kids will be getting off school soon and I need to do a few errands before I go pick them up."

"Yes, oh, planning goddess. We're done for now. After all that talk about what a hot man you are cohabitating with, I've got to take a cold shower before the kids get home. So off with you and I'll talk to you tomorrow."

As she watched Tegan pull away from her house, Patti found herself wondering if she would ever find someone to complete her as well as Tegan and Alexander suited each other. Then she shook herself and reminded herself, "I'm the optimistic one. If *she* can do it, then I can too. I'll just have to wait until it's my turn." Resolutely, she shoved the paperwork to the side and got up to start creating something interesting for dinner.

~ * ~

Plans were finalized, clothes were bought and accessorized. Relatives from out of town arrived and were ensconced in the local hotels and motels. The rehearsal dinner was at The Party House, and since J.T. was working as a bouncer that night, everyone got to meet him. He spent time talking in Spanish to some of Alexander's family, who had lived in the areas in Texas and Mexico that J.T. had visited. He charmed all of the relatives, who were now eagerly awaiting a chance to try the cooking he told them he and Patti were going to provide.

When the big day finally arrived, Patti was up at the crack of dawn, busy in her catering kitchen, with J.T. at her side. They chopped, cooked and assembled more food than she had ever seen at one time. The day had started out cool and rainy, but as a tribute to the happy couple, the sky cleared well before their wedding was scheduled. By the time the guests began to arrive, even the grass was mostly dry, and the sun shone warm with an early fall glow, giving a special light to the festivities. Patti and J.T. got all of the food to the house and Patti left J.T. in charge of the set-up while she went into the house to do her maid-of-honor duties. These mostly involved calming Tegan down, making sure she knew how beautiful she looked and sneaking her a half-glass of champagne so they could have their own private toast to her future happiness.

Nine

Many hours later, Patti sighed with pleasure as she sat back in a comfortable wicker chair on the back porch and kicked her shoes off to wriggle her hot, tired toes. She had resisted J.T.'s orders to sit and rest the first few times he had tried to get her to relax. But finally, when he gently pushed her into a chair and handed her an open bottle of champagne along with a glass, she realized just how tired she was. She sat down to watch as he organized the kids into a mass "clean-up" army. She was amazed to see her own kids, as well as Tegan's, Juanita's and even the out-of-town visiting cousins all helping. They all liked J.T. and wanted him to see what a good job they could do. Kids who normally would argue about *why* cleaning even needed to be done when it would just get dirty again were now racing around trying to clean up more than each other. Patti shook her head in wonder, and leaned back in her chair with her feet up on the step stool in front of her. She thought over the events of the day trying to figure out which part had been her favorite.

The cooking in the early morning hours had been fun, despite the stress of knowing just how many people were going to be eating the food. J.T. was a good companion in the kitchen. They chatted amiably, or just worked in harmony quietly, and the food was quickly and efficiently prepared. They had gotten it delivered to Tegan and Alexander's house, figured out where they were going to put everything and gotten it all set up for serving. Then the guests had begun to arrive and the speed of the day picked up immediately. Tegan was beautiful, but a mass of nerves, and it took all of Patti's skill at calming her friend down to get her to stop quivering with excitement. Patti had repeatedly reminded Tegan how much in love she and Alexander were and how happy they already were together. Patti was exhausted from the mental strain by the time the music signaled she was to follow Katie down the aisle between the folding chairs. The huge expanse of two backyards had been decorated for the occasion with fall flowers and streamers.

When Patti saw Tegan's face, as her father walked her slowly down the aisle, and her eyes were only on Alexander's face, she knew all her work in calming her friend down was worth the effort. The light of love that illuminated Alexander's face was so warm with hope and anticipation she knew anything she had done to help bring these two people together was something to be proud of. They had both spoken their vows clearly, looking only at each other. When they put the rings onto each others' fingers, they had both started to cry, as if it was a moment they had been waiting for their whole lives, and now their joy was become the reality of total bliss. It was so obvious to everyone there these two people belonged together, that the cocoon of love they created had made everyone else feel warm and loved as well. In fact, after they had kissed, Alexander had turned and addressed the gathering, in both English and Spanish, thanking everyone for contributing to the joy he and Tegan felt by coming to witness their marriage. Then he had welcomed everyone to their home and invited them all to "eat, drink and make merry." The thunderous applause that followed allowed for a catharsis of emotions, as the union of these two people made family of everyone who was there.

J.T. and Patti had moved into high gear then, with Patti immensely grateful for J.T.'s experience in serving such large crowds of people. They had been a good team, each anticipating the other's needs, and looking to lend a hand, when needed, in order to keep the serving dishes full and the food available. They had been too busy to do much talking, but once again, they worked together so well, Patti felt relaxed enough to have a few glasses of wine, allowing her to join in many of the frequent toasts to the newlyweds' future happiness.

At some point, the DJ, who was one of Alexander's cousins from Aurora, had begun playing music. At Alexander's request, the first song was Santana's "Game of Love," and since Patti knew just what kind of games Tegan and Alexander had played with each other during their courtship, she was probably the only spectator to really understand just *why* that was their song. They started out doing a simple slow dance, but it didn't take long for their passion to make them forget their audience, and there were many cheers, whistles and catcalls when Alexander held his new wife close and kissed her repeatedly while they moved to the music.

After that song, everyone joined in dancing, even the smallest children and the oldest grandparents got up to celebrate by moving around the dance floor. Patti found herself being grabbed by one man after another as the music had them all anxious to show off their dancing skills. But the biggest surprise was when Patti turned to see who her new partner would be and J.T. took her hand and led her in a spirited polka to the mariachi band music that was blaring out the speakers. She was so out of breath afterwards she collapsed into a chair and gratefully drank the large glass of ice water J.T. poured for her.

"I had no idea you were such a good dancer," Patti panted while she tried to catch her breath.

J.T. smiled, "We Romas learn to dance before we learn to walk. And polkas are one of our specialties. Anything else and I could have resisted the urge to join in, but I love to hop around to a good polka beat, and besides Polacks, no one does polka music like a good mariachi band."

J.T. patted Patti's hand, "So thanks for indulging me, boss. You sit and catch your breath and I'll get back to refilling the food for this ravenous crowd."

The rest of the reception was taken up with more eating and drinking, more dancing and finally, cutting of the cake and tossing of the wedding bouquet. Patti tried to duck away from the crowd of single women that urged Tegan to, "Aim for me!" and "Make me lucky!" But Chelsea and Jake pushed her back into the crowd and she had to dodge to avoid the bouquet she was sure Tegan threw directly at her. It was caught by Rosa, who had just turned fifteen and she blushed when her father, Alexander's brother Edgar, started to lecture her on how she had better *not* be the next one in the crowd to get married. His cousins then crowded around him and reminded him just how old Juanita had been when he met her while they were still in high school. Much teasing and laughing followed, and when Rosa's boyfriend caught the garter, Patti suspected a fix, since she knew Alexander had known about Rosa's boyfriend before her dad did.

Tegan and Alexander had gone into their house to change for the drive into downtown Chicago to the hotel they were staying in for the night. When they emerged quite a while later, looking sheepish, they were once again teased unmercifully. Everyone went out front to wave to them as they drove off to start their married life together.

That was when J.T. pushed Patti into the chair, handed her the open bottle of champagne along with a glass, and encouraged the children to show him just who could do the best job cleaning up from the crowd. As she sipped the sparking wine, Patti was suffused with feelings of happiness. Her best friend was now happily married to the man of her dreams, who was also the father of her baby due in three months. The children were doing so much of the cleaning there wouldn't be too much to finish up tomorrow. The guests who were still there had finally stopped eating everything in sight, so Patti didn't have to worry anymore that they would run out of food. And she had her feet up and a bottle of chilled champagne to drink. Life was good.

As she watched J.T. joking around with all the kids who were trying to impress him, Patti thought about how glad she was he had walked into her kitchen, and how much he was adding to her enjoyment of life lately. She decided, as she caught his eye and he smiled back at her, that life was possibly going to be even better in the very near future.

Ten

There were so many bills to pay, and so many itemized lists to justify with receipts, Patti spent most of the week after the wedding doing what she hated the most: the paperwork. She knew Tegan would be happy to help her with it, but she felt doing it was a part of her wedding present to her partner. Since she was not spending any time soliciting business, she was surprised and delighted to find she got a few calls about doing birthday parties for some of the local kids. She even got a call asking her to do a retirement party for the father of one of the women in her playgroup. So almost the entire month of October was booked by Patti, with at least one party a week, while Tegan was still on her honeymoon. The only week Patti turned down a party was the last week of October, since her fortieth birthday was on the twenty-ninth and she wasn't about to risk having to work on her own big day.

When Tegan and Alexander returned from their honeymoon, they were positively glowing with happiness. It wasn't long before Patti felt she had to remind her partner they still had work to do together that didn't involve Tegan's new husband.

"Hey, what do you expect?" Tegan asked her when Patti remarked on her lack of interest in their upcoming parties. "I'm a new bride, seven months pregnant, both of my kids are acting up to show Alex they can take my attention away from him any time they want to, and I'm trying to plan a big, secret, surprise party for my best friend's fortieth birthday, but she's so busy nagging at me to help her with other parties she committed us to when I was gone, she isn't giving me the time to plan the party of a lifetime, which is what she so richly deserves after the fortieth birthday party *she* threw for me earlier this year!" Tegan stopped to breathe.

Somewhat mollified, Patti remarked, "You know I'll be happy with whatever you plan. Even if you just do what I did, and take me out to The Party House for food and drinks. Not that *you'll* be able to do any drinking, but for once, I'll know I have a secure ride home with my own personal designated driver."

Looking at Patti closely, Tegan asked, "Are you sure? I mean; I lots of ideas for super-colossal merry-making when I realized I would have to repay *you* for my party. But I never figured I'd be almost eight months pregnant and unable to drink you under the table to celebrate. It kind of cuts down on my options...for instance, limbo-dancing is now out of the question. So is bar-hopping downtown, since even if I drink only cokes, I'd still be exposed to all that sugar and it would be *so* unhealthy for the baby. He'd probably start playing soccer with my belly button again, from the sugar-buzz and the loud music he'd be hearing. He's a party-boy, all right, and he hasn't even been born yet. He's going to be a whole lot of trouble when *he* gets older. Alex says *he* was trouble, too, so he'll know how to handle it. But still…I don't want to disappoint you. Can I save the really *huge* party for next year? Or whenever I'm fixed and no longer nursing anyone, so we can *really* party down? Like maybe for your forty-fifth birthday?"

Patti smiled, then hugged her best friend. "Yes, I can wait for the big boffo party until you stop popping out Alex's babies. And really, dinner and drinks, as long as you and the girls from the neighborhood are there, is a good enough party for me."

Tegan smirked at Patti, "Since J.T. is a bouncer at The Party House, maybe I can ask him to be your personal bodyguard for your birthday? I mean, he'll have to pay *close* attention to your body, because the best way to keep other guys from making passes at you is you being too busy clinching with a big, hairy, tattooed biker to even notice they are there, right?"

Patti sighed dramatically, "I don't know about that. I know he's the man of my dreams these days. Sometimes I can feel him watching me and I think he's interested. Other times, he acts like we are just friends, or boss and employee, so I never know what to think. Just make sure no guys start trying to feed me shots, like what happened to you, and I'll be okay. There's no Alex to ride to the rescue for me, and even though my kids are more open-minded than your Katie; even they would draw the line at mom bringing home a bunch of guys to celebrate with."

Tegan rolled her eyes, and they both laughed. They got back to discussing business and the parties they would be running for the rest of the month.

Eleven

For his part, J.T. was enjoying every chance he got to work with Patti in the kitchen. Without ever discussing it, they both realized that for them, cooking and eating food together was a way to express inner emotions. When Patti had learned J.T. was a passable carpenter also, she had enlisted him to help her work on the restaurant part of the storefront. They would spend time putting up drywall or painting walls, then cook for each other afterwards, eating in the back kitchen. Gradually, they were learning each other's recipes and sharing food acted as an aphrodisiac for both of them.

J.T. had initially been attracted to Patti's physical looks, since she was everything he looked for in a woman: much shorter than him, with womanly curves that made his mouth water. But her naughty sense of humor let him know that as much as he was spending an inordinate amount of time fantasizing about having sex in many different ways with her, Patti was doing the same thing. Her wry, self-deprecating sense of humor had been the final note in convincing him he couldn't possibly leave town without taking this woman to bed. But wary of the employer-employee dynamics, J.T. was ready to take as much time as needed to make Patti feel comfortable with the idea. As the days passed, he found himself hoping she wouldn't take *too* long letting him know she was ready. Always the gentleman, he was prepared to wait her out, but gentleman or not, it had been a *really* long time for him and his patience wasn't going to last forever.

When Patti had mentioned her birthday party was going to be at The Party House two nights before Halloween, J.T. had decided to ask for that Thursday night off so he could be there as a guest and not as a bouncer. But the manager had explained to him the entire week before Halloween was one of the busiest weeks of the year for him, and *no one* was allowed to take off during that time. There was money to be made and people to keep in line, and J.T. had to plan to work every night. With a sigh, J.T. resigned himself to waiting a little bit longer to let Patti know how he felt about her.

~ * ~

Patti dressed for her party, knowing J.T. was going to be there, but working and not as a guest. She wanted to look sexy, but not too much, so other guys in the bar would leave her alone. She also wanted to be comfortable, so she chose black gauchos and an orange cammie, in honor of Halloween week's colors. She decided to wear a see-through black blouse over the cammie, and as a joke, she used one of the fake tattoos that came with the costume make-up kit her son Jake had bought, to make it look like she had really done something wild and crazy in honor of her fortieth birthday.

She had hustled the kids over to Tegan's house, since they were going to spend the night there, with Alexander promising to treat them to a horror-show of movies he rented from the local video store, all hand-chosen by Katie and Kevin. When she saw what movies they were planning on watching, Patti rolled her eyes, and said, "Just so you know, if they wake up with nightmares anytime in the near future, I'm going to feel free to call you no matter what time of night it is, to thank you for showing them all of this crap!"

Alexander laughed, and said, "Hey, I watched all kinds of junk like this when I was their age and it never did me any harm!" Then he grabbed at Tegan, who had just been walking by him, growled and pretended to bite her neck.

Patti rolled her eyes and said, "Let's just get out of here and go party, okay? Before he convinces you to stay with him, and I have to drive myself home."

Tegan peeled herself free from her husband and said, "Not a chance, girl. We have to go celebrate your joining me in old age. You are now officially on *this* side of the hill, and the ride for the rest of the way is going to move faster. Us oldsters have to stick together. So let's get going, gum some food while you drink away your troubles and I jealously watch you, then drive you safely home."

When they were on their way out to the car, Tegan smiled at Patti and said, "Oh, by the way, nice cleavage. Is that for J.T.'s sake? Or just a defiant move to let old age know you won't 'go quietly into the night'?"

Patti smiled back, "Girl, you know I have cleavage even in a turtleneck. I just wanted to show a little skin…

and this!" With that, she theatrically pulled off the shirt on the one side, to show off the fake tattoo.

Tegan looked closely, "That's not real, is it?"

Patti shook her head, "No, but I am thinking about getting a real one. This is a test drive, if you will."

Tegan shook her head, "First cleavage in public...looks like you're wearing a wonder-bra."

Patti shook her head, smiling.

"Fine, you have such big boobs you don't need one. But first this huge expanse of cleavage, that even being eight months pregnant I can't compete with. Then a fake tattoo, to prepare you for a real one? What is happening to my innocent, sweet, best friend Patti?"

Patti snorted as they both laughed. "Innocent? In your dreams! Not since I was seventeen and gave it away in the back seat of a Chevy with a cutie named Bob. Sweet? Maybe to a vampire due to high blood sugar from all of the carbs I eat all of the time. But best friend? You betcha! Now let's get to where my presents are, and start celebrating. Par-tay! Par-tay!"

Twelve

Just as the manager had said, J.T. found the entire week had been a busy one at The Party House. Thursday, two nights before Halloween, was the worst one yet. In fact, he was so busy checking ID's and making sure customers looking to be over-served knew he was watching them, he almost missed Tegan and Patti walking in. He had seen when Juanita and some of the other neighborhood women he had met at Tegan's wedding arrived. But he was in the middle of an argument with a man trying to sneak his under-age girlfriend into the bar area when Patti tapped his arm. He turned to see her and promptly forgot what he was in the middle of saying.

"Black suits you well, boss," was all he could think of to say, when what he really wanted to do was grab her, kiss her and drag her off somewhere to tear off all of her clothing and help her celebrate her birthday with a bang.

Patti smiled at him, saying, "It's too bad you have to work tonight. I'd like to see what other kinds of dancing you do, since you were such a live wire doing the polka. Not that I expect to hear a polka in here, but I'm sure I'll be feeling like dancing after a few drinks."

J.T. smiled ruefully, "Well then, I'll just have to take you out dancing some other time, and we can celebrate your birthday together then. How about that?"

Patti nodded and smiled. At that moment, Tegan returned and grabbed her hand to pull her over to where their other friends were sitting with a pile of gifts on the table and balloons tied to the chairs.

"Come on, birthday girl. We have some serious partying to do and we can't get started without the guest of honor. Yak with the big, tall and hairy one some other time. Now's the time for eating, drinking and making whoopee!"

After that, J.T. only got to see glimpses of Patti while she enjoyed being roasted by her girlfriends and laughing at the outrageous gifts they had gotten for her. Many gave her gag gifts, like reading glasses, a cane and vitamins for senior citizens, along with a gift card to buy things for herself she would *really* like.

After enough time had passed, and with enough alcohol consumed, Patti did indeed start dancing. At first she danced only with her girlfriends. Then a few guys asked her to dance and J.T. had to swallow his jealousy watching other men trying to make a pass at Patti, while he had to stay at his post at the door. When the time came for shift change, he was partly relieved he wouldn't have to keep watching Patti dance with other men and partly annoyed he wouldn't be able to keep an eye on her and be sure the more ardent among the dancers kept their hands where they belonged. With a sigh, he went back outside to card the crowd of people who expected their costumes and make-up would make them look old enough to get in, even when the guys obviously weren't even shaving yet

By the time J.T. got rotated back into the room again, it was after eleven and less than an hour until closing time. The first thing he did was look for Patti and he was very unhappy to see her dirty dancing with a smarmy-looking sleaze-ball. He looked like the kind of guy who would proposition every woman in the place in hopes that one of them would say "yes," and it really wouldn't matter to him which one agreed, since all he wanted was "a" woman and he didn't care "who" she was. J.T. tried to focus on everyone else in the room, but his eyes kept returning to the woman he had such hopes for. He felt his anger and jealousy build as he saw the man groping Patti in places he had not yet worked up the nerve to try to touch.

He was watching the unpleasant scene so intently, he jumped when he felt a hand on his arm. It was Tegan.

"Can't you stop that?" she said, inclining her head in the direction he had been staring.

"Stop what?" he asked. "She seems to be having a good time. I work here. And I work for her. I don't think it's my place to interfere in her party."

"She's *not* having a good time," Tegan hissed. "She must be drunk or high or something. I wouldn't put it past him to have slipped something into her drink."

J.T. looked quickly at Tegan and asked, "Why?"

Understanding crossed Tegan's face, "You don't know *who* he is, do you?"

J.T. shook his head.

"That's Jake the Snake, the asshole who made her life a living hell for so long."

"That's her ex?" J.T. asked in surprise. "I thought he spent all of his time telling her she was too fat to be sexy." He looked more closely at them now. "He seems to have changed his mind about her, for now anyway."

"That's what I can't figure out," said Tegan. "I don't know what his game is, but he must be planning something. What's really bothering me is why she's letting him get away with it. She hates his guts. Why is she letting him touch her?"

"I've got an idea. I'll be right back," J.T. left his post for a minute, conferred with the bartender, then returned with an angry look on his face.

"I was right. The first drink he bought her was a triple, and he's been feeding her doubles ever since then. Has she been letting him get her drinks?"

Tegan nodded sadly, "Yes. He told her the first one was his present to her for her birthday, the cheap-ass. Then he asked her to dance and he's been all over her since. She was talking to all of us gals for a while, but he's been monopolizing her since forever, and I'm worried he's going to get her to let him take her home."

J.T. shrugged, "Well, he *is* her ex. I don't like the idea any more than you do, but if that's what she wants to do, she's a big girl."

Tegan shook her head, "You really don't get it, do you? She may be horny, but she's not crazy. If she wakes up next to him in the morning, you are going to hear the screaming all the way across town in your apartment. It'll be deafening in my house. Then I'll get a call a little while later, asking me to come and bail her ass out of jail, when he's found with one of her fancy butcher knives sticking out of his heart."

Tegan paused dramatically, "Then, when I get her out of the slammer, she's going to beat the shit out of me, pregnant or not, for being the sober one who allowed her to be so stupid as to take him home with her. This is a disaster in the making and we have to do something to stop it. Now do you understand?"

J.T. nodded, "But what?"

Tegan nodded her head towards Patti, "You're a bouncer here. Can't you just throw him out? For being excessively obnoxious and slimy? For pawing the birthday girl? For anything?"

J.T. shook his head, "Not and expect to still have a job here tomorrow, after he calls and complains to the boss."

At Tegan's exasperated look, he frowned, "Honestly, Tegan, if I threw every guy out of here who was desperately pawing a female after getting her drunk in order to spend the night with her, there'd be no one left in the bar. No one with a penis, anyway, except me and a couple of bartenders." He sighed. "I agree with you we need to do something, but I'm just not sure what we *can* do."

Tegan gave him a speculative look. "It's close to closing time? How close?"

J.T. looked at his watch, "It's eleven-forty. We close at midnight. They will be announcing it's time to go home in about five minutes. It usually takes at least fifteen minutes to clear everyone out."

Tegan nodded, "Then I'm going to go get her now, and do what she did to me last year."

At J.T.'s questioning look, she continued, "I'm going to tell her she has to come into the bathroom with me. Then I'm going to pretend I'm dizzy or something, anything to get her to stay in there with me. In the meantime, you clear everyone out, and I *do* mean *everyone*! Make sure the Snake leaves. Tell him he has to go. Tell him I took Patti out the back door. Tell him anything you can think of. But get him out of here!"

J.T. nodded.

"Once everyone else is gone, we can come out, gather up all of her presents and I'll drive her home. Only thing is, if she passes out in the car, I won't be able to get her into her house. Plus I'll be worried the Snake might be waiting outside of her house for me to bring her home. Can you ride in the car with us? Then help me get her into her house?"

J.T. nodded again, "But won't he just be able to get her to let him in once we leave?"

Tegan shook her head, "He doesn't have a key anymore. And she'll *never* let him into her house once the spell is broken. I'm hoping once she's home, she'll realize she doesn't want *him* in there. Or she'll pass out. Either way, we'll have saved her from a fate worse than death."

J.T. smiled now. "Okay, Tegan. You do your part and I'll do mine. I'll watch from here, to be sure he doesn't try to stop you. Just be sure you keep her in there until midnight. I don't want him complaining I hustled him out of the door early. But once it's midnight, I'm being paid to be sure the place is empty and they don't care *how* I do it."

J.T. watched as Tegan slowly walked over to the table where Patti was being mauled by her ex-husband, and saw Tegan's whole demeanor change once she was close enough for them to see her. Dramatically she grabbed her belly and swayed, holding onto the back of Patti's chair with her other hand. J.T. was too far away, and the noise level was too loud, for him to hear what was being said, but the instant Patti saw the look on Tegan's face, she solicitously jumped up and held Tegan's arm, while she staggered towards the ladies room. J.T. smiled in appreciation of Tegan's performance and enjoyed the look of displeasure on Jake's face as he watched the two women walk away from him.

At that instant, the lights blinked off and on twice and the sound system went dead, as the manager's voice said, "It is now eleven-forty-five and we will be closing in fifteen minutes. We ask that you please finish your drinks and head out to your cars. Please ask us to call you a cab if you don't feel able to drive home safely. Designated drivers can ask for a coupon for a free appetizer during your next visit here. We hope you all have a safe journey home and hope to see you here again soon. Don't forget the next two nights' Halloween parties… no cover charge for anyone in costume. And closing time is one a.m. on Friday and Saturday nights. Y'all come on back soon, ya hear?"

Amid the shuffling of guests out of the doors, J.T. managed to keep an eye firmly fixed on Jake, who sat at his table and waited. He drummed his fingers on the table. He lit another cigarette. And he waited. So did J.T.

When it was two minutes before midnight, and Jake was the last person still sitting down, not moving to leave, J.T. walked into the seating area and tapped him on the shoulder. "Time to leave, mister. You have to be out of here in two minutes. You should get moving now."

Jake glared at him, "I'm waiting for someone to get back out of the ladies' room. I'll leave when I'm good and ready."

J.T. inclined his head in the direction of the rest rooms, "If you mean the gal you were dancing with, she and the pregnant one left out the back door already. They asked me to collect the gifts and keep them here until they come back for them."

Jake bristled in his anger, "Did they say anything about me?"

J.T. couldn't stop his lips from smiling, "Hey, man, you don't want to hear what they said about you. You just need to get going, now."

Jake stood up now, and despite being a half-foot shorter than J.T., looked like he was about to pick a fight. The manager appeared behind J.T., and asked, "Is there anything wrong here?"

Jake angrily pointed at J.T. "This big ape of yours says the woman I was waiting for already left. I think he's lying."

The manager looked at Jake coldly, then said, "I don't think so. And it's closing time. You need to vacate the premises or I'm going to have to have you removed."

J.T. nodded, "And I'm just the big ape who will do it."

Jake looked from one to the other of the larger men, and decided to abandon the fight. He shrugged, slammed his drink glass down on the table so hard it cracked the glass, then he turned and angrily strode out of the door.

The manager turned to J.T. "Well?"

J.T. said, "The woman he was waiting for is taking care of her very pregnant friend in the ladies room. They didn't want him to be here when they got out. These are her presents, since it was her birthday. You know how some guys are; they won't take no for an answer."

The manager nodded. "Fine. I take it you will walk them out? To be sure he's not out there waiting for them?"

J.T. nodded. "I'll take them out the side door, okay?"

The manager nodded, then moved over to the bar to confer with the bartenders and close the registers.

J.T. went over to the ladies room door and knocked on it. Then he poked his head in the door and asked, "Are you two all right in here?"

Upon seeing him, Patti got up from where she was sitting on the couch next to Tegan, and said, "I'm feeling a whole lot better now you're here. Want to dance with me, big guy?"

Tegan rolled her eyes, and J.T. smiled, both at her over Patti's head, and at Patti herself, who was sashaying up to him, provocatively swaying her hips.

"Nah, not tonight, boss. It's closing time, and I'm going to escort you two ladies home. Tegan said you got a lot of presents and you might need some help getting all your stuff home. So I'm going to ride home with you and help you get it inside your house. Then I'll get a ride from her back to my Harley."

Patti draped herself on J.T., saying, "Why don't you just give me a ride back home on your hog, big boy? I'd love to feel your engine between my legs."

Despite an instant hard-on that threatened to split his jeans open, J.T. forced himself to remember the condition Patti was in: so drunk she had been in danger of allowing her hated ex-husband to go home with her. So he put his arm around her and helped her to walk back into the bar area, with Tegan following behind them.

Once in the bar he said, "But you need to get all of your gifts home. I'm not taking the chance you'll pass out and fall off the back of my bike. After all, honey, you're not wearing one of those biker shirts that tells people if they can read the shirt, you've fallen off the bike, and they should put you back on it. We don't want to lose you on the way home."

Grousing slightly, Patti tried to help gather up her presents, but J.T. grabbed most of them and Tegan got the rest. Patti even gave her purse to Tegan. They walked over to the side door with J.T. in the lead, followed by Patti then Tegan. Once outside, Tegan said, "Wait here; I'll go get the car."

Patti used that opportunity to press herself against the front of J.T., whose hands were busy holding bags of presents. "*Oooh*, you smell so good! Can I open your shirt and see your tattoos again? Did you see mine?"

With that, Patti leaned back and pulled her shirt off the side with the fake tattoo and the strap from her cammie went down. J.T. almost stopped breathing at the sight of more of the breasts he had been fantasizing about for months. Patti now leaned back close to him again and slurred, "I'm thinking about getting a real tattoo. Don't you think it would look good on me?"

J.T. nodded slowly and was considering dropping the packages and crushing Patti to him, when Tegan drove up, parked the car right next to them then hopped out of the driver's door.

They got the presents into one side of the back seat of the car. Patti slid into the back seat, patted the tiny space left next to her, and looked meaningfully at J.T. He shook his head and laughed, "I'm afraid not, boss. There's no leg room back there, and if I tried to get in, I'd probably never be able to get out. I'll have to ride up front with Tegan." He slammed the door shut and got into the front seat.

"Suit yourself," said Patti, who asked Tegan to put the CD they had been listening to on the way to the party back in and turn it up. She then began to sing lustily along with the music, and J.T. and Tegan smiled at each other as they drove the short distance to Patti's house, listening to her rendition of some of her favorite songs at the top of her voice. They stopped at a light a couple of blocks from their destination and Tegan poked J.T. and pointed to the back seat. He turned around to see Patti's eyes were closed and she resembled a rag doll, slumped over on her presents.

J.T. smiled. "At least she's not singing anymore," he said conversationally.

Tegan nodded, "But you are going to have to get her into her house. It doesn't look like she's going to be able to walk in...at least, not without someone holding her up."

J.T. nodded. "No problem."

Tegan smiled. "You don't think there's going to be a problem? Then you've never seen Patti drunk before. Hold onto your belt buckle, because she's probably going to try to get your pants off the minute you're in her room."

J.T. looked quickly at Tegan, "Why? We don't have that kind of relationship."

Tegan looked at him closely, "*Duh*! And why not? She's been hot for your ass since she met you. Are you gay?"

It was such an unexpected question J.T. laughed despite himself. "Uh, no. I've been trying to wait for a good time, but either we're busy working on food together, or her kids are around, or something else comes up. Believe me; I'm not any happier than she is that we haven't gotten around to it yet."

Tegan nodded. "Well, don't keep on waiting forever. She's even talked about firing you if her being your boss was stopping you."

J.T. nodded, too. "Thanks for the heads up."

Tegan swung into Patti's driveway and parked the car up next to the garage door. J.T. got out and opened the back door to slide Patti closer to him across the seat. Tegan grabbed the bags of presents, then proceeded to use Patti's key to open the front door. She went in and put the presents on the floor by the front door, then held the door open for J.T., who was carrying the semi-conscious birthday girl through the door.

He turned to Tegan expectantly, and when she just looked at him questioningly, he asked, "Bedroom?"

Tegan smiled, "Oh, I forgot you haven't been in here before. Her bedroom is that way, down the hall and to the right of the kitchen. Do you want me to lead the way and turn on the lights?"

J.T. shook his head, "No, but I think you should drive home and get Alexander to come back to give me a ride to my Harley. You're too pregnant to be out so late at night. You need your rest. Go on now and I'll get her to bed, then go wait out on the front stoop for him."

Tegan smiled again, "Okay, J.T. Thanks for your help. You know you really are a gentleman. Your mother should be proud. See you later."

J.T. grunted as he shifted Patti's weight around and carried her through the darkened rooms, down the hall and into her bedroom. He was able to see where the bed was from the light of the moon coming through the open blinds. He carefully placed her onto the bed, then looked around for a lamp. Instead, he saw the door to the master bathroom, reached in and found the flipped on the light switch. He turned around to tuck Patti into bed.

As he pulled the covers back, moving her around to do so, Patti opened her eyes and smiled at him broadly.

"Hey, big guy. Are you finally going to stay the night with me?"

J.T. smiled at her and shook his head, "Not tonight, honey. I'm just tucking you into bed, then heading back for my Harley."

Patti made a face at him. "But it's my birthday! Don't I get to have what I want for my birthday?"

When J.T shook his head again, Patti suddenly looked sad and vulnerable and asked, "Why not? Don't you want me? Am I too old? Too fat?"

J.T. inwardly cursed the man who had torn her self-confidence to shreds during their marriage. He sat on the side of her bed and caressed her face with his right hand, while he took her hand in his left hand.

"No, Patricia. You are just right to me. You are everything I want. I've wanted you since the first time I walked into your place."

When she tried to interrupt him, he placed a finger on her lips and continued, "But I want our first time to be something *both* of us can remember. I fully expect it to be better than anything I can even imagine."

He shuddered, almost losing his control, when she licked, then sucked on his finger.

"I'll remember it, honest I will!" she protested.

J.T. shook his head. "No, you won't. Honey, you were almost ready to let your ex-husband come home with you. That asshole was feeding you doubles all night. That's why you passed out in the back seat of Tegan's car on the drive home."

Patti's eyes widened. "I did? Jake was there? I vaguely remember seeing him."

J.T. smiled, realizing how little attention she had been paying to the man he had been so jealous of.

"But really, Jules. If I don't remember, we can do it all over again in the morning and I guarantee I'll remember that!"

J.T. shook his head again, "No, Patricia. Not tonight. But soon, *really* soon. I'm going to take you out dancing, then keep you up all night afterwards, until I've had my fill of pleasuring you in as many ways as I can think of."

Patti closed her eyes and sighed in anticipation. "Are you sure I can't talk you into it tonight?"

J.T. smiled, "Patricia, you'd be passed out before we even got naked."

Patti smiled at him, her eyes barely open, "You'd be surprised just how quickly I can get naked when I want to!"

J.T. tucked the covers in around her and got up with a long sigh. As he turned to head out of the room, Patti asked, "Can you do me one more favor then, before you go?"

J.T. stopped and turned to look at her, "What?

"Can you get me a can of coke and a glass of ice cubes? That always settles my stomach; and I have a feeling I'm going to be *really* thirsty when I wake up."

J.T. smiled and went out in search of the kitchen. He found the coke in the fridge and a glass in the cabinet next to it. He got the ice cubes into the glass, then returned to Patti's room.

As he entered the room, Patti appeared to be already asleep. He put the glass and the can on the nightstand next to the bed and turned to leave once again.

He put his hand on the doorknob, then was surprised when he heard Patti say, "Oh, Jules?"

He turned and stopped breathing. No, all of the oxygen left the room. He could hear and feel all of the blood in his body rushing down to the one part of his body that least needed more blood.

Patti had thrown off the covers to reveal she had stripped while he was gone and she lay there naked, her hands moving slowly around on her ample curves.

"Jules," she crooned, "are you absolutely positive you won't stay?"

Summoning every ounce of will he had, J.T. forced himself to shake his head, despite the magnetic force from her naked body that drew his every body part to want him to throw himself on top of her and take her as she was asking him to do.

"My mother raised me to respect women," he began, "Not to take advantage of ones who have had too much to drink. Especially a woman I respect so much, no matter how much I want her."

Patti sighed, "Okay, Jules. Good night. And remind me to let your mother know just what I think of how she raised her boy if I ever get to meet her."

Reluctantly, J.T. walked out of the door and closed it behind him, then rested his forehead on the door. His inner struggle raged. His mother's words told him to walk out of the house, that he was doing the right thing. But his own body threatened to take the choice away from him and urged him to go back into the bedroom to take what he wanted so badly from the woman in there that he was choking on the taste of his own desires.

He was taking deep cleansing breaths, sucking oxygen deeply into his lungs, trying to relearn how to breathe, but his hand was moving of its own volition to the door knob, when he heard the car horn beep twice from the driveway. Partly relieved and partly irritated, he realized Alexander must be in the driveway waiting to give him a ride back to his bike. He shook his head and realized the choice had been taken away from him. He poked his head back into the bedroom to say "Goodnight," and heard the gentle snoring coming from the bed. That let him know he had been right. She would have passed out on him...he had made the right choice.

With a long sigh, he said quietly, "Soon, Patricia. *really* soon! That's a promise!"

He walked out of the house, locking the door from the inside, then pulling it shut. He got into the waiting car and sat looking straight ahead of him for a minute. Alexander smiled as he started backing out of the driveway.

"Yeah, Tegan said you'd probably have a rough time getting out of there," he said conversationally.

J.T. sighed, "Just drive me back to my bike. Then I'm gonna take a long ride along a highway somewhere, and try to convince myself leaving was the right thing to do."

Alexander nodded. "Sometimes it's really hard to know when to leave them alone. But if it's meant to be, well then...." He drove in silence for a while, then said, "For what it's worth, everyone who knows and loves Patti is rooting for you. She's a whole lot of woman, with a personality as large as her heart, but I think you can handle it. Your leaving her alone tonight just supports my opinion of you. She hasn't been treated very well by the men in her life. I think you two will be good together. And that's all I'm going to say."

Alexander pulled his car up next to J.T.'s Harley. As J.T. got out of the car, he asked. "Are you sure you don't want to take the bike for a ride and let me try out your car?"

Alexander shook his head and smiled, "Let's wait until after Tegan has the baby. Then, from what I've read, she will be so mellow from the nursing hormones she won't get so angry if I take you up on your offer. Deal?"

J.T. smiled and nodded, "Yeah, man, deal. And thanks for the ride."

Alexander nodded back, "Anytime. Good night."

After he watched the car drive away, J.T. looked up at the moon and the stars in the sky. "Lord, I want that woman so bad. Let me have this one, at least for a little while, please?" Then after his impromptu prayer, he climbed onto his bike, revved the engine and rode off to find a stretch of highway to soothe his soul.

Thirteen

The next morning, Patti woke up late with a king-sized hangover and a parched throat. She was glad to see a half-drunk glass of coke next to her bed and marveled at her own foresight in bringing it into the room with her. She opened the drawer of her nightstand, took out a couple aspirins and downed them with the coke. She lay back down and moaned for a while. When she was able to sit up without feeling nauseous, she staggered into her kitchen and got another can of coke out of the fridge. Food was not a possibility yet, so she sat down at her kitchen table and put her head down on the table to stop the nausea that once again threatened her. She picked up her phone and called Tegan.

"Hello?" Tegan said when she answered the phone.

"Did the kids get off to school all right?" Patti said, noticing her tongue was lumping in her mouth, making her a bit hard to understand.

"Hey, Patti! How are ya doing, partner?" Tegan asked brightly, sounding more amused than she should be.

"Don't take pleasure in my pain. Be merciful and speak a little quieter, okay?" Patti managed to say, before she had to take another long drink of coke to wet her throat and enable her to continue speaking.

"Okay, *is this better now*?" Tegan laughed.

"*Ow*! I'm not sure what hurts more…talking loudly, or listening to it," Patti moaned.

"To answer your question, yes, the kids got off to school on time. I even fed them breakfast, though boxed cereal isn't really all that hard to serve," Tegan chuckled. "But I did cut up some fruit for them, so everyone got a big dose of antioxidants this morning. Do you want me to bring you over some of the leftover fruit salad? Or are you too nauseated to even think about eating?"

"Come on over," Patti managed to say, "I may be passed out on the kitchen table when you get here. Come to the back door, and if you knock loudly enough, I'll probably hear you."

"Coffee?" Asked Tegan.

"Are you trying to make me barf?" Patti whined. "Just the fruit salad."

"See ya in a few," Tegan said, then she hung up the phone.

Patti laid her head down on the table again and immediately fell asleep. She was wakened a few minutes later by the loud pounding of her head…no, it was the loud pounding at the back door. She staggered over to the door and let Tegan in, then fell back into her chair. She stared ashen-faced as Tegan carried a serving dish into the kitchen, found a couple of bowls and spoons and ladled out some fruit. Tegan turned to carry the bowls over to the table, sat across from her and started to eat her fruit salad.

"So," Tegan began conversationally, "How much do you remember of your party last night, old friend?"

"Not much," Patti replied, as she tried to quiet her stomach, which was not sure it approved of the smell of the fruit salad so close to her nose.

"Do you remember getting home?"

Patti shook her head, then closed her eyes from the pain.

Tegan continued, "Do you remember I had to ask J.T. to come with us, because I was afraid, and rightly so, you would pass out in my car and I wouldn't be able to get you in the house by myself?"

"No," Patti said, putting a single tiny piece of cantaloupe in her mouth and sucking on it. "About the last thing I remember is opening my presents. Then I was dancing for a while with you gals and with some guys who asked me. They kept trying to grope me and I kept hitting hands away. Sheesh! You'd think they'd treat a forty-year-old woman with more respect, wouldn't you?"

Tegan smiled, "Well, one of them treated you with lots of respect, even though you pushed him to the limits!"

Patti looked puzzled. "Who?"

Tegan smiled tauntingly. "Well, it wasn't the snake, that's for sure. He was major-ly disrespectful! You *do* remember he was there, don't you?"

Patti made a face, "Who told him my party would be there? Or did he just figure it out and crash it? I vaguely remember him being there and buying me a couple of drinks. Then he danced with me. I blew him off, right?"

When Tegan shook her head, smiling even more broadly, Patti moaned. "Oh, God, tell me I didn't let him touch me, please!"

Tegan nodded, smiling even more widely.

Patti put her head in her hands and moaned again, "I thought it was just a terrible dream…a nightmare! Whatever possessed me to allow that asshole to touch me and in public yet?" Patti looked up hopefully, "Was I legally insane?"

Tegan smirked now, "No. But you *were* legally intoxicated. In fact, he was the one who got you so drunk. Every twinge, every pain, every bit of nausea you feel right now, you can blame on the snake. He bought you a triple for your birthday present, then followed that up with doubles all night long. He said he knew what you liked, better than we did when we tried to object. And of course, the drunker you got, the more you agreed with him. When he started to make moves on you and we objected; he told us to piss off, then he got serious about groping you."

"I'm going to kill him the next time I see that smarmy, slimy son-of a bitch!" Patti said, gritting her teeth from the pain and the effort of speaking.

"No, don't," Tegan said conversationally. "I'd just have to come and bail you out of jail. In fact, that's how I convinced J.T. to help me get you away from the sleaze-ball you used to be married to."

"How?" Patti asked, putting another piece of cantaloupe into her mouth and chewing slowly.

Tegan smiled, "He didn't know *who* was groping you, but he was mightily upset, let me tell you. There was so much smoke coming from his ears as he watched you being groped, he almost didn't hear me start to talk to him. I asked him to help me rescue you, and he said he figured he shouldn't interfere. You appeared to be having a good time, and it was your birthday, after all. Once I explained it was the snake who was touching you, he found out from the bartenders about the mickies you were being slipped. He helped me plan your escape. I told him if he didn't, the whole town would hear you screaming this morning when you woke up with the snake next to you. I'd soon get a call to come and bail you out of jail when you stuck a butcher knife into his conniving heart."

Patti was continuing to eat, but the action of chewing was painful, so she chewed slowly as she listened.

Tegan warmed to her subject. "I faked having pains in my abdomen and got you to come with me to the ladies room." She leaned over and patted her friend's hand. "Even drunk, darling, you were concerned about me. That's so sweet of you. Anyway, I dragged you into the bathroom with me and made you sit with me on the couch. I heard the announcement for the place closing, but you didn't. You were too busy complaining that J.T. hadn't tried to have sex with you yet. You seemed to have forgotten all about the snake out there waiting to pounce on you again. Once the place was emptied, J.T. stuck his head into the bathroom and let us know it was time to come out. He carried your presents to the car; then you passed out on the drive to your house."

"So he had to carry me in?" Patti asked, horrified. "I must weigh a ton! The poor guy! I hope he didn't get a hernia."

Tegan chuckled, "He didn't seem to mind. I left your presents on the floor by the front door and took the car home. At J.T.'s suggestion, I sent Alex back to give him a ride back to his Harley at the bar." Tegan leaned over conspiratorially, "He's such a gentleman. He was concerned about me being so pregnant and being out so late at night. What a nice guy!"

Patti made a face. "If he's such a nice guy, how come I woke up naked?"

Tegan smiled, "Alex said when he picked J.T. up, he looked pretty shook up. My guess is you propositioned the lad in a *big* way. I'm thinking you probably stripped to try to convince him to stay and have his way with you. But he took the ride from Alex, so chances are you didn't have time to do anything with him that you'd want to remember!"

Patti laid her head down on the table and moaned again. "Oh, God! Now, in addition to being embarrassed I let my ex touch me in front of my friends, I have to be humiliated by facing the guy I'm lusting for, knowing he knows how I feel about him."

Dramatically, she paused, then continued, "And to think I figured when I woke up, I couldn't possibly feel any worse than I did at that moment. Now I have to add abject humiliation to hungover. This day is just getting better and better by the moment. Next thing I know, you'll be telling me Jake Jr. had a camera in my bedroom and the whole town is going to know what a pathetic, horny housewife I am, lusting after my much-younger employee. Do me a favor and just kill me now, okay? If you love me, end my pain."

Patti jumped when the phone rang.

Tegan, closer to it, answered then smirked as she said, "No, she's right here. I'm sure she'll be glad to talk to you." She handed the phone to Patti.

"Hello?" Patti said.

"Hey boss, you doing okay this morning?" J.T. asked solicitously.

Patti fought her desire to slam the phone down, "Yes, thanks for your concern. And thanks for putting me to bed last night. Tegan has just been telling me how much of a big help you were to her. I don't remember anything after opening my presents, so I'm glad my friends took such good care of me."

There was silence for a heartbeat, then J.T. said, "Well, I'm going to head on over to your place to put another coat of primer on the drywall, okay, boss?"

"That's why I gave you your own key," Patti said. "Of course it's okay. If I'm feeling up for it, I may come in later today."

"Don't worry about a thing. I'll take care of the work that needs doing," J.T. said, "If you're still feeling too hung over to work, I'll be fine. You have been working like a dog. You needed a blow-out. You just rest, and I'll see you soon, Patti. Bye."

Patti hung up the phone and looked at Tegan, who was smiling.

"You could have told him I was still asleep or something."

"But who would have let me in, then? You're going to have to face him, sooner or later. Maybe now that he knows how you feel, he'll let you know how *he* feels."

At Patti's surprised look, Tegan smiled again, "He was awfully jealous of the snake, for being a guy who was just concerned about his employer. I'll bet he's just being the respectful guy he is, waiting until it's the right time for him to make his move. You're not used to being treated with respect. So that means he's waiting for you to let him know when the right time has arrived. I think the ball's in *your* court now."

Tegan got up and put her dishes into the sink. She put the rest of the fruit salad into Patti's fridge, then turned to say, "I'm gonna head home now. You need to get some more sleep. You look like hell and I'm sure you feel even worse than you look. Call me if you need anything from me to help you feel better."

Patti smiled weakly, "Okay. And thanks for everything."

Tegan smiled back at her, "And happy birthday again!"

After Tegan left, Patti slowly got up, leaving her bowl on the table, and made her way back to her bed. She snuggled under the covers and sighed. "J.T., you are the most frustrating man I have ever met. But the longer you make me wait, the more I plan to enjoy you."

She fell back asleep and didn't wake up again until she heard the kids get home from school.

Fourteen

Appetizers Lead to Ethnic and Exotic Main Course

Monday morning found Patti and J.T. in the front of the business building, painting the walls of the restaurant's dining room. They were working in companionable silence, much to Patti's relief, since she still was not sure how to approach the subject of her no-longer-secret attraction to her employee. Suddenly the front door was slammed open and Tegan burst in, marking up the wall that had already been painted with the first coat of color and almost knocking the nearest paint cans over.

"Patti! What the hell are you thinking? Are you even using the brains you were born with? Explain yourself, before I smack you upside your head to knock some sense into you!"

Patti looked instantly guilty and J.T. looked at Tegan then at Patti and said,

"Maybe I should take a break now, boss? This sounds like you two need to talk, maybe in private?"

Tegan shook her head, "Why? It concerns *you*, too. Or it should." She turned to glare at Patti.

"So?" shouted Tegan, "What do you have to say for yourself?"

Patti shrugged, "What is there to say?"

"So it's true then? What Chelsea said when I saw her waiting for Katie in front of their school?" Tegan kept glaring at Patti as if that would make her see the error of her ways.

"If it's my business, too," began J.T., "what *did* Chelsea say?"

Tegan continued to glare at Patti as she answered J.T. "She said that the snake moved back into the house over the weekend. She said he was supposed to pick them up for his weekend visitation, but he used some sob story about being tossed out of his apartment and needing a place to stay. She said you agreed to let him stay until he can save up some money. Are you *insane*?" This last she shouted in Patti's face, forcing her to move backwards to avoid Tegan's advance on her.

J.T. had been looking at Patti while Tegan spoke. He picked his paintbrush back up and began to assault the walls with it, painting with a vengeance as if he had to punish something for his feelings.

Patti spoke to Tegan, but looked alternately at her and J.T.'s back. "I had to do it. He had no place else to go. His last bimbo moved out and she was paying half the rent and bills. He couldn't afford to live there anymore, so the landlord tossed him out. He said he just needs a place to stay for a few weeks. I told him he had to be out before

December. He said he might have to stay through the holidays, but he'd be out by the beginning of January."

Tegan snorted, "And you believed him? For crying out loud, he's a lying scum! He just wants a home base to use so he can go out drinking and whoring again. He'll try to get you to take him back on the nights he can't get anyone else to let him in their bed…he's *not* in *your* bed, is he?"

"*No!*" Patti yelled, and J.T. looked up in surprise at her vehemence.

"Then where *is* he sleeping?" Tegan asked nastily. "On the floor next to your bed?"

"On the couch in the living room. I told him that was the only place he was welcome to sleep. I told him the kids need their rest and their space, so he has to be the one to sleep on the lumpy couch. He agreed and that's where he's spent the last couple of nights. I swear it." Patti said to Tegan while she looked into J.T.'s face as he had turned to watch her as she spoke. After a few seconds of looking into her eyes, he turned silently back to the wall he was painting.

Tegan sighed heavily. "Patti, Patti, Patti. What am I going to do with you? It took you forever to throw that cheating jerk out the first time. A leopard doesn't change its spots. He's just going to do the same thing to you again. I thought you had gained enough self-confidence so you wouldn't let him play you for a fool again. And now? I don't know what to think."

Patti sighed. "The kids wanted me to let him move in…well, Jake did, anyway. Chelsea isn't so crazy about the idea. But he asked me in front of them, since he had just told them he had to cancel their visit to his place because he didn't have a place anymore. Jake says we need to give his dad a chance to save up enough money so he can get a place by himself. Chelsea just rolled her eyes. As the older one, she's more aware of what a user her dad is."

Tegan sat down heavily on the nearest chair, "Well, at least the kids are home after school, so once he gets home from work, you will be chaperoned for most of the evening. I'd suggest you start going to bed really early and lock yourself in your bedroom. Like I told you, I'm not looking forward to that call from a jail cell when they find the snake with one of your expensive gourmet knives in his heart. But that would actually be preferable to finding out you let him talk you into giving him another chance. *Yuck!*" She made a face, "Promise me you won't do anything stupid like that or I won't be able to sleep at night!"

"I promise," Patti said solemnly.

Tegan continued, "I wonder if I can talk Alex into paying for a motel room for that jerk, so he can save his money without compromising *your* integrity?"

Patti shook her head, "No, this is *my* problem, not yours. It can't be solved with Alex's money or with anything anyone else can do. I'm the one who let him move in…temporarily. So I'll have to deal with it. I'm not charging him any rent and I really do expect him to be gone as soon as possible. Cut me some slack and give me credit for remembering what he put me through the last time. I don't intend to give him a second chance. Like the saying goes: 'Fool me once, shame on you. Fool me twice, shame on me.' I don't think it will take long on that couch before he will want to move out. At least that's my plan."

Tegan sighed heavily again, "I hope you're right." She shook her head. "And I hope you can stay strong, girl. Because I'm going to be too busy with the new baby to be much help to you, since I'm due the second week of December." Tegan continued, "Hey, since Alex won't be getting any after that, I can send him over to work out his frustration by kicking the crap out of the snake if you want me to. That's about all I can offer to you in the way of help."

Patti shook her head, "No, that won't be necessary. Like I said, this is my mess and I'm going to have to deal with it."

Tegan pushed herself to her feet. "I have to get going. I have my OB appointment in less than an hour. But I had to storm over here and yell at you first. At least if my blood pressure is high again, this time I'll know why."

Patti moved over to help Tegan maneuver around the paint cans and Tegan grabbed her for a big hug. "I hope you know what you are doing, girl. Just promise me you'll be careful and watch your back."

Patti smiled. "I'll watch my front, too. I don't trust him at all…but he *is* the father of my kids, so I feel I owe him a warm place to crash until he gets back on his feet. That's all there is to this. I promise."

Tegan turned as she went out the door, "Okay. But remember, I have my ways of finding out what's going on with you, even if you don't tell me the instant things happen!" She waved at J.T., "And bye, you good-looking hunk of biker-dude."

Patti closed the door behind Tegan, then turned to look at J.T., who was studiously applying paint to the wall in front of him.

"I'm really sorry you had to find out this way," she began.

J.T. shook his head as he turned to look at her.

"Why? There's no reason for you to tell me about your private life, is there?"

He looked seriously at her.

Patti nodded, "Yes, there is. I do remember enough from my birthday to know there's unfinished business between us. I feel ridiculous talking about it like this, but you already know how I feel about you, right?"

J.T. regarded her, his light blue eyes intent on her face. "Do I? I thought I did; but now, with your ex in your house again, I guess anything I might have been planning is going to have to be postponed indefinitely."

Patti looked miserably at him. "You're not going to leave town on me, are you? I mean, before we get a chance to find out what we'd be like together?"

J.T. carefully put his paintbrush down and walked over to stand in front of Patti. He was so tall, when she was wearing flats she didn't even come to his shoulders. She looked up expectantly at him and he put one finger under her chin and lifted her face up to look at him. Slowly he bent his face down and his lips lightly brushed hers. One kiss, another kiss, another...then with a groan, Patti melted against him and wound her arms up and around him, pressing herself against his hardness and feeling the danger and excitement of trying to control a man so much bigger than herself.

J.T. groaned too, and used one large hand to fondle her butt, pressing himself into her, so she could feel the length of the hardness she had been imagining for months. He moved his other hand up and down her curves; now holding a breast, now rubbing her hip, then he wound his fingers into her hair and used the two contact points of lips and groin to make her feel his desire. He moved his head slightly. His lips kissed along her face to her ear then to her neck. His tongue licked a trail along the curve of her face to her chin, then he kissed her once more. Reluctantly he moved away from her and smiled at the expectant look on her face.

"Nope," he said simply, then he turned to go back to his paintbrush.

Trying to catch her breath, Patti stammered, "Couldn't we have just a little taste right here? In my place? Just to take the edge off for both of us?"

J.T. shook his head. "No, Patricia. I told you on your birthday, I want our first time to be something special. Something we both will always remember. Better than what I have been imagining every night since I met you."

He smiled at the look of disappointment on her face, "Not that I haven't had my share of getting down and dirty in public places, but I don't want to be worrying about someone walking in on us until we get a chance to really enjoy each other. After that, I'll christen your restaurant with you, in the back kitchen and the front serving area, with and without customers being in the place. I don't care."

Patti sighed heavily, "But I can't ask you to stay over while Jake is in the house, can I?"

He shook his head, "No, I think that would be asking for trouble. He already won't like me because I was the guy to throw him out of the bar when he was trying to get you drunk enough to take him home with you. I don't want to have to worry about trying to keep one eye open if I happen to fall asleep in your bed."

Patti rolled her eyes, "Figures, I get the one biker in America who has high moral standards."

J.T. smiled again, "No, you got a Rom biker. We Romani are very morally straight people. We don't have much of a culture, but we do hold our religion very sacred and dear to us. We are superstitious and old-school in a lot of ways. I told you, my female relatives taught me to respect women at all times. I'll respect you right up to the first time you allow me to touch you; after that, you will belong to me. That's the way I am and that's the way it's got to be."

With a heavy sigh, he picked his paintbrush, saying, "So now, we have work to do. But don't get too close to me, okay? I'm trying very hard to control myself. If I have to smell you right under my nose too often, well…even I have my breaking point."

Patti smiled suggestively, "You won't be doing anything I'm not thinking about myself. But if that's the way you want to play it, I guess that's what we'll do. For now."

They resumed their painting, with only occasional brushes against each other, making them both shudder with barely-concealed desire. The sexually-charged atmosphere kept them at peak excitement and as Patti told Tegan later, "Honestly, I don't think I've ever felt so alive. So aware of every cell in my body being fully awake and expectant. I don't know how long his control is going to last, but if I have anything to say about it; it won't be too much longer. All I can think about is how his body felt while he was groping me. I was hot for him before…now I'm burning up!"

~ * ~

Despite Patti's attempts to get J.T. to lose his cool, the weeks before Thanksgiving passed uneventfully. True, they were both busy, since the restaurant had to be completely finished before the inspectors gave it the okay for them to open. They planned on opening right after the holidays, so they both worked during the school hours, occasionally being joined by an electrician or plumber. Patti would go home to feed her kids and to work with Tegan on the parties they were hired to plan and run. J.T. would go to his second job as a bouncer, which kept him busy at least four or five nights a week.

For his part, Jake was behaving himself, only occasionally staying out late at night and he agreed with Patti he didn't need a key of his own, since there was always someone, either Patti or the kids, home when he was. On the nights he did stumble home drunk late at night, Patti would let him in, then immediately go into her bedroom and lock the door. Three weeks flew by in a blur and only occasionally did Patti get the feeling Jake was regarding her speculatively, as if he was trying to figure out when he could make his move. Most of the time, he acted politely grateful for being allowed to be there. He even helped occasionally with the dishes.

The fact that life was rather routine was comforting in a way, but also aggravating, since Patti was anxious to have a chance to be alone with J.T. The only real glimpse she got of Jake's true feelings came when she told him, in addition to Tegan and her family, she had invited J.T. to join them for their traditional Thanksgiving dinner at her house.

"Why?" he had angrily asked her. "It's not like he's family or anything. He's just the hired help at your little restaurant thing. Why can't he go somewhere else? Where he's more welcome?"

Patti narrowed her eyes. "Excuse me? Where he's *more welcome*? He's always welcome in *my* house! Actually, more welcome than you are. Which reminds me, when are you moving out? How much money have you saved during the last three weeks?"

Jake shifted in his chair, finally answering, "Not nearly enough. I mean, I have some. But I need a big chunk of change to have first and last month's rent, so I can get a half-way decent place, close enough to be able to see the kids for visitation. You're just going to have to give me some more time."

He got up and slowly approached Patti, saying softly, "It hasn't been that bad, having me around, has it? I've been behaving myself, acting like a perfect gentleman, even though being this close to you all of the time is starting to get to me."

Jake leaned close to Patti and inhaled her hair, then said, "It was always good between us, wasn't it, Patti? Remember? We had some really good times, didn't we?"

Patti moved back quickly, saying, "You mean when we weren't fighting? Yeah, I guess I remember one or two times it was good. The rest of the time, when you even bothered to come home at night, you were usually too drunk to be any good in bed. And I've never been one to be happy with sloppy seconds, so no, I don't remember many really good times."

Jake made a grab for her and Patti stepped deftly out of his grasp. The door slammed open and Chelsea strode in, followed by her brother.

"Oh, did we interrupt anything?" Chelsea said, "I hope so."

Jake glared at his daughter, "What do you mean by that, young lady? And don't use that disrespectful tone with me!"

Chelsea did a major eye-roll, "Oh, puh-leeze! To get respect, you have to earn it, even when you are a parent. What have you done lately, besides force yourself in here, to sponge off my mother?"

Jake moved forward to hit her, but Patti was quicker and moved between them. "No, Jake. Leave her alone."

He glared at Patti. "Why? I'm still her dad. She's still a kid. She has no right to talk to me like that."

Patti stared him down. "She has every right. She's thirteen and growing into her own person. You may not like her opinions, but she's got a right to have them and even to express them. Whether you like them or not."

Jake glared at Chelsea over the top of Patti's head. She glared back. Jake Jr. was the one to break the silence, saying, "Hey Dad, come upstairs and see the new computer game I got from Kevin. It's one Bill gave to him and he's letting me borrow it."

Jake sneered. "Oh goody, a game the fags down in boys-town all like to play? I can hardly wait to see it."

Mindful of Patti's intake of breath, signaling an explosion to come, both of the Jakes headed upstairs quickly, leaving the females in the kitchen.

Patti looked at Chelsea, who asked. "When is he leaving, Mom?"

Patti sighed, "I don't know, honey. He says he needs more time to save his money."

Chelsea shook her head, "Exactly *why* is that your problem? Are *you* the one who can't save any money? You're not even charging him rent, for crying out loud! He's been here over three weeks already. How long does it take to save when you're not paying any bills?"

Patti looked at Chelsea closely. "Don't you want him to stay?"

Chelsea shook her head. "No. I don't really even like going to stay with him, since he's always got some female around. It's always obvious he can't wait for us to be gone so he can go back to doing whatever it is he does with her when we're not there. It makes me uncomfortable...and I feel like I'm just in the way. Can't he move out after Thanksgiving?"

Patti hugged her daughter, "We'll see, Chels, we'll see."

She started to move around the kitchen, saying, "Let's see what we have around here to put together for a dinner, okay?"

Both of them tried to lose themselves in dinner preparations, knowing neither of them had much control over the present situation.

~*~

"Are you sure this will be okay?" asked J.T. once again, when he called Patti to verify when he was supposed to arrive to do his part of the cooking for the Thanksgiving dinner.

"Why wouldn't it be?" Patti asked, distracted by her search for the pumpkin pie recipe she wanted to make next.

"Well, the main reason is your ex-husband is still in your house, and won't be happy to see me," J.T. replied.

Patti sniffed, "So what? You're going to be in the kitchen with me, doing the cooking. He's going to be out in the living room with Alex and the boys, watching football. The only time he has to be polite to you is when we eat. I think even *he* can manage that much. And if not, too damn bad. You and I will be too busy cooking to care about any hissy fit he might throw. So come over about eleven, like I asked you. The pies should be coming out of the oven by then, so you will be able to get the sweet potato casserole and your sour-dough rolls going then. See you later."

J.T. sighed when he hung up the phone. "I hope you are right, Patricia. I really don't want to have to fight your ex on a family holiday like this."

He changed into a nicer pair of jeans and put a flannel shirt on over his tee shirt, rode out to the grocery store to soak up the atmosphere while he picked up the ingredients he needed to bring. On a whim, he also picked up a bouquet of seasonal flowers in a green vase as a hostess gift. Then he headed over to Patti's house, to join her in creating a gourmet feast.

Since Patti was busy in the kitchen when J.T. rang the doorbell, he was not surprised to find Chelsea answering the door.

"Hey, J.T. Good to see you!" Chelsea said, "Happy Thanksgiving and all…"

Her eyebrows shot up when she saw the flowers. "Are those for Mom?"

J.T. smiled and nodded, "Hey yourself, Chelsea. And yes, the flowers are to thank your mom for inviting me so I didn't have to spend yet another Thanksgiving eating greasy burgers, wishing I was back home, cooking and eating with my family."

The younger Jake was sitting on the couch, watching the pre-game shows that endlessly fill the time before the football starts. He said, "Hi", when he saw J.T. and looked surprised at the flowers.

"Dad has never given Mom flowers," he said to his sister while they exchanged a significant look.

J.T. shrugged, "It's not such a big deal. I really like your mom and she has been really good to me, giving me a job and treating me like family by inviting me over here." He smiled at them both, "So I expect she's in the kitchen?" He inclined his head towards the back of the house.

Chelsea smiled and Jake made a face as the clattering of pots against each other could be heard, along with shouting. "Don't you guys ever put my stuff back where it belongs? I pay you to wash the dishes and pots, not to hide them from me!"

J.T. nodded at the kids, then moved towards the noise. When he walked through the door into the kitchen, his heart skipped a beat. Patti wasn't wearing anything special, but her jeans were just tight enough to outline her curves, and the cami she wore bared an expanse of cleavage that made his mouth water. She had put her hair up earlier, but the exertion of cooking and baking, and in general bustling around the room, had made some tendrils work themselves loose. They fell in gentle curves around her face, which looked sweaty and exasperated. When she saw J.T., she broke into a wide smile. When she saw the flowers he held out wordlessly to her, the smile was replaced by a look of shock.

"What are those for?" she gasped.

J.T. smiled, "To thank you for being such a kind-hearted woman that you took pity on this poor Rom so far from home, gave me a job and invited me into your home to celebrate the day as if I was a part of your family. Usually I'm alone or eating burgers in some dive. Today, I'm looking forward to helping you create a feast to remember. So please accept these as a token of my feelings for you."

Patti moved forward to take the flowers, and as she took them in one hand, her other hand reached up to J.T.'s neck to pull his head down so she could give him a quick kiss. He obliged, then had to clear his throat to swallow the lump that had appeared in it before he could speak again.

He forced himself to focus on the food. "I take it the bird is in the oven?"

Patti nodded as she placed the vase holding the flowers on the ledge in front of the window. "The pies are done; the bird is stuffed and in the oven and I'm working on the cranberry sauce now. I got a new recipe that has cayenne and cilantro in it, so we can taste-test it soon. But there's room in the oven for your sweet potato casserole and room on the counter by the stove for your dough to rise. What do you need to get started?"

J.T. put the bag with the ingredients he had brought with him onto the counter and asked for the bowls and utensils he needed. They spent the next couple hours companionably working in the kitchen, which was a familiar and welcome routine for them. Chelsea and Jake drifted in and out a few times, poking their fingers into foods, getting their hands rapped with wooden spoons and being allowed to walk out only with something in their hands so the appetizers were gradually put onto the table in the combination living room/dining room.

When J.T. carried the crock-pot with the mini meatballs out to set up on the card table being used as a buffet table, he had to spend some time complimenting Chelsea on the table cloths and napkins she had made and the fancy name-tags she had arranged, so everyone would know where to sit. He was amused to see she had put him between her mother and herself, with her dad further down the table between her brother Jake and Katie. When she saw him looking and he raised his eyebrows to look at her, she defended her choice, saying, "Hey, you and mom have to be able to easily get in and out of the kitchen.

You're the cooks, after all! Besides, I'm hoping to avoid any unpleasant scenes between my parents, so it's better to separate them."

In a quiet tone, J.T. asked, "Where *is* your dad?"

Chelsea shrugged, "Who knows? He said he was going out this morning to get some beer for dinner. He said he had some other errands to run also. But I figure he's probably in some bar somewhere, and he'll get back in time for the football games with some lame story about why he's late."

J.T. looked closely at her, "How has he been treating your mom?"

Chelsea shrugged again, "Okay, I guess. No major fights...*yet*," she added significantly. She smiled at him conspiratorially. "But he never brings her flowers, so you've got that going for you."

J.T. smiled back at her, "I treat her like she deserves to be treated. Don't you ever forget that, young lady. You deserve to get the same kind of treatment from any boy who wants to catch your eye. If he doesn't make you feel special, he's not worth wasting your time on."

Chelsea rolled her eyes, "Thanks, *dad*. Now aren't you supposed to be in the kitchen?"

As J.T. headed back into the kitchen, he didn't look out the window Chelsea was facing, so he didn't see her father was heading up the sidewalk to the front door. The door was unlocked, so Jake Sr. let himself in, then headed into the bathroom. Chelsea and Jake Jr. exchanged looks and headed into the kitchen so there would be too many people in the kitchen for their dad to want to stay for long. Their plan worked, since Jake Sr. didn't seem to want to cause any trouble in front of his kids. He barely acknowledged J.T. with a grunt in his direction, then complained about the lack of room in the fridge for his beer. He shoved it into the fridge, slammed the door hard and opened his beer on the way into the living room, following his son who had told him the game was starting soon. Chelsea and Patti both seemed to let out a breath when he left the room and J.T. was too polite to comment on it, so he busied himself punching the sour-dough and getting the counter cleaned and covered with flour so he could make the rolls.

When Chelsea left the room, Patti said, "It'll be good to be able to relax in my own home again once he leaves."

J.T. shot her a quick look, but any comment he was planning was forgotten when Tegan burst through the back door, waddling as only a pregnant woman in her ninth month can, rubbing her belly and saying, "Is there anything to eat in this house? I have plenty of room in this pup tent of a dress, so I plan to eat so much the kid wants to be born early since his space will get overcrowded by my full stomach."

Laughing, Patti hugged her, then Alexander, who followed her into the room, saying, "But my darling, you are so ravishing as a pregnant woman. You are positively glowing with happiness. I will truly miss that, as well as the Mount Everest your belly has become. Though it *has* become increasingly difficult and awkward to express my love without worrying about the trauma it must be causing to our son."

Katie rolled her eyes in the classic teenager manner on her way in the door, saying, "For God's sake, *Tío*

Alejandro. Can't you two talk about anything else, *ever*?"
She hugged Patti briefly, got herself a can of coke out of
the fridge, said, "Hey, J.T.", then went into the living
room, yelling, "Chelsea! Where are you?"

Kevin entered the kitchen holding a couple of new
computer games in his hand. He nodded and smiled at
J.T., hugged Patti, grabbed himself a coke out of the
fridge, then followed his sister into the next room.

Tegan said brightly, "Hey, Patti, did I tell you the OB
said it was okay for me to have a glass of wine with
dinner?"

Patti smiled, saying, "Really? Good, since I got a few
bottles of the Nouveau Beaujolais I liked the best at the
tasting."

Tegan leaned closer to Patti and asked conspiratorially,
"How big is your biggest wine glass? Half a bottle, I
hope?"

Alexander said warningly, "Tegan, my love. One glass,
not one bottle. We don't have much longer to go now. It's
not any easier on me than it is on you. Just a few more
weeks."

Tegan sighed, "Yeah, I know." She brightened again,
saying, "Then it will be okay, since a glass of wine helps
bring the milk down." Then she saw the flowers in the
vase by the window.

"*Wow!*" Tegan turned to look at J.T. "I take it this is
one of *your* contributions?"

J.T. smiled and nodded while he rolled out the dough
to make his rolls.

Tegan exchanged a significant look with Patti, inclining her head towards J.T. and raising her eyebrows. Patti smiled ruefully in return while shaking her head.

Tegan continued, "Thanks for planning dinner for so early, Patti. This way, we get to eat with you then head on over to Edgar and Juanita's house to eat more over there. Now you see why I'm so glad about the pup tent I'm wearing?"

Patti smiled broadly at her. "No problem-o. I know much better than to upset a woman so extremely advanced in her pregnancy…and I'm really happy you are eating here as well as there. It just wouldn't be Thanksgiving without you here."

Alexander grabbed a coke for himself and went through the door into the living room to watch the omnipresent football coverage and sample the appetizers he knew would be there.

Tegan followed him, then returned with a couple of plates piled high with a variety of appetizers, which she set on a counter. She perched as gracefully as she could on one of the bar stool-type chairs in the kitchen and shared her food with her hosts. She chatted amiably with Patti and J.T. as they worked on finishing the last of the foods for the Thanksgiving feast. They were all laughing heartily at a dirty joke J.T. had just told when Jake walked into the kitchen.

"Sorry to interrupt the hen party," he sneered, glaring at J.T. as he grabbed another beer out of the fridge. "When do we eat, or are you all just planning on partying in the kitchen all day?"

Patti sniffed haughtily, "Oh, the appetizers in the living room aren't enough for you? You were planning on eating dinner,too? How ever will the local bars stay in business without you there to plump up their bottom line?"

Jake turned to Patti and said sarcastically, "I could say something about how you know all about plumping up bottoms..."

J.T. turned from checking on the food in the oven and drew himself up to his full height, making the kitchen suddenly seem more crowded, saying simply, "Don't."

"Why not?" Jake glared at J.T. again, while moving towards the door to the living room. "What are you going to do? Make a scene at the family's Thanksgiving dinner, defending your boss? Like the good little minimum-wage employee you are?" With an evil grin, Jake went into the living room and the door swung shut on the sounds of crowds cheering on football.

There was silence for a moment.

Tegan shook her head, "How does he do that? How does he manage to suck all of the joy out of any occasion and make everyone feel as nasty-tempered as he is?"

Patti shrugged, but J.T. was the one who answered. "He's a small man with a small ego, and even less self-confidence. I've run into lots of guys like him. He baits everyone, then backs off with his hands up, saying *What did I do?*, acting as if he's the injured party when he's the one who started it all just for the fun of watching other people squirm or get uncomfortable. The only way to deal with guys like him is to ignore them."

Patti sighed, "Easy for you to say."

J.T. smiled at her, "You didn't let me finish. If ignoring doesn't work, then I just like to squash 'em like a bug."

Tegan interjected, "Yay! Can I watch? And will you do it *before* dinner so I don't have to miss a thing?"

Patti smiled back at J.T. "You'd do that for me? What a sweetie!"

The kitchen timer went off and J.T. and Patti turned their attention back to getting all of the food ready to be served at the same time. Tegan was enlisted to announce to the people in the living room that dinner was going to be served imminently, so the TV had to be turned off and the wine opened.

Alexander came into the kitchen to get the wines and the corkscrew and to kiss his wife, saying, "I've been bereft without you by my side, my love." He rubbed her belly fondly, then added, "I don't think I could take much more of the strain of trying to make pleasant conversation with such an unpleasant man."

He turned to Patti, "However did a wonderful woman like you end up with a jerk like him?" Alexander asked, adding under his breath, "*¡Él me da un dolor!*"

J.T. was the only one who laughed, then added, "*¡Usted tomó las palabras de la boca!*"

Tegan frowned at her husband, "*¡Hablas inglés, por favor!*"

Alexander bowed to her, then to Patti, saying, "*¡Lo siento!* Sorry, ladies. I was saying the snake, as you two so accurately refer to him, gives me a pain. And J.T. was agreeing with me." He winked at J.T., adding, "It's so nice to have someone around who can speak *español* besides me."

He turned to Patti to ask, "Am I to open the *gewürztraminer* wine also, or just the Nouveau?"

"Both," answered Patti distractedly while she spooned the mashed potatoes into a bowl. "That way we can drink what tastes best with each course. And take the carbonated grape juice and open that so the kids can join us in our Thanksgiving toast."

"Your wish is my command, *senora*," said Alexander, as he went back into the dining area with the bottles Patti had waved at, as well as the corkscrew.

There was a flurry of activity as the kids were enlisted to help carry all of the dishes of food to the dining room table and J.T. carried the turkey in along with the carving knife. Jake glared at him again, then went into the kitchen to get himself another beer.

J.T. shrugged, asking Patti, "Should I let him do the carving?"

"Oh, God, no!" said Patti, adding, "The last time he tried to carve a turkey, it ended up on the floor because he stuck the fork into the leg, which broke off, and the bird went flying. Remember?" She laughed, and was joined in her amusement by Tegan and all four of the kids, who had been witness to the disaster of their last Thanksgiving before the divorce.

J.T. commenced with the carving and did an excellent job, making sure there was enough cut for everyone to eat their fill before he sat down at the table. At that point, Alexander proposed a toast, "To the cooks!"

Everyone joined in the toast, although Jake didn't join in the chorus.

Patti said, "I want to propose a toast also. Since it has been said a family is a circle of people who surround you with love, I want to toast to our family being together once again."

Tegan said, "I'd like to propose a toast to the new people who have joined in our family since last year." She coyly winked at Alexander, then blew him a kiss, right before she drank her toast. J.T. was surprised to feel Patti's hand on his thigh, but he managed to smile as he raised his glass to toast.

Not to be outdone, Alexander said, "One last toast... to the new family member who will be soon with us. We look forward to including you in our family!" Everyone tipped their glasses once again.

Jake grumbled, "Aren't we done yet? Can we eat *now*?"

Patti laughed, "You're worse than the kids. Yes, dig in, everyone."

Conversation was sporadic as everyone passed dishes around, eating their fill of whatever they decided they liked best. Tegan nursed her one glass of wine and made it last all through dinner, but she allowed Alexander to have a glass of each of the two wines, telling him, "Go ahead, my love, splurge!"

After a while, everyone began to slow down; then the eating finally stopped as people began to push themselves away from the table rubbing their bellies.

Tegan groaned. "I may have the roomiest clothing on, but believe me, the kid is playing soccer in there again. I'm going to have to pass on dessert if I expect to be able to eat anything at Juanita and Edgar's house."

J.T. got up from the table. "I'll start the coffee, Patti, so you can sit and enjoy your company. Chelsea, Jake, want to help me get some of these dishes into the dishwasher?"

Jake, the snake, glared at him as all four kids jumped up to help get the table cleared. He grabbed the nearest wine bottle and poured the last of it into his glass. Patti, Tegan and Alexander were talking about the grand opening of Patti's Place and the logistics of advertising a new restaurant. Jake watched them for a while, then announced. "I'm going out for a smoke. I'll be in for dessert." He stalked out the front door, spilling wine as he carried his overly-full glass with him.

There was a moment of silence when he left. Patti let out a breath, "Phew, I thought he'd never leave."

"Speaking of leaving, when *is* he?" Tegan asked. "It's been a month since he moved in and you're not charging him any rent. Doesn't he have enough saved yet?"

Patti shook her head slowly, "I don't know. I asked him the other day and he made some excuses about having to save up first and last month's rent, 'blah-de blah, blah'. It can't be soon enough for me."

Alexander leaned over the table, doing an impression of a mobster, saying, You want I should *make* him leave?"

Tegan giggled, "You don't do a very good job of sounding scary, my love!"

Patti shook her head, "Maybe not to you, but I seem to remember him doing a good job on those guys in the bar at your birthday party last year!"

Alexander covered Tegan's hand on the table with his own. "I was protecting my woman. A man will do anything, even things he doesn't want to do, to protect the one he loves."

He leaned over to kiss Tegan and Patti rolled her eyes at them. "I'm beginning to see why Katie always tells you guys to get a room. But then, you have a whole house." She shook her head as their kiss grew more passionate, "Hey, do I have to throw a bucket of water on you two? Come up for air! After that dinner you just ate, you'd both barf if you tried."

Tegan and Alexander laughed and they were all still chuckling when J.T. walked back into the room, saying, "The coffee is done and I've got the whipped cream whipped. Do you want to come in there to get dessert, or should I bring it out here?"

Patti said, "Why don't you sit and relax, too? I didn't invite you over here to be the hired help. Leave the dishes for later and come join us."

J.T. shook his head then inclined it at the kitchen door. "The kids have all of the dishes in the dishwasher already. I told them to get it going, then come out here for dessert." He sat down next to Patti and smiled at her, "So, do we go get it, or should I bring the pies out here?"

She smiled at him, "Can I just whisper in your ear what I'd *really* like for dessert?"

Surprisingly, J.T. blushed, then smiled back at Patti, "Honey, not now. We have company. And think of the children."

Tegan snorted. "Haven't you heard Katie? Mine, at least, are used to it. I'm trying to teach them by example what a good, healthy relationship looks like. My first marriage was *not* the model I'd like them to follow…but *this* one is."

The front door slammed and Jake strode back in, smelling not only of tobacco, but of pot as well.

Patti glared at him, "You'd better not be keeping any of *that* in my house, mister! I'm not getting busted for your bad habits."

He shrugged at her. "No problem-o, Patti-o. It's in the car. When's dessert?"

J.T. got up. "I was just going to bring the pies in, and…"

Jake interrupted. "Then get to it, big boy. You're not being paid to sit around and chat with the boss. Holiday, or no holiday," he said, smiling at his own wit.

J.T. went into the kitchen and the kids emerged next, carrying the coffeepot, a tray with mugs and the creamer, two pies and the bowl with whipped cream. J.T. was the last one back out with the dessert plates and the forks. After everyone had admired Patti's pumpkin and French Silk pies, she cut up the pies into sections and put slices onto the dishes as J.T. handed them to her. Then there was quiet again, as everyone, even Tegan, enjoyed Patti's pies.

The coffee was poured and passed around and everyone sat back to rub their bellies and digest their food. Jake Jr. and Kevin asked if they could be excused, then went upstairs to play one of Kevin's new computer games. Chelsea and Katie asked if they could be excused and when Patti said, "Yes," she and Tegan looked at each other and rolled their eyes.

"Who knows what thirteen-year-old girls do when no one is watching?" Patti said, laughing, as Tegan yelled after the kids, "Remember, we are leaving in an hour to get to Juanita and Edgar's house!"

J.T. got up and started carrying the dessert plates into the kitchen, "Don't," said Patti. "Sit and chat with us. It's your holiday, too, you know."

J.T. smiled at her. "I'll be right back, I just want to get these plates into the sink, soaking. They'll be easier to clean later that way."

Jake followed J.T. into the kitchen and Patti and Tegan shot each other worried looks, but Jake emerged quickly, carrying another beer. He was smirking. "What a good little minimum-wage slave you have there, Patti. He's really good with the dishes. Does he do windows?" He gave a nasty laugh, as J.T. came back into the room. "Are there any more dishes out here?"

Patti shook her head, "No, J.T. Sit down and relax."

"Yeah," Jake started, "Do this, do that, then do this, too. She's got you really well trained, hasn't she?"

J.T. turned to look at him, as Patti and Tegan held their breath. "What's that supposed to mean?" he asked pleasantly. "She's my boss. I don't mind."

Jake sneered at him. "But you're a man. Grow yourself a pair! Don't you ever get tired of following her orders?"

J.T. gave him a long look, as if he was studying a bug. Then a slow smile spread over his face as he drawled, "Well now, it *does* get kind of tiresome sometimes, since I don't really like doing the dishes..." he winked at Patti, "But then, who does?"

He turned to give Jake a serious look, "But then, some orders I really don't mind following. Like when she says, 'Get your tongue out of my pussy and get back up here and fuck me hard again, big guy!' Now *those* are the kind of orders I live for!"

Alexander spit his coffee out as he started to laugh. Tegan's jaw dropped open. Patti smiled a secretive smile as she blushed a delicate shade of pink. Jake got up without a word, strode over to the door, grabbed his jacket off the coat tree and he walked out the front door, slamming it behind him. There was the sound of his car starting, then his tires squealed, as he quickly drove away.

Patti looked at J.T. and smiled at him. Then Alexander started to clap, Tegan joined him, and laughing, Patti did too. J.T. stood up and took a bow.

Patti grabbed his hand as he sat down, "That was a stroke of genius. He'll be gone for hours while he drinks some bar dry. And the rest of us can relax now."

J.T. shrugged. "I didn't know it would make him leave. But he was being a real asshole. I told you, if you can't ignore them, then you squash them. He was trying to be *muy* macho...he has no idea how well I can play *that* game."

Tegan laughed, "I'd think the tattoos should have given him a clue, don't you?"

"Or that big hog of yours in the driveway?" suggested Alexander.

Patti smiled, "Or the fact you look like such a huge bad-ass? Face it, J.T., you may be the nicest, most polite and soft-spoken man I have ever met, but that's not what you look like. If I was a man, you'd make me want to hide my wife as well as my daughters. Maybe even my mother!"

Alexander nodded, "I agree. As I have gotten to know you, I've realized what an honorable and decent man you are. But Patti's right…that's not what you look like."

J.T. shrugged. "When you spend your life wandering around, you kind of have to look intimidating or you have to keep proving yourself, over and over again and that gets really tiresome. I got tall at an early age, but it wasn't until I got a lot of tattoos and shaved my head when I started going bald in my late twenties, that other guys stopped trying to fight me where-ever I went. The beard helped too, but that doesn't seem to matter so much anymore. Maybe I've just got enough attitude now, the mustache is enough."

Patti patted his hand on his coffee cup as she said, "I'm glad you didn't shave the 'stache. I really like it. It's kind of erotic!"

Tegan rolled her eyes, "TMI! Too much information! I mean, I could go on for hours about how much I love to feel Alex's facial hair on the insides of my thighs, but really, people. We do need to remember we're in polite company."

Alexander drew his eyebrows up to his hairline, "We are? Since when?"

Everyone laughed, then they had more coffee and spent a bit of time chatting about Patti's baby, her soon-to-be-opened restaurant, and Tegan's actual baby, whose arrival they were all happily anticipating.

Before long, Katie came down the stairs, saying, "Hey, Mom, I just got a text-message from Rosa. Isn't it about time to be getting over to *Tío* Edgar's house?"

Tegan looked at her watch and started to push herself up from the table. Alexander solicitously put an arm around her and helped her get up from the chair. He was rewarded by a kiss, which led to an embrace, which led to Katie rolling her eyes again, saying, to no one in particular. "You see what I have to put up with? They never stop."

Patti laughed. "Doesn't it make you feel all warm and fuzzy to see your mother so happy with her new husband?"

Katie made a face. "No, it makes me feel all weird and yucky and glad our sex ed classes at school only teach abstinence. I'd be totally embarrassed if we had to watch videos of stuff like this with boys in the room! *Eww*!"

Tegan yelled for Jake to come downstairs and there was a flurry of activity as those leaving got their coats and jackets on and said their goodbyes to all who were staying. They had driven over, as Alexander had explained, because Tegan was entirely too pregnant to walk on icy sidewalks.

Once the car had left the driveway, Jake asked, "Mom, is it okay if I just keep on playing Kevin's new game? He left it here for me."

Patti smiled at him. "Sure thing, honey."

Chelsea said. "I'm going back upstairs, too. I want to watch more of that DVD I rented, from the first season of *Desperate Housewives*. I'm just going to grab another coke first and then you won't see me again." She gave a significant look to her mother, went into the kitchen, reappeared with a can of coke and a glass of ice and then she went back up the stairs, smiling broadly.

Patti laughed, "Do you think they could have made it any more obvious they are giving us time to be alone?"

J.T. smiled at her, sat down on the couch and patted the place next to him. "I think it's kind of sweet of them. So let's take advantage of the first opportunity we've ever had to be alone in a private place."

"They really like you, you know," Patti said, as she grabbed their two wine glasses and the second bottle of Nouveau Beaujolais. She sat down next to J.T., poured wine into two glasses and handed him one.

"I really like you, too," she said, as she kicked off her shoes and put her feet up on the coffee table. "You know," she began companionably. "Last year, Tegan passed out right after dinner, since she and Alex were a new item, but keeping their relationship secret from everyone. Separately, him at Edgar's and her here, they both drank way too much because they were already having feelings for each other they were not ready to acknowledge. After I put her to bed in my room, I came back out here and toasted the night spirits that had made her go crazy that night. I asked them to be more gentle with her. And now look at them: only a year later and they're married and expecting their first child in a couple of weeks. What a difference a year makes, huh?"

J.T. was quiet for a moment. "I don't really want to share where I was last year for Thanksgiving. Let's just say, I was *not* in a place I wanted to be."

Patti looked up at him and smiled, "I wasn't trying to get you to tell me anything. I was just kind of leading up to how much happier Tegan and Alex are this year...and how much happier I am, too. I'm really glad you came to share Thanksgiving dinner with us this year. And I'm really glad you came into my life."

J.T. took the wine glass out of Patti's hand and put both of their glasses on the table. He used one finger to lift Patti's face up and gently kiss her lips. She leaned into him and sighed, as she ran her hands up his chest and opened her mouth to taste the passion on his tongue. He moaned, as the feelings he had been restraining for so long forced their way to the surface. His hands sought to explore where they had not dared go before. His one arm was around her shoulders and that hand was in her hair, holding her head so he could continue to kiss her, their tongues in a passionate duel that both would win. His other hand was tracing her curves, down her shoulder, her arm, then back up to her breast. The cami she was wearing gave little resistance as he cupped her breast in his hand, then licked his way down her neck to her chest. He lifted her breast out of the top of the cami and drew in his breath in admiration.

"Silver dollar nipples. They're huge! Just the way I like them!" Then his mouth was on the nipple he was admiring and Patti almost stopped breathing as he licked and sucked, drawing his tongue and mouth almost all of the way off her most sensitive areas. He drew the whole thing back into his mouth and began the assault all over again. Sometime during this ultimate pleasure, J.T. got her other breast up and out of the cami also, and his attentions were split between the two breasts, alternately teasing one then the other, making her moan and shift around on the couch, increasing her arousal until she tore his shirts off. The flannel was removed, then the tee shirt. She licked her way from one tattoo to the other, taking a few moments to lick each of his tiny hard nipples, to repay him for his ardent attention.

J.T.'s hands were busy opening the zipper on Patti's jeans, then pushing into her pants, as he slid them off of her ample hips. Patti lifted her butt off the couch and he used one hand to slide her jeans off, then he resumed his assault on her breasts. "Oh, God," she murmured, as his one hand slid into her panties and his fingers explored her.

"You're so wet," he muttered as he licked his way back up to her face and she opened her eyes to look at him as she gasped, "That's what you do to me!"

He smiled at her smugly, saying, "Let's see how much wetter I can get you," as he began to twirl the tip of one finger around, using her own moisture to tease her tiny nub of pleasure. He slid one wide finger into her and resumed the slow, lazy circles again. Patti felt herself beginning to climb a hill, then she fell off the other side. She bit her lip as she moaned, trying not to be audible to the kids upstairs, but losing control of herself as she had her first orgasm with a man in over five years.

J.T. chuckled softly, saying, "I wonder just how loud I can make you yell before the kids hear you."

Patti shook her head to clear it, the sweat of passion making her hair stick to her face and neck as she reclaimed his lips while she worked at his belt buckle and zipper. He tried to stop her with his hand, but she pushed it away.

"No!" she told him, "It's *not* all just about me. I want to pleasure you, too. I want to feel you inside of me. I'm burning up for you, Jules. I need to feel your hardness."

Once she had his zipper opened, she slid the top of his jeans down and found he didn't have anything on under them. "*Yes!*" She hissed, as she took his swollen member in her hand and stroked it, enjoying the size of it as she hiked one thigh over his lap to end up with one knee on either side of him. She stroked herself with him, feeling her slick wetness joined by his until with a groan, he took the decision way from her and thrust himself into her in one quick movement that took her breath away. She screamed as she arched backwards, then used the back of her own hand to stop the sound.

J.T. stopped moving. "Did I hurt you? God, what an idiot I am! I know how big I am and you're so small. I didn't hurt you too much, did I?"

Patti opened her eyes to look deeply into his eyes, shaking her head urgently, "*No*! Not pain! More pleasure than I can take without screaming."

Then she began to move on him, riding him back and forth, then sideways, then in a circle, using him to stir herself up into a frenzy. All of the while her muscles were squeezing him so tightly he had to fight himself not to explode with pleasure. He fought for control while she spiraled off into another orgasm, gasping and panting, licking him on his shoulder and neck, then she bit the side of his neck and that was the end of his control. With a howl, he pushed himself into her faster and faster, deeper, until he felt himself come to the end of her and knew she had taken all of him deep inside of her and still she rode him, letting him know she could take whatever he had to give and use it to give them both extreme pleasure. He felt himself ready to burst...then he exploded, the spasms so intense they almost hurt as he pushed himself into her again and again, until they both collapsed, panting; her screaming now reduced to a whimper.

Patti lifted her head off of his shoulder to smile at him, asking, "*Now* will you come and join me in my bed?"

He smiled back at her, "I guess so…but I'm not staying the night. Not while there's a chance he'll be coming back." Then he stopped smiling, saying, "Oh, God, Patricia, I didn't use a condom. I'm so sorry!"

Patti shook her head, her damp hair clinging to her face, and tickling his chest, starting to arouse him all over again. "No need to worry, darlin'. I went on the pill a couple of months ago, hoping for just such an opportunity. And may I say, Jules, you are really, really, *really* worth waiting for."

He kissed her deeply, thrusting his tongue into her mouth, then withdrawing it. "So are you, Patricia. But in case you are worried about AIDS or anything else, I got a clean bill of health from a doctor back in July, right before I got to town."

She smiled at him. "Good. I'm too aroused to worry now, but tomorrow when I wake up, I'll be really glad you told me that tonight. Now as much as I don't want to do this…" she pushed herself up onto her knees, and drew herself up and off of his lap. "The sooner we get into my bed, the sooner we can get back down to business."

She grabbed the two wine glasses and the bottle and began to sway her hips, saying, "Last one in the bedroom gets to go down on the other one first."

He laughed, then jumped up as if to race her. She giggled, and made a mad dash for the bedroom, putting the glasses and the bottle down, then heading for the adjoining bathroom. "I'll be right out, but as you can plainly see, I made it in here first!" Then she closed the door.

A few minutes later, she came back out and J.T. said, "My turn." They both grabbed each other's various parts on their way past, then Patti settled herself down on the bed, sitting up against the headboard, sipping her wine. When J.T. came back into the room, he grabbed the other wine glass and took a few sips as he moved to the other side of the bed. He put the glass on the table next to his side of the bed and crawled across, as if he was a lion on the prowl, sniffing and growling.

Patti giggled, "What's going on?"

He gave her a look of passion, with humor behind it. "I'm smelling an aroused female. There's nothing I like more than to taste something that smells so good."

He moved his head down to her stomach, then he licked his way down her belly. Gently, he spread her thighs and began to assault her senses in yet another way. Patti barely got the wine glass put down before she was writhing and twisting, moaning out her feelings, as he brought her to new levels of pleasures, making her know what it felt like to be cherished and enjoyed. She found she got extreme pleasure not only from his mustache on her tender skin, but from the scratchiness of his chin, when the tiny hairs let her know a man was touching her. When she lost all control of herself and was merely a boneless, whimpering, thrashing animal, he drew himself up to his knees in front of her, lifted her hips off of the bed, and pushed his way into her again. This time, layer upon layer of sensations played off of each other and Patti felt like she finally understood what it meant to be madly in love, as she felt herself losing control over her own body. She knew she would follow this man anywhere in the world just to feel him inside of her again.

As he pounded himself into her repeatedly, pulling all of the way out, then pushing all of the way back in again, until his balls rested against her, J.T. realized he had in his hands a woman who could take whatever he could dish out, a woman who was a match for him in passion and intensity. As he fought himself and the burning desire to explode into her again, he watched her face and thought he had never seen a more beautiful woman in his life. To honor her, he gave up his control and lost himself in a pleasure more intense than anything else he had ever felt. He collapsed onto her and breathed her name with the last vestige of strength he had.

As her arms encircled him, gently stroking his back and arms, then his head, J.T. felt as if he had finally found a home to belong. And that was wherever this woman was.

Eventually able to move, and thirsty once again, they both drank more wine, then spent the next couple of hours enjoying each other in as many ways as they could think of, with each time more thrilling than the last time. The room got dark as time passed, and they both eventually dozed off, overcome with physical exhaustion and the kind of lassitude that comes from a total-body satisfaction.

J.T. was the first one to open his eyes, and since he was lying on his back with Patti lying next to him, her head on his shoulder, his arm holding her close to his heart, he had to lift his head to see the clock on the nightstand. As he put his head back down, Patti sighed, then leaned forward to inhale deeply, then to lick at his chest hair that was tickling her nose.

"You're going to leave me now, aren't you?" she asked in a groggy voice.

"Yes," he answered, stroking her back and shoulders, then working his hand up into her hair. "But not because I want to, I'd rather sleep here all night and wake up to go another round with you before breakfast. But I'm not taking the chance your ex will stumble back in drunk, and find my bike is still in your driveway. I'm sure I could take him, but that's not how I want to spend even a part of my first night with you."

"Yeah," Patti sighed. "I'm sure you can fight almost as well as you make love. But I don't want to see you getting hurt in any way, and like Tegan says, I'd probably put a knife through his heart, then we'd have to wait years until I got out of jail for another chance to spend the night together."

J.T. regarded her seriously for a moment. "So, you'd best let me get up now, Patricia. Before I change my mind and decide to take my chances."

Reluctantly, Patti sat up and watched as J.T. got up, then began to search for his clothes, which he had carried into the bedroom. He quickly got dressed, then sat on the nearby chair to pull on his boots.

Patti licked her lips as she watched him, then smiled guiltily when he smiled at the look on her face. "You look hungry, my love," he teased. "Didn't you get enough for one night?"

Patti sighed heavily. "After as many years as I've waited for any man to want to touch me again, if I had my choice, you wouldn't leave here for a week...or at least until neither of us could walk anymore!"

J.T. chuckled, "I'd love to take you up on that challenge in the very near future. Now that I know just how well we fit together, I'm going to have even more trouble keeping my hands off you...even in public!"

Patti walked naked across the room and stood in front of J.T. to kiss him. He groaned as he ran his hands on her curves and she rubbed herself on him. Their kissing grew more passionate, until he gently pushed her back, saying, "Enough. Patricia, have mercy on me. I had enough trouble getting my jeans zipped back up...don't make it impossible for me to think clearly enough to ride home."

With another sigh, Patti backed away, then sat back down on the bed. "I guess you're right. I don't want to have to worry all night about you getting home safely. Call me when you get back to your place, okay? Just so I know you're all right?"

J.T. nodded. "I will, sweetheart."

Patti gave him an odd look, "Jules... do I belong to you now?"

When he nodded gravely at her, she smiled back at him. "Good."

She got up, walked over to the bathroom, grabbed a robe off the back of the door and belted it while she walked over to the door and unlocked it. "I'll walk you to the door, so I can be sure to lock it after you. That way, I can have one more chance to kiss you and grope you before you leave."

J.T. shook his head and smiled, "Patricia, you are the woman of my dreams."

They walked slowly in the dark to the front door.

Patti opened it. "Now for my goodbye kiss and fondle!"

They spent a few sweaty moments, groping and kissing, then with a shake of his head, J.T. let her go and walked out of the front door into the cool night air.

"Call me," Patti said.

"I will," J.T. replied.

He got on his Harley and rode off into the night. Patti watched until he turned the corner. She closed the door, locked it and walked back into her bedroom to wait for his call. She was just drifting back to sleep, when the phone rang.

"Hello?" she murmured.

"It's me, Patricia. I'm home, so you can go back to sleep. Good night, darlin'."

"Good night, Jules," she answered. "See you very soon." She hung up the phone and instantly fell back asleep.

J.T. looked at his phone after he heard her hang up. "Yes, Patricia, you're mine now. I have no idea for how long, but I intend to enjoy you for as long as you'll let me."

With a sigh, he took off his boots and lay back on his cot to stare out of the window at the moon. Eventually, he fell asleep to spend the night dreaming of the many different positions he had not yet had Patti in, and that he fully intended to try at his very first opportunity.

~ * ~

Hours later, Patti moaned as she slept, dreaming J.T. had come back and was pressing himself against her backside. She wriggled against him, then realized something was very wrong. As she fought her way to wakefulness, she realized the part of him he was pressing against her was not the size it should be. With a start, she realized she knew that organ only too well and she woke up and twisted around to yell at the intruder.

"Jake, what the hell are you doing in my bed?" She was outraged enough not to care how loudly she was yelling. "And how the hell did you get back into the house, let alone into my bedroom?"

He stared at her with glassy eyes, as he grabbed for her again, slurring, "You didn't really think I gave back *all* of the keys, did you? Without making any copies first?" She inched back even further away from him on the bed. "Come on, baby, get over here and let's do the wild thing again. You know you want to."

Mortified, she shook her head. "*No*! I most certainly *do not*. Not with you, you slimy son of a bitch. Get the hell out of my bedroom before I call the police on you, and report an intruder in my house."

He moved towards her again. "It's *my* house too, you know. I'm still paying half the damn mortgage. The kids are mine. And this is my bed. You belong to me, too. So get back here and I'll give you something to give thanks for." He chortled at his own wit.

Patti got up and grabbed the robe on the chair near the bed, shaking her head. "No way, asshole. I wouldn't let you touch me if you were the last man on earth. And you most certainly are not. What's wrong, couldn't you find any bimbo willing to take you in for the night? You must be losing your touch."

It was obvious this barb hit home. Jake sat up and glared at her. "I don't want any other woman tonight. I want you. If you were trying to use that bald, ball-less biker to make me jealous, it worked. You're mine. So get over here and let me make you scream."

An evil look came over Patti's face as she thoroughly enjoyed what she was about to say. "Oh, I don't think that would be such a good idea, Jake. You know, I never even knew what sloppy seconds were until you used to come home smelling of another woman while you tried to get me in the mood. But I'm more polite than you, so I'll tell you ahead of time. I've already done all of the screaming I want to do for one night, thank you. And I did it with J.T. hours ago, while you were out wasting your time drinking."

The shocked look on Jake's face helped her enjoy what she was saying even more. "And quite frankly, even if *you* don't care about having sloppy seconds, I do. After the good time I had with him, I have abso-bloody-lutely *no* interest in any mediocre sex you might have to offer. So you just get your fat ass out of my bed and out of my bedroom right now, or I really *will* call the police."

Dazed, he got up and started to walk towards her as she kept on talking, "And another thing, tomorrow morning you will take your things and get the hell out of *my* house. I'm pulling in the welcome mat and sending you on your way. You get out of here, or I'll throw your shit out in the street the next time you leave here and I'll change the locks."

Jake sputtered. "You can't do that to me!"

"Oh, yes I can and I am. Goodbye, Jake. I've had enough of you to last a lifetime."

Now he wheedled. "But Patti, honey, I don't have nearly enough money saved. Where am I supposed to go?"

"I don't know and I don't care. Out of here is all I care about. The rest is *your* problem, not mine."

He shook his head. "You're throwing me out right before the holidays? Even *you* can't be *that* cold!"

Patti smiled at him, nodding. "Just watch me. Take your clothes and get back out to the living room. But first, give me the keys."

Jake advanced on her then, as she held her hand out for the keys. He raised his hand as he got closer, and Patti watched with a sickening sense of déjà vu, as he got ready to hit her.

"Mom, Dad, what's all of the yelling about?" asked Jake Jr., who stood in the doorway and rubbed his eyes.

Jake stopped in his tracks, and his eyes were wild. "You just go on back up to bed, son. Your Mom and I are discussing where I'm going to live. She just told me I have to be out of here tomorrow morning, but I'm trying to explain to her I can't leave just yet. You really want me to stay around for the holidays, right?"

Their son regarded Jake for a long moment, before he slowly shook his head. "No, Dad, I think you should leave. It's been really hard on everyone, having you back in the house. You and Mom are divorced now. You don't belong here anymore. I'm sorry, but you really should get yourself a new place somewhere else."

With that, he slowly walked over to hug his Mom, then turned to look at his dad defiantly. "Mom's right, Dad… the sooner you move out of here, the better."

Jake's bluster all seemed to leave him, as he looked at his son, at ten years old, as tall as his mother, standing next to her and presenting a united front with her, refusing to be the trump card Jake had planned to use him as. Wordlessly, he picked up his clothes off the floor and searched through the pants pockets, then dropped a ring with two keys onto the nearby bed stand. He turned and walked through the door back into the living room. There was the sound of squeaking as he threw himself heavily onto the couch.

Patti hugged her son again, and said softly, "Thanks, Jakey."

He looked at her intently. "Was he really going to hit you, Mom?"

She shook her head as she regarded him gravely. "I don't know. I just don't know. But he couldn't do it in front of you. I'm sorry we woke you up, but I'm really glad you came in when you did."

He continued to look at her. "Will you be all right now? Or do you want me to stay in here with you until he passes out?"

She sighed heavily. "I sure wish you didn't have to know what that meant. But quite frankly, he's probably already passed out. I think you should go back up to bed and I'll see you in the morning."

He started towards the door, then turned back to look at her. "Mom?"

"What, honey?" she asked.

"I don't have to be like him when I grow up, do I? Just because he's my dad doesn't mean I will treat people like he does, does it?" The concern on his face made her want to weep, but instead Patti smiled at her son.

"No, sweetie, you don't have to be anything like him. You get to choose what kind of man you will be when you grow up."

He looked at her for a long moment, then sighed with relief. "Good, because I'd rather be the kind of man who brings you flowers than the kind who hits you because I'm drunk and nasty."

She smiled at him. "You are too sweet and thoughtful to be any other way, my love. Now go up to bed and sweet dreams, my prince."

He smiled at her, then left. She heard him walk back up the stairs, close his door and, uncharacteristically, lock it. She poked her head out of her room, and was reassured to hear Jake was indeed passed out and snoring loudly from the couch. She closed and locked her door and crawled into bed. Sleep was elusive for a while, as she rewound the events of the night in her mind. Eventually, she fell asleep, remembering how good she had felt when J.T. had his arms around her. Once again, she dreamed of being with him in a biker bar, wearing a leather bustier that allowed her to display all of her tattoos.

Fifteen

The next morning, Patti called J.T. soon after she woke up.

"This better be good, man, it's way too early," is what he said as he answered the phone.

Patti smiled into the phone. "Hey, J.T. It's me. I need you to do me a favor."

Instantly awake, J.T. said, "Sure, anything for you, Patti. What's up?"

"Remember that electrician who needs to hook up the smoke and fire alarms in the dining room before we can get inspected?"

"Yeah, isn't he supposed to be there this morning? What happened, did he cancel?"

"No, but I won't be able to be there. Could you take my place and sign the paperwork showing the work was done?"

"Sure, but why?"

"I'm going to be busy for a while. As soon as I get off the phone, I'm going to pack up all of Jake's shit, then put his bags out the front door. I'm throwing him out today. I don't want him in my house anymore."

There was silence for a moment.

J.T. asked slowly, "What did he do when he got back last night?"

Patti answered, "I'll tell you later. Once he's gone, I'll swing by to be sure everything went okay."

"Do you need some help with him? Like someone to bodily throw him out?"

"No, I need you to be there so the wiring gets done as scheduled. We've been waiting weeks for this guy to show up, remember. I hope he does and doesn't use the excuse of holidays to blow us off."

"How about you call me when you're done, so I know you're okay?"

"Fine. I don't think I'll have any trouble. I figure once I've got all his stuff packed, I'll wake him up and remind him he's being evicted. If I'm lucky, he'll be so hung-over he won't know what's happening until he's out the door looking at his stuff in the driveway. Hopefully, the keys I made him turn over last night are the last copies he had, so once he's out, he's not getting back in."

"Patti, are you sure you're all right?" J.T. asked, while he fought back his desire to rush over and make good on his promise to squash her ex like a bug.

"Yes; just get over there and go ahead and sign any paperwork for me, okay?"

"No problem. Consider it done. And Patricia?"

"What?"

"Watch yourself. If he gives you any trouble, call me and I'll come over and throw his ass out into the street, along with all of the other pieces I tear him into."

Patti smiled into the phone. "Thanks, J.T. But the kids are up and I don't think he'll try anything in front of them. I'll talk to you soon. Bye."

J.T. looked at the silent phone in his hand. He realized that, as much as it was a comfort Patti said the kids were awake and she didn't expect any trouble from her ex while they were around, her saying that meant she *had* had trouble with him in the past when the kids were *not* around

As he got himself ready to head out the door, J.T. promised out loud, "If he hurt you last night, or tries to today, I'll rip his heart out after I pull his head off." He sighed as he went out the door to go wait for the contractor to show up.

As Patti had hoped, Jake was not in any condition to argue with her at first when she shook him awake. She had found all of his things and packed them, including the dirty laundry, into his two suitcases he had stashed in the front coat closet. She put both pieces of luggage outside her front door on the stoop; she proceeded to wake up her ex while their children were both sitting at the table, picking at their cereal.

"Jake! Wake up! It's time for you to leave. Get your ass up and out of here, right now!"

He struggled to sit up, while grabbing for the cup of coffee Patti was waving in front of his face. He got his hands around the cup, then took a quick sip and looked around with a bewildered look on his face.

"What? Where am I going? And stop talking so loud."

"*No!*" Patti told him. "I don't care where you go. But you are being evicted from my house, so you need to get up and get out of here. I told you last night when I discovered you had lied to me and kept copies of my keys."

He looked guiltily around at the family he had had so little use for when they were his. "I'm still having half of the mortgage taken out of my paycheck every week, along with child support and alimony. So I have a right to be here, even if you don't want me here. Don't I, kids?"

He looked hopefully over at the table, and was dismayed when Chelsea shook her head vigorously. He turned to look at his son and their eyes met for a moment. Then Jake shook his head also.

"No, Dad. It's time for you to leave."

Grasping at straws, Jake said, "But I won't be able to find a place big enough for you two to come and visit me. How am I going to be able to afford Christmas presents if I have to get myself a new apartment in December?"

When only stony silence greeted his remarks, he turned back to Patti, "Can't a guy make one little mistake? Just let me stay until the end of December. I promise I'll clear out right after the holidays. Have a heart, Patti. If you want me to beg, I will. But you need to give me a little more time."

Patti shook her head. "No, Jake. No more time. I'm all out of patience. Having you in the house has been a real strain on everyone. We can't relax while you are here…we're all walking on eggshells, waiting for you to misbehave or abuse someone again. I'm tired of it. I've packed all your things and your luggage is on the front stoop. You need to get up and get out."

Getting angry, Jake shot a murderous look at her. "Why the big rush? Is that biker moving in? That's what this is all about, isn't it? You want me out of the way so you can have him and all of his biker friends move in, so you can have orgies, probably in front of the kids. I'll take you back to court, you whoring bitch! I'll tell the judge what the hell you're up to and we'll see who gets to keep the house and the kids."

Shocked silence greeted his words. He looked around to see outrage on Patti's face, disapproval on Chelsea's face and disappointment on the face of his son.

Jake Jr. cleared his throat and spoke next. "Dad, we are old enough to talk for ourselves, not like when Mom had to throw you out the last time. I don't want you in the house anymore. I'm too scared I will turn out to be the kind of man you are, who hits his wife and tries to terrorize his children into doing what he wants..." He stopped talking, because his eyes had filled with tears and his voice broke. He turned his face away from his father.

Jake cleared his throat. "Well, I need to pee first. Then I'll go, seeing as how I'm not welcome around here anymore."

He lurched towards the bathroom and slammed the door shut. No one spoke while he was out of sight. He opened the door and strode back into the room, looking around and speaking to no one in particular.

"You'll all be sorry when I'm gone. You'll miss your old dad when you don't have me to kick around anymore. You'll see."

He walked over to the front door, threw the empty coffee cup onto the stoop, shattering it, and picked up his bags. He got out his keys, threw his bags into the car, got in and drove off, his tires squealing on the pavement.

As one, all three of the witnesses to his temper tantrum let out a breath of relief once his car had turned the corner. Patti started to tremble and her children both rushed over to hug her, as they all shed tears of mourning for the husband and father they wished they had.

They were all still holding each other when the phone rang. Chelsea was the first to move and she ran to answer it.

"Hello?" she said in a tentative, shaky voice. "Yes, he's gone."

She listened for a moment, nodding. "Mom? J.T. needs to talk to you." She held out the phone.

Patti nodded while she wiped her eyes then cleared her throat. Taking the phone, she said, "Hello? What's up?"

J.T. felt his blood boil at the tone in her voice. He longed to pull her into his arms to comfort her, after he pounded out his anger on the man who had hurt her so much it sounded like she was crying. Instead, he forced himself to speak clearly.

"The contractor guy is done, but he won't take my signature on the paperwork. He says it has to be you, since you are the owner. I've given him a sample of some food I made, but you need to get here to sign the papers. Are you okay? Do you want me to come and get you?"

Drawing in a shaky breath, Patti said, "No, I'll drive right over." She thought about what he had said, "Did you say you made some food? Is there enough for me to have some, since I didn't have any breakfast?"

J.T. managed a small chuckle. "Honey, you know how I cook. Bring the kids with you. In fact, if you wanted to, you could bring everyone on your side of the block with you, and there would probably *still* be leftovers!"

Smiling into the phone, Patti said, "Okay. We'll be right there. Bye."

She turned to her kids. "Let's all head on over to my place. J.T. says he did some cooking and there's enough for all of us "

Chelsea smiled. "I'm gonna wash my face first. My eyes are puffy from crying. And I really need to blow my nose."

Jake nodded. "Me, too. And I have to find my shoes."

Patti smiled at her kids, "Okay, five minutes, then we're leaving. In case I haven't told you two lately, I really love you both. Marriage to your dad was an ordeal, but I got you two out of it, so it was worth it."

They both gave their mom a quick hug, then they all went into their various rooms to get ready to leave the house. As she splashed cold water on her own face, Patti made a face at herself in the mirror. "Well, he's gone. I hope I don't look so scary J.T. runs in the other direction without giving me a chance to enjoy him some more." Sticking her tongue out at herself, she turned and yelled, "Time to go! Get in the car or walk!"

A few minutes later, Patti pushed open the door to her business and was assailed by the smells of spices and chocolate. Her kids followed her in the door and both immediately sniffed the air appreciatively.

"Hey, J.T. What smells so good? What did you make this time?" asked Chelsea.

Jake walked over to the table next to the one the electrician was sitting at and fingered the flower petals of the bouquet in a vase in the middle of the table.

"Flowers again?" he asked J.T., then they smiled at each other as an unspoken message flashed between them.

J.T. spoke. "Patti, this is Joe Garcia, the electrician. He's got the paperwork you need to sign on the table by that pen there."

Patti smiled as the man put his fork down and stood briefly to shake her hand, then sat back down and got back to eating his food.

"Did everything go okay?" she asked. "Is the wiring all done now and ready for us to be looked over by the state guy next week?"

"Yes, Ms. Johnson. And may I add this cook of yours really knows his Mexican cooking! If this is the kind of food you will be serving here, I'm going to drag my family here as often as we are in the neighborhood. I'll be here for lunch take-outs as often as I can."

Patti smiled, looking at J.T., then she examined the paperwork. "Do I need to sign in more than one place?"

The electrician showed her where to sign and then stood up to leave after giving her copies of the paperwork. "I hope I didn't inconvenience you, but I had no idea who this man was and I'm new on the job. I didn't want to chance not having the correct signature, which would have slowed down your approval. I hope you understand."

Patti nodded. "No problem. I was on my way here anyway. Thanks for coming out on the day after Thanksgiving. Have a nice holiday. We should be open early in January for lunch almost every day, and we will be available for party bookings at other times. See you then."

"That you will," he said, as he put the paperwork into his toolbox and went out the front door.

Patti turned to J.T. "What did you make that smells so good? And why? I only told you to wait for him. You didn't have to cook anything."

J.T. looked at her solemnly. "Yes, I did. I couldn't just sit around here, doing nothing while I waited for him to get here. I was fighting myself not to rush over to your house and see for myself that you were all right. I had to take my mind off of worrying about you, so I picked up a few ingredients on the way over here, and I got to cooking to distract myself."

"You picked up some flowers, too," Jake said, smiling approvingly.

J.T. nodded. "You all just sit there and I'll go get you some of what I made. I think you'll like it."

He went into the kitchen and reappeared a few minutes later, balancing three plates on his arms, along with a bottle of hot sauce.

Patti looked at the plate he put in front of her, sniffed it, then smiled. "What is it?"

J.T. smiled back at her. "Guatemalan black beans with rice and corn relish with tomatoes and peppers. Go ahead, eat."

"Aren't you going to have any?" Patti asked.

"Yeah, I'm going to get myself some now and bring in the bottle of coke with four glasses of ice."

After he got back from the kitchen and had poured everyone some soda, J.T. sat across from Patti at the table with the flowers and began to eat.

"J.T, this is excellent! Just when I think you can't surprise me with new recipes, or even better food than the last time, you do!" Patti said.

Chelsea and Jake nodded their head, then Jake asked, "Is there any more in the kitchen?"

J.T. nodded, then started to get up.

"No, don't bother," said Chelsea, "We know where the kitchen is. You just sit and eat. I want to find some more cheese to put on mine."

Once both kids were in the kitchen, J.T. leaned closer to Patti and reached for her hand. She gave him the one she was not using to eat and smiled at him.

"He didn't hurt you, did he? I mean, last night, or this morning?" he asked her, searching her face for some sign that would tell him, without words, what he wanted to know.

Patti shook her head. "No. He had a copy of the house key and one to my room, though. I woke up a couple hours after you called last night to find he was in my bed, naked, expecting me to be so horny I'd take even him."

J.T. looked angry, but Patti smiled at him. "It's okay. I told him he had to get the hell out of my room or I'd call the police and report him as an intruder. We argued for a while, then I pointed out to him I had already had enough good sex for one night and didn't have any intention of giving in to him."

Patti gave J.T. an arch look. "He was *so* not happy about finding out you and I had spent time together. I told him he had to leave first thing in the morning and I demanded he give me his keys, then go out to the sofa to sleep. Which he did."

Jake came back through the door, his plate piled high with another helping of food and Chelsea was right behind him.

"He almost hit her then," he said to J.T., "but I walked into the room, since I had heard them arguing, and he didn't want to do it in front of me. He tried to use me to get her to agree to let him stay, but I told him it was time for him to leave. I told him none of us could relax with him in the house."

Chelsea nodded, as she sat down at the table and watched her brother dig into his food. She turned to J.T. "Then this morning, he had the nerve to call Mom a whore and tell her he would take her back to court, to tell the judge all about her biker boyfriend and the orgies you two would be having in front of us kids." She made a face at J.T. "As if, huh?"

J.T. had put his fork down when Jake started talking. When he raised his glass to take a drink, his hand shook. When he saw the others noticing, he put his glass down. He looked at his plate then raised his eyes to look at Patti.

"He has hit you before?"

Patti sighed. "It's all over now. He's not ever getting back into my house again. Just drop it. I don't expect we'll be seeing him in the near future, since he went on about how he won't be able to find a place big enough for the kids to stay to visit him and how he won't be able to afford any Christmas presents or anything. I don't think we need to worry about him showing up anytime soon."

J.T. looked Patti in the eye for a long time. Then he said, slowly, "Give me one good reason not to give that asshole an object lesson in why you don't hit people who are smaller than you...mainly because there is always someone bigger than you who might not be happy about your actions. And you never, I repeat, *never*, hit a lady."

Patti met his gaze, then smiled at him. "No, J.T. This is my battle, not yours. And I won this time. I threw him out and he's not getting back in, ever again. I appreciate your wanting to be my Prince Charming, but there are some things a woman has to do for herself. Let's just say after last night, there's no more doubt in my mind the divorce was the best thing to do." She looked around at her kids who were nodding. "For all of us."

Patti got up, walked over to J.T., turned his face up to hers and kissed him. Then he wrapped his arms around her and held her close to him, his face buried in her breasts. They held onto each other for a long moment. Then Patti smiled, her eyes a bit shinier than they had been, as she said, "I'm going out to the kitchen to make some coffee. You all finish out here."

After she took her plate out to the kitchen, J.T. cleared his throat then reapplied himself to eating his food. After exchanging small smiles, Chelsea and Jake did the same and the only sound was the scraping of forks on plates.

Patti came out into the dining room as J.T. got up, grabbing all of the plates off the table.

"Are you all ready for some dessert now?" he asked, while all three turned to him in surprise.

"Dessert?" asked Patti, "You had time to make all of that great food *and* dessert? Or is it just ice cream or something?"

J.T. smiled. "You'll see. I'll be right back."

Patti sat down and smiled at her kids. "I could get really used to this kind of treatment." They both nodded, and smiled at her.

J.T. reappeared carrying a tray that held the coffeepot, some mugs and some dessert plates and forks, as well as a round chocolate thing and a bowl.

Meeting the surprised look in Patti's eyes, J.T. smiled. "Flourless chocolate cake, with raspberry and almond compote."

When she smiled at him even broader, he looked guilty. "Well, I told you I was worried about you. I had to do something to pass the time and cooking relieves my stress."

Then he sat down, cut the dessert into portions and they passed the compote around. The adults and Chelsea poured themselves some coffee and they applied themselves to dessert.

After they had all eaten their fill, Chelsea and Jake offered to clean up the kitchen and the dishes, so they cleared off the table and went into the kitchen.

J.T. had leaned back on his chair balancing on the back two legs, while he watched Patti stir some milk into her coffee.

"I really wish I didn't have to work tonight, so I could come over and be with you," J.T. said.

Patti looked up at him and smiled, "You could come over after you get off work, you know. I could wait up for you."

J.T. shook his head. "No, I'm not looking for just a booty call. I want to take you out to dinner, maybe dancing and make you feel special."

Patti gave him a serious look. "You *do* make me feel special. You cook this delicious food for me. You worry about me. You offer to beat the crap out of my ex for me." She gave him a lecherous look. "And you rocked my world last night, I might add. I don't think I've *ever* made any noises like that during sex. But last night, I couldn't seem to shut up. A couple times, I think you actually made me pass out from sheer pleasure. What else could I ask for?"

J.T. smiled, leaning forward in his chair and covering her hand with his. "If you think of anything, honey, you just let me know and I'll see about doing it."

Patti leered. "I can think of a few things we haven't tried yet."

J.T. patted his lap and Patti got up and stood in front of him for a long, satisfying kiss. He pulled her onto his lap, and they spent a few sweaty moments, groping and kissing. J.T. groaned when Patti wriggled her hips back and forth, causing his engorged organ to become larger and more painful, trapped as it was between the zipper and his abdomen.

He growled. "If your kids weren't here, I'd take you right here, right now!"

Patti giggled. "And if they weren't here, I'd let you!"

Trying to focus, J.T. now regarded her seriously. "Do you think they will mind if I stay the night with you?"

Patti looked deeply into his eyes and felt herself begin to get lost in their gaze. "No, I don't think so. But we can ask them, if you are worried."

His eyebrows shot up to his forehead, "Really? Isn't that kind of weird?"

Patti shrugged, "I don't think so. I've never had to worry about this before, because I haven't been with any man since Jake."

The door swung open and Chelsea strode back into the room followed by her brother, saying, "See? I told you they would be kissing by now. Pay up!"

Sighing, Jake reached into his pocket, pulled out a coin and handed it to his sister.

Chelsea gave an arch look to her mother, as she told her brother, in a patronizing tone, "You have a lot to learn about women, dear boy!"

Patti laughed. "That's a good way to bring up what we wanted to talk to you guys about. J.T. wants to know if you two will mind if he stays the night at our house after we go on a date tomorrow night."

Chelsea and Jake both looked seriously at J.T., who shifted in his seat, as well as he could, with their mother on his lap. She got up, stood behind him and rubbed his neck. "Well? Would you mind?"

Slowly both children shook their heads, with Chelsea saying, "Actually, I was hoping you would be asking us if you could move in."

J.T. and Patti both regarded them with surprise, as Jake nodded in agreement with his sister.

"We've both had to live in two places for the past few years and it's not fun, trying to remember what color your toothbrush is, in two different houses. Then you have to remember where you changed your clothes to get them all washed." Chelsea's voice trailed off and her brother chimed in.

"You told us you were only staying with some friends temporarily, since you were sleeping on a cot in their living room. If you move in with us, you can share a real bed with Mom and have a better place to sleep. And somewhere to put all your clothes. And a garage for your Harley. There isn't enough room for a car in it, but you could probably put your motorcycle in there, at least when it snows or rains."

Chelsea nodded. "Then you can take turns doing the cooking with Mom and she won't have to cook every night, but we can all get to eat excellent food every night of the week. We won't even mind if you get tired of cooking and order a pizza every now and then, since we all like the same stuff on our pizza."

With both kids looking at them encouragingly, J.T. became even more acutely aware of Patti's hands on his neck, massaging his shoulders and the tension he could feel tightening muscles all around his body. Patti obviously felt the tension and spoke next.

"I don't think J.T. wants to move in, kids. Remember, he's not the kind of guy to stay in any one place for too long. He told me that when I hired him."

She withdrew her hands and began to walk to her seat. J.T. grabbed her hand and held it, while he looked into her eyes.

"I don't know about that," he began, smiling at the surprised look in her eyes. "As long as I'm in town, I might as well be staying somewhere I'm more comfortable." He looked at Chelsea and Jake and winked. "Somewhere I'm more welcome to stay as long as I want to. I'm kind of tired of moving around all the time. I feel real at-home around here, especially since I'm enjoying getting a chance to cook what I want to, instead of what I'm told to. I could see myself staying in town for quite a while, if I had a place to stay."

Patti realized she had stopped breathing and her heart was pounding. J.T. reached up and traced down the side of her face with one finger, then he looked into her eyes and smiled at her. "What do you say, Patricia? Should we give it a try?"

Patti looked up quickly, to see both of her children smiling broadly at them as she spoke, "You two don't have to worry. I won't let your dad move in again, if that's what you are worried about."

Chelsea made a face at her mom, then rolled her eyes, "Mom! It's not that at all! We just really like J.T., and like having him around. We won't be the first ones in the neighborhood to have a man move into the house. Even Tegan moved into a house with *Tio* Alejandro before they got married. So it's no big deal, really Mom."

Jake spoke up. "But Dad won't dare come back and ever try to hit you again if he knows J.T. is living with us, will he?"

J.T. stood up. "Let's not pressure your mother right now, okay guys?" He cleared off the table, putting the few remaining dirty dishes and the dessert onto the tray he had brought.

"Patti, we can talk about this tomorrow night. Give you some time to think it over. I need to get going, so I can change and get to work on time today. I'll call you tomorrow, to discuss when I'm going to pick you up for our dinner and dancing date tomorrow night, okay?"

Patti watched J.T. go through the door into the kitchen, then she followed him.

"I don't want you to think I'm not happy about the kids' suggestion…" she began.

J.T. stopped rinsing off the dishes and turned and held his arms out for Patti to come closer. She did and he enfolded her in his arms. She breathed out a shaky sigh.

"I think you've had a bit too much emotional turmoil for one day, honey," J.T. said, as he rubbed her back. "I'll admit I was staggered by their casual suggestion and acceptance of the idea of my moving in, but it really does make a lot of sense, when you look at it from their point of view. They gain the security of having a big man around to protect them and their mom and, just incidentally, twice the good cooking to eat!"

He chuckled, and she heard it rumble from low in his chest. She sighed again and snuggled closer to him. He held her tighter, then kissed the top of her head.

"But how do you really feel about the idea?" she asked him in a small voice.

She turned her head up to look into his eyes and he was almost undone by the love that was hiding behind the fear in her eyes. His face softened as the warmth in his eyes melted her fear and they looked deeply into each other's souls.

"Patricia, I want to make you happy. Seems I've fallen in love with you and so I have no intention of leaving anytime in the near future. Maybe not even in the far future."

He lowered his face to press his lips against hers, softly at first, then with more urgency, yet still he restrained himself

"If you are not comfortable with the idea, then I won't pressure you. But if you think there is room in your heart for a lonely Rom biker who is tired of wandering around looking for what he thinks he may have already found, then I think we should seriously consider the idea of me moving into your house. And soon."

He wrapped his arms more tightly around her and lowered his head to kiss her again. Their passion ignited and he picked her off the ground and held her effortlessly in his arms as he leaned back against the sink in the kitchen they shared. It was a long, sweaty, groping while before she pushed herself back, and he reluctantly let her feet touch the floor again.

She looked into his eyes. "I want you in my bed every night, Jules. I want to fall asleep in your arms and wake up next to you in the morning. I want your name tattooed on my heart, since you already own it."

She shook her head, as if to clear it. "So, I guess since you have already moved into my heart, you might as well move into my house."

He smiled and put his hands on either side of her face then moved them slowly back into her hair, as he lowered his face and kissed her gently.

"I love you," he said simply.

"I know," she said, smiling. "And I love you, too."

"Should I call you tomorrow when I wake up?" J.T. asked.

Patti shook her head, "No, we wake up earlier than you. Just bring your stuff over when you are ready and we'll be there."

J.T. nodded. "Our date is still on for tomorrow night. I plan to take you downtown to a place I know that has hot food and even hotter blues. I want to show you off to the entire world. Then I plan to take you home and make you scream so loud your kids will have to wear headphones. In fact, maybe that's what I'll buy them for Christmas so they won't hear you shouting all night."

Patti laughed. "That's what they get for suggesting this whole thing. 'Be careful what you wish for, you just might get it'!"

J.T. gave her a serious look. "You are what I have wished for, for months now. I'm still not over the shock of having you to myself, but I'm going to work really hard on that. Starting tomorrow."

He shook his head. "But right now, I think I have to get the last of the dishes going, then head out of here to get ready for work."

Patti shook her head. "No, you get going. The kids loaded everything else into the dishwasher and you did all of the cooking, after all. I'll load the dessert plates into it; then we'll go, too. I'll bring the leftovers home with me.

I'm going to go home and change the sheets. Maybe give myself a pedicure and shave my legs, so I'm all ready for our date tomorrow night."

J.T. smiled at her. "You always look beautiful to me, Patricia. You're sure you don't want me to help with the last of the dishes?"

When she shook her head again, he said, "Okay, then I'm going out through the front, so I can say goodbye to your kids, and just incidentally, thank them for bringing up something I wouldn't have had the guts to suggest for months."

Patti laughed, then waved as J.T. walked out of the kitchen. She turned to finish off the dishes and her first thought was, "I've got to call Tegan! Have I got news for her!"

She hummed to herself, thinking about what kind of design she wanted to get tattooed on her left breast with the name of her man in it.

Sixteen

Tegan insisted on rushing right over to hear all of the particulars in excruciating detail, when Patti called to tell her the news. The kids disappeared upstairs to their rooms when Tegan arrived, and left the two women alone to talk in Patti's dining room over a pot of coffee.

"I knew it! I knew that asshole had hit you while you were married," Tegan was saying angrily. She shook her head, "But J.T. wanted to kill him for you. Now there's a *real* man for you."

Patti nodded, "I guess that's why the kids want him to move in. They figure Jake won't dare try anything again if he knows J.T. is living here."

Tegan looked at her best friend closely. "Maybe they just really like him. Maybe they can sense how good he is for you." She thoughtfully stirred her coffee, then looked into Patti's eyes. "But how about you? How do you really feel about this? I mean, not how do you feel about how the kids feel, but how do *you* really feel about him moving in?"

Patti met her friend's eyes. "I'm not sure. I really do care about him; I just hope this doesn't kill our relationship. I'd hate for all of us to get used to having him around, then he decides it's time to hit the road again and we have to deal with another hole in our lives." She sighed.

Tegan nodded, covering Patti's hand with hers. "That would hurt worse than throwing Jake out the first time, wouldn't it?"

Patti gave Tegan a small smile. "Yes and no. It would hurt for him to reject all of us; but on the other hand, I really want Chelsea and Jake to see what a good relationship can be like."

"You mean like," Tegan then mimicked her daughter. "*Honestly, Mom, can't you two ever talk about anything else? O-M-G, can't you keep your hands to yourself, at least in public?* You mean like that kind of good relationship?"

Both women laughed and Patti patted her friend's hand, "Well, maybe not *quite* like that. My kids do seem more used to the idea of physical affection being a good thing. Hopefully, they won't agree with Katie about the horrors of having too much of a good thing."

Patti got up to answer the phone. "It's for you...your main squeeze...he must be missing you, eh? You've been here, gosh, at least an hour or so."

Tegan looked guilty as she took the phone, then made some excuses into it. She hurriedly handed it back to Patti. "The doctor told me not to drive anymore, since I'm so huge I can barely reach the pedals without squishing my belly into the steering wheel. Alex was at Edgar's when you called, so I just jumped into the car and came over. He's walking over here; then he'll drive me back home."

Patti smirked at her friend, "You bad girl!"

Tegan nodded ruefully, "I know. And I'm *way* past ready for this pregnancy to be over. I'm counting the hours now, but not for the same reasons as Alex. He's just anxious to see his first child for the first time. I'm ready to beg *you* to do the c-section for me, right here and now, just so I don't have to be pregnant anymore."

Patti smirked at Tegan. "Well, that's *one* thing I don't have to worry about. I went on the pill a couple months ago, so there's no danger of anything unexpected happening here."

Tegan looked at her friend closely. "What if J.T. wants to have a baby with you?"

Patti looked at her in alarm. "God, I hope not! How would I run my restaurant? You, at least, enjoy your pregnancies, for the most part. I always hated being pregnant, since I got as big as a house…probably since I started out the size of a duplex anyway. And the morning sickness? For someone who likes to eat as much as I do? *Bleah!* I couldn't even enjoy cooking, since I got so nauseous just smelling certain things."

Tegan pointed out. "He *is* younger than you, you know. He might still want kids."

Patti shook her head. "Then he's going to have to have them with someone else. I'm done with that. Don't get me wrong… I'm looking forward to babysitting for you as much as I want; but then I'm looking forward to coming back to my diaper-free house and relaxing somewhere far away from *where babies cry*."

"Tegan?" Alexander yelled as he walked in through the front door. "Oh, *there* you are, my disobedient beloved one." He strode over to stand in front of her, hands on his hips, shaking his head in disapproval.

"Whatever am I going to do with you?" he asked her, only half in jest.

Tegan shrugged, then used the arm rests on the chair to push herself up to a standing position. "I don't know. Get yourself fixed, so I don't have to go through the ninth month ever again?"

Alexander sighed, but the look he gave her was full of love and pride. "Maybe don't eat so much and the next one won't be quite so big right before you deliver?"

Patti snorted, "With you as big as you are? And her an Amazon in her own right? I don't think that's possible! You two are doomed to make huge babies. Take it from me: if you want her to pop you out another one, you should knock her up again before this one turns a year old. She'll be too baby-brained and full of nursing hormones to object. It'll be too late for her to complain and she'll be able to get herself fixed after the second one. You'll have to take her to some really phenomenal place for a second honeymoon, like on your third anniversary. But by then, there'll be no danger of another pregnancy and you can screw happily ever after."

Tegan sighed, "We will be able to screw again? And really enjoy it, without having to worry about squishing the baby?" She gave Alexander a hungry look and both he and Patti laughed.

Alexander bowed to Patti. "Thanks, dear lady, for your suggestions. I now have my life mapped out for the next few years. Can I help you with yours? Maybe throw that no-good ex of yours out of your house?"

Patti smiled back at him. "No. I already did that…as of this morning, he's history. But thanks for offering. Now I just have to worry about how things will change around here, once J.T. moves in tomorrow. There's never a dull moment these days."

Alexander's eyebrows shot up, as he exchanged a look with his wife. He nodded, and turned to Patti. "Then good luck…to all of you."

At Patti's questioning look, he continued. "As I have been privileged to learn, a relationship with a woman who has children does not just involve the two of you. It involves *all* of you. And having extra dance partners makes the steps involved a lot more complicated. Of course, it increases the potential for love, but it also makes mistakes unavoidable, and people's feet are bound to get stepped on."

Alexander smiled fondly at Tegan, then turned to smile at the look on Patti's face. "I didn't say it wasn't possible, Patti. I just said it was more complicated. J.T. is a good man. You are a good woman. And your kids are good kids. You should be fine. Just remember to laugh often, and give your kids really good headphones, so they won't hear what you are doing in your room. Make love as often, and as vigorously, as you can manage!"

All three of them laughed and Tegan said, "See, Patti. You got him so philosophical, he's forgotten to be angry with me for driving. Thanks!"

Alexander shook his head, "No, I didn't forget, my love. I intend to punish you as soon as I get you home. Remember, the kids are already on their way to their dad's place for the weekend." He leered at her, "No one is home to hear you scream."

Tegan gave him a look of mock-terror. "Please sir, can I have some more?"

They all laughed again and Patti said, "Okay, you two. Out of here. I'm going to order a pizza for tonight and spend some time making sure my kids really are all right with this new move. And Tegan? I'll call you, but probably not until Monday. We can trade stories and decide who had the most exciting, sex-filled weekend, okay?"

Alexander raised his eyebrows. "Excuse me? You two will trade stories about intimate moments?"

Tegan smiled at him, "Yes, but don't worry your pretty little head about it, my love. Just think of it as being your way to pleasure two women. Me first, then her when I tell her all about it." She and Patti exchanged smiles.

Alexander looked from one to the other of them. "But I don't get any pleasure out of the second time. Don't I get to hear any details, too?"

Patti sighed exaggeratedly. "Well, I'm sure Tegan has already told you how much I've been fantasizing about J.T. Yesterday, after you all left, we finally got a chance to be alone together, since my kids obligingly hid themselves upstairs. After such a long man-fast, any sex would have been appreciated. But not only was J.T. a sensitive and creative lover…but what I was *really* thrilled with, was the size of his…"

"¡*Basta*! *Enough*!" Alexander looked horrified. "Tegan, I'll be waiting in the car. When you and Patti are through with whatever you were talking about, we can leave. And try not to share *too* much of our love life with others."

He turned to Patti. "Goodbye, you depraved woman."

Patti snickered. "How do you think you got to be number one on our playgroup's top five fantasy men list? It wasn't just on your good looks, though that sure helps!"

Alexander rolled his eyes in exasperation, turned and walked to the front door. Both women made a big deal out of watching his butt as he walked. He turned, when he got to the door, and he waggled his finger at them both. "Naughty, naughty! I can hear what you are thinking. Ladies, behave yourselves."

They both laughed and Tegan hugged Patti. "Good luck, partner. I hope things work out, for all of you. Now, if you'll excuse me, there's something I just remembered that I *really* have to get home to do, right now!" She leered at her husband. "Isn't there, dear?"

He leered back at her. "Yes. Get in the car, NOW!"

Patti shut the door after she waved at them. As they drove off, she yelled, "Chelsea! Jake! What kind of pizza, what size and from where?"

~ * ~

Patti hadn't been asleep long when the phone rang. She had been sitting up in bed working on a crossword puzzle to unwind after her long, emotional discussions with her children over what they all wanted out of life. Since she had half expected J.T. to call, she had the phone close to her so she didn't have to get out of bed to answer it.

"Hello?"

"Hi, Patricia. It's me," J.T. said. "I'm sorry to wake you, but I had to talk to you. I've been thinking about you all night, even while I was growling at under-aged and drunken troublemakers."

"That's okay," Patti said. "I thought you might call. I was up late talking to the kids. We had pizza, then talked about life in general and you in particular."

There was silence for a moment.

"Are you still there?"

J.T. swallowed hard. "So, are they still okay with me moving in tomorrow?"

Patti smiled. "Of course, you goof! They are the ones who brought it up, remember?"

J.T. let out the breath he had not realized he was holding. "I know. But I was afraid they might have changed their minds, after really thinking about it."

"No," Patti answered. "In fact, if anything, they are even more convinced this is a good idea."

There was silence for another moment. "And you?"

Patti took a deep breath. "I want you in my bed, Jules. I'm not making any promises about forever...I don't think you want any. But I like sharing my life with you; you make it more interesting. We complement each other, in the kitchen, and in the bedroom." Patti smiled into the phone again. "And quite frankly, those are the only two rooms I care about, anyway."

J.T. smiled into his phone. "Then I'll see you tomorrow, Patricia. I'm not sure how early I'll be up, but as soon as I am, I'll pack up and come over. I won't have much to bring, since I travel light."

Patti yawned. "Okay, then. We'll be up and I'll try to clear some space in my dresser and in the closet for you.

We can reheat the leftovers from what you made today for lunch."

J.T. smiled again. "Good night, Patricia. See you soon."

"Good night to you too, Jules."

After he hung up his phone, Jules lay in his cot and stared through the window at the stars in the sky for a very long time. "What has happened to me? I have never moved in with any woman...I've never stayed anywhere for long enough to want to." He thought about what it felt like to hold Patti and make love to her. He remembered the sounds she made and the pleasures they had shared together. Then he got up and removed his jeans, which had become uncomfortably tight, and he pulled on a pair of sweat pants and sighed heavily as he lay down.

"Tomorrow starts a new phase in my life, I guess. Good luck to all of us."

With that prayer in his mind, he finally fell asleep.

~ * ~

Patti and the kids were all up early, as usual, on Saturday morning. Patti went to an early morning Jazzercise class, since she felt the need to work off some of the Thanksgiving calories, as well as her stress. She had stripped the bed and put the sheets into the wash before she left, so she put them into the dryer when she got home, then got to work cleaning out a couple of drawers in her dresser. As long as she was at it, she vacuumed and cleaned her entire room and was putting the sheets back onto the bed, when Jake yelled. "He's here, Mom. J.T. is in the driveway."

"Just let him in and tell him I'm in here," she yelled back. With dismay, she realized she had not changed, so she was still in the spandex she wore to exercise. She hated how she looked in it, so she used that as an incentive to keep herself going to class. She figured if she just went often enough, maybe she could remove some of the bulges that annoyed her so much, when not held in by heavier fabrics, like denim.

Patti was in the process of grabbing some clothes to change into when J.T. walked into the room and stopped when he saw her. Suddenly shy, she was not sure what to say, so she just looked at him.

"Patricia, you are a sight for sore eyes," J.T. said, as his eyes shone with admiration and lust. "It's way too early in the morning for me to even be awake, but you are worth waking up for."

Patti giggled. "Even with spandex on, so you can see all of my bulges?"

J.T. shook his head. "I told you, honey, I like a woman with meat on her bones." With an evil leer, he began, "Or was that, I like to bone a woman with my..."

"Hey, J.T.," Chelsea stuck her head into the room. "Mom, do you want me to start reheating that yummy food J.T. made yesterday?"

J.T. blushed, and Patti laughed at his discomfort. "Mister, you are going to have to get used to watching what you say around here. It's a small house, so there are always kids in hearing distance."

Chelsea rolled her eyes. "The *kids* that you refer to are certainly old enough to understand what kinds of perversion you two are talking about. And if we had a problem with it, we wouldn't have invited you to move in here, now, would we?"

J.T. shook his head and smiled at Chelsea. "All the same, the last thing I want to do is make you feel uncomfortable in your own house. And your mother is right...I think the last time I lived in a house that had children in it, I was one of the children."

Mollified, Chelsea walked in to give J.T. a hug. "Then I'm extra glad you are moving in with us. Mom needs another grown-up around to talk nasty with. Now that her attention will be focused on you, maybe we will be able to get away with more, since she'll be busy with you?"

With mock disapproval, Patti asked, "And just what kinds of things are you planning on getting away with, young lady?"

Chelsea rolled her eyes again. "Nothing, Ma. Just yanking both of you, that's all. Trying to break up the tension in the room. Shoot me for trying! I'll just head into the kitchen to get lunch started and you two can go back to being awkward and uncomfortable with each other, okay?"

Snickering, she left the room. J.T. and Patti were left looking at each other. Patti started to smile, and J.T. did, too.

"She's right, isn't she?" Patti asked. "I wonder why?"

J.T. gave her a serious look. "Maybe because the last time you let a man move in, it did not lead to any pleasant experiences?"

Patti nodded.

"And for me," J.T. continued. "This is a totally new experience. I haven't lived with a woman since my divorce, and that was almost fifteen years ago. I've been traveling around ever since and never found anyone else I even thought about moving in with."

"You were married?" Patti asked. With disapproval in her voice, she continued. "Why didn't you tell me?"

J.T. smiled at her. "Because it just never came up. It was a very long time ago and I was just a boy. I could barely even grow facial hair back then. And besides," J.T. gave Patti an arch look, "We are going to have lots of time to learn everything there is to know about each other, now I'm moving in, right?"

Patti smiled back at him, "Well, okay. Let me show you which drawers I emptied for you to put your clothes into. Then you can get unpacked."

J.T. moved closer to her and Patti started to breathe faster, even though he wasn't touching her at all. All the same, she could feel heat radiating from his body to hers.

"How about if I throw you onto the bed that you just put clean sheets on and we can mess them all up?" he growled at her, then blew at a wisp of hair that had fallen into her face.

In a breathy voice, Patti said, "Not now, J.T.! The kids are awake and surely listening, to see how we are going to handle this new situation. We *are* going out tonight, right? We'll just have to wait until then."

J.T. leaned closer to her and inhaled. "You smell all nice and sweaty," he said in a low tone. "Promise me someday you'll let me tear your spandex off you with my teeth?"

Patti giggled. "Jules, you are such an animal. I can hardly wait!"

Chelsea called out. "Lunch is ready! Come and get it a-
fore I slop it to the hogs."

J.T. raised an eyebrow as he looked at Patti, and she
shrugged. "I grew up on a farm in upper state New York.
We didn't raise hogs, but it was one of my favorite
sayings when I was a kid!"

J.T. nodded. "See, I didn't know you grew up on a
farm, or even what state you were born in. That's the kind
of stuff we can look forward to learning about each other,
now that we have the time."

Patti nodded, too. "Okay. But the first thing I want to
learn about you is all of the details about your marriage.
You know all about mine. Then we can move on from
there."

J.T. rolled his eyes and, using a high falsetto voice,
mimicked a centerfold model. "My favorite color is red;
favorite turn-ons are holding hands while walking along a
beach, reading poetry and drinking beer while shooting
pool in biker bars."

Patti smiled. "Quite a juxtaposition there, mister!"

Jake stuck his head into the room and made hog-
grunting noises.

Patti threw a pillow at his head. She and J.T. followed
him into the kitchen to eat their lunch.

While they ate, J.T. brought up a subject he was not
sure how to broach. He cleared his throat. "My buddies
were really cool with me moving out so suddenly, and
they gave me back the rent money I had given them for
December. So how much do you want me to pay you for
rent?"

Patti gave him a studied look. "Why don't we wait and see if this is going to work out all right for all of us first? Then we can start with you paying some of the bills in January."

"Instead of rent?" J.T. asked. "I guess that would be fair, as long as the bills are big enough to help you out. We can grocery shop together, then I'll pay you back for a quarter of that, okay?" He looked concerned. "Maybe I should pay for more than a quarter, since I eat more than all of you?"

Jake laughed. "He really *hasn't* been around growing kids lately, has he? Wait until he sees how much pizza we can put away on a good night."

J.T. smiled. "No, but I remember eating all of the time, whenever I had a growth spurt, once I was a teenager. So maybe a quarter of the grocery bill will be just about right." He chewed for a while. "Since I don't have to pay any rent in December, I'll have more money to buy Christmas presents with; so if that's okay with all of you, that's what I'll do."

Patti smiled at him. "J.T., you don't have to buy us anything."

He smiled back. "I know. But I want to. I already know what I'm going to get for all of you. And you and I are going to blow a chunk of my money tonight, going out celebrating."

Patti gave him a questioning look. "What are we celebrating?"

He patted her hand. "I seem to remember promising you, since I had to work on your birthday, I would take you out for dinner and dancing and we would celebrate your birthday then. And I, personally, want to celebrate having found people who like having me around. And having a real place to live...a house that doesn't have wheels on it. RVs can be nice, but growing up, I spent a lot of time wishing I lived in a real house like other kids did."

"You lived in an RV?" Jake asked, "Cool! You must have seen a lot of the country. Did you move around a lot?"

J.T. nodded, adding ruefully, "It was fun, when I was younger, like you are. We have relatives in almost every state in the country, so we always had somewhere we could park it and live for a while. But once I got to Chelsea's age and was a teenager, I *really* just wanted to be like everyone else and have a permanent home. I wanted to stay in one state long enough to finish a year of high school and not have to always be the new kid who got made fun of for being different from everyone else."

Chelsea nodded. "That must have been really hard for you. I know I always feel like I don't fit in, because my mom is divorced and my dad is such a jerk. I hear other kids complaining about how strict their dads are, or how nice and I can't say anything because the less I have to do with mine, the better I feel."

Patti gave her a stricken look. J.T. covered Chelsea's hand with his while he nodded. "What doesn't kill you makes you stronger, huh, girlie?" He patted her hand. "You just remember while they are talking about their dads, that the biker dude who lives in *your* house, can beat up their dads anytime!"

Chelsea gave him a grateful smile and Jake chuckled. "*Our* guy can beat up *your* guy, anytime. *Great*!"

Patti rolled her eyes. "Well, I'm not sure that's the kind of thing I would advise you to go spreading around your school, though."

Chelsea smiled. "We won't have to! Anyone who has ever seen J.T. will know who he is and just how big and mean he looks. We won't have to say anything else. "

"Not to change the subject too much, or anything…" Patti made sure everyone saw the disapproval on her face, "But where are we going tonight, J.T.? And when are we leaving, and when do you think we will be getting home?"

Chelsea gave her a horrified look. "*Mom*! You're *not* thinking that we need a babysitter, are you?"

Patti looked taken aback. "Well, if we are going to be gone for a long time, then…" her voice trailed off as Jake glared at her too.

"*Mom!* Chelsea is old enough to *be* a sitter. We will be just fine. We know the neighbors on both sides and Tegan lives so close she and *Tío* Alejandro would be here in a heartbeat if we called them. Get real!"

J.T. smiled at Patti. "Well, it looks like they have let you know what's what."

Patti made a face at both kids. "I'm just concerned, that's all. I've never gone anywhere at night and left you two alone. This is new for me."

J.T. answered. "As for your question, we can make the dinner reservations for anytime, but I'd advise not much before eight, since blues bands are notorious for being late. They are usually scheduled to start about ten, but that's just a suggestion, and usually they start later than that. If we want to hear any music, we'll have to stay until at least midnight, maybe one."

Patti nodded. "How should I dress? Is this a fancy place, or what?"

J.T. made a face at her. "Fancy? Nah. This is a place I checked out the last time I passed through Chicago. One of my second cousins owns it and like I told you, the food is hot, but the blues are hotter. It's in a changing neighborhood…it was pretty rough a few years ago, but it was already starting to gentrify then. I'm sure it's more upscale now. I called a few weeks ago and talked to my cousin to be sure things haven't changed. He said for Saturday nights I should make a reservation. But he said to use his name and tell them I'm a relative. That way, they'll give me a good table. So you tell me what time you want to get there and I'll do that."

Patti gave him a funny look. "Is there anywhere around there to get a tattoo?"

J.T. looked at her, surprise evident on his face, "Why? Are you really planning on getting one?"

Patti nodded. "Uh-huh. I've been dreaming about it lately, so I figure it's time."

J.T. smiled. "As a matter of fact, I've had some ink done at a place in the neighborhood. The owner does good work, although he's kind of pricey. Maybe I can get one, too, and we can get a volume discount?"

Chelsea now jumped in. "Really Mom? That is *so* cool! Wait until I tell Katie! She thinks that 'cause she has a new brother coming, she's the coolest."

Patti laughed nervously. "Let's wait until I see if I chicken out or not, okay? I mean, Tegan can't chicken out…the baby's coming, whether she's ready or not. But just because I have myself psyched out to do this doesn't mean I won't turn tail and run when the guy brings a needle close to my skin."

J.T. smiled at her affectionately. "Hell, I've had it done lots of times. It's like a bee sting, until the outline is done. Then your skin makes endorphins and you don't hardly feel the color going on. I'll hold your hand, if you hold mine."

Patti smiled at him, and nodded. "Deal." She gave him an arch look, "Hey, why don't you come and take a look at my clothes with me, and tell me what you think I should wear for tonight?"

Jake said, "I'm going over to Bill's house, remember, Mom? We have that science project to work on."

Chelsea added, "I'm going over to help Rosa watch the kids while her parents are doing some Christmas shopping. Remember? Katie's in the city at her dad's place, so Rosa asked me to do this last week. She's paying me, too."

Chelsea gave them all a secretive look. "There's this holiday coming up that I might need money to buy gifts for, right?"

Patti looked at her watch. "What time are you both going to be home, then? I don't want to leave the house until you are both back and I know the doors are locked for the night."

Jake shrugged. "I don't know how long it will take us to get done. But it's not even one now, Mom. I'm sure I'll be home in plenty of time."

Patti nodded. "Just be sure you get home before it gets dark, okay? That means by about four or so."

Chelsea nodded. "Rosa said she'd need me there from about one to about four. So I'd better get going. Leave the dishes for later, Mom. I'll do them when I get back."

There was a flurry of activity as both kids headed out the door to their various destinations. J.T. sat quietly and watched. When the house was quiet and Patti came back into the kitchen, he held out his hand to her and smiled.

"Looks like we have some time to kill before we head into the city, huh, darlin'?" He waggled his eyebrows at her. "And you, still in your spandex."

Patti smiled at him from across the room. "Race you to the bedroom!" She shrieked with laughter as he jumped up and chased her there.

Later, while they lay panting on the bed, J.T. spoke. "Patricia, my love, I finally feel like I have a real place to belong."

Her voice hoarse from screaming, Patti said, "You mean in my house?"

He smiled at her, and moved his hips, making her bite her lip and moan with pleasure.

"That, too. But mostly, in you. This is where I belong."

Patti smiled at him. "So stay for a while. Stay and be my man."

J.T. nodded. "I will." He kissed her to seal the bargain.

They both sighed with pleasure and exhaustion and drifted off for a mid-afternoon nap wrapped in each others' arms, secure in the knowledge Patti had set the alarm for three-thirty.

~ * ~

Much, much later, Patti giggled as they strolled down the street to where she had parked her car so they could have dinner and dance to blues music from a live band. They were holding hands and at irregular intervals, J.T. would pull her into his arms for another kiss and another session of groping...each time left her more excited, and more disheveled.

"Hey, Jules. Why don't we find a biker bar? I'm sure there's some around here somewhere, huh? Then I can show off my new tattoo!"

J.T. smiled indulgently at her. "What a bad influence I am on you already, Patricia. I've been living in your house for less than a day and already you have a tattoo with my name on it..." He traced the heart on her left breast, then rubbed the nipple under the design. Patti shuddered with pleasure.

"And now, even though we have been drinking and carousing and dancing until all hours of the night, you want me to take you to a biker bar? What's next?"

Patti giggled again. "I don't know. Orgies in the street?"

J.T. pulled her close again and pressed himself against her firmly, "*No!*" He growled at her, while his tongue traced a line around her mouth, then he kissed her roughly. "I don't share. You're mine now, remember? No one else touches you."

Patti twined herself around him, rubbing herself against his throbbing erection and running her hands under his shirt to trace the outline of his new tattoo, the one over his heart that had her name on it.

"Okay. But I really like to shoot pool and I haven't been able to for years. Jake didn't know how to play and a woman can't go into a pool hall by herself without looking like she's there to play with more balls than are on the table."

He smiled at her fondly. "Honey, we have your car, remember? You can't go to a biker bar driving a car."

She shook her head. "Why not? You have a Harley in my garage."

He patiently explained. "But if you don't ride up on it, you are not a biker. You are a poser. And posers are not welcome in biker bars."

Patti pouted. "Even with tattoos?"

He nodded solemnly. "Yes. But wait until the weather gets nicer. I'll take you and show you off in all the places I know. I'm going to take you camping, too. There's a lot of great places in Wisconsin where you can set up your tent and ride the back roads all day, feeling the wind in your face. When we get back to the site, I'll make you camping food that will knock your socks off; then you can thank me by blowing me away with your sexual skills. Nothing beats sex in the great outdoors."

Patti sighed. "I haven't been camping since I was in college. Jake didn't like doing that either."

J.T. used his finger to lift her face up to look him in the eye. "Sounds to me like this Jake guy didn't know what he had. His loss is my gain. I intend to get down on my knees every day, and thank God you are mine."

Patti giggled. "Okay. And Jules? While you are down there…"

He growled at her and kissed her, his tongue tasting of beer and his love. They got into her car and drove out of the city to the house where they both now lived.

After checking to be sure both kids were all right, they retired to their bedroom and made luxurious love lasting half of the night. J.T. was used to staying up later than Patti, so afterwards, when she was fast asleep in his arms, he lay and thought about what his life had been and what it had become. He gave thanks for everything about this woman who had changed his world. Then he closed his eyes and slept his first night in a real house.

Seventeen

The days in December were busier than usual. Not only was everyone rushing around, decorating, baking and buying and wrapping presents for Christmas, but Patti was trying to keep to her schedule and have the restaurant ready to open up for lunches and booked parties only, right after the holidays. She and J.T. continued to spend their days there, getting all of the loose ends taken care of, then J.T. would go to his night job and Patti would go back home to work on any parties Pat-Teg had booked. By agreement, since Tegan was due the second week of December, they had only booked a couple of kids' birthday parties for the first week in December. Then they put a hold on parties until after the holidays.

Tegan had scheduled her c-section for the second Saturday, the thirteenth. This meant arrangements had to be made for her kids to get a ride to the hospital from Patti, since Alexander was going to be in the delivery room with his wife. J.T. had made a deal with his boss at the Party House, so he worked every Friday night, but had every Saturday night off. He had added an extra weekday to make up for that. He was home and sleeping when Tegan and

Alexander dropped the kids off at Patti's house on their way to the hospital.

"Good luck, you two," Patti said, as she ran out to the car and made Tegan get out so she could hug her. "Or should I say, you three?"

Alexander smiled weakly. "Thank you."

Tegan inclined her head towards him, sitting in the car behind the wheel, and winked at Patti. "I sure hope he doesn't pass out in the delivery room. You know what they say about the bigger they are, the harder they fall."

Patti peered into the car and waved at Alexander, saying to Tegan quietly, "Yeah, he looks kind of green around the edges."

She smiled at Alexander and spoke loud enough for him to hear. "You'll be fine, all of you. Call me when you are ready for me to bring the kids to meet their new brother."

Tegan got back into the car with great difficulty and they drove off. Patti walked slowly into the house, then smiled at the kids who were arguing about who got to play what video games in which rooms. She left them to their own devices, and went into the kitchen to create something interesting for lunch from some new recipes she had found on the internet. She had been using all four kids as taste-testers for her cooking for years and she knew they would be flattered to be asked their opinions and would be honest with her.

Since the c-section had been scheduled for ten, Patti didn't expect to get called until some time later in the afternoon. When she had not heard anything by two, she began to wonder what could be taking so long, so she called the hospital. She was informed there was not yet a room number assigned to her friend. She was told to be patient, so she told the kids what she had learned and tried to keep herself busy baking some oatmeal pecan chocolate chip cookies, which were Tegan's favorites, as a welcome-home gift.

The phone rang just before three. At first she didn't recognize the voice; then she realized it was Alexander, who sounded as if he didn't know whether to laugh or to cry. He might have been doing both at the same time.

"Patti," he began, "Bring the kids over to meet their brother. *¡Dios mio!* I must give the phone to Tegan…"

Patti waited patiently, then heard Tegan's voice. "Patti! He's here! He's huge! And he's hungry! I finally got my nipple out of his mouth, so his daddy is holding him now. I'll tell you all about it when you get here."

"We'll be right over," Patti began, "What room number are you in?"

"Who the hell knows? I've still got the epidural in me, so I can't walk yet and I'm trying to talk them into giving me something to eat, but they are being all pissy about it, since it hasn't been long enough since the surgery, or some crap like that."

Patti giggled. "Should I smuggle in some cookies?"

"Patti, you are a life-saver. Hell, yeah! And bring my kids on over here!"

"Okay, partner. See you soon." Patti hung up, and yelled, "Everyone who wants to see Tegan's new baby, get in the car now!"

J.T. came into the kitchen and asked, "What about the cookies still in the oven and the ones you haven't baked yet?"

Patti shrugged, "Uh, I'll finish them later?"

J.T. shook his head, "I'll stay home, honey. There isn't enough room in your car for me to go too, anyway. I'll finish the cookies, then throw something into the oven for dinner, okay?"

Patti got up on tiptoe to kiss him. "Are you sure?"

He nodded, then pulled her closer for a longer kiss.

Patti put the already-done cookies onto a plate, rounded up the kids, then drove to the hospital.

Since Patti was the first one Tegan had called, she and the kids were the first visitors. She found Tegan alert and chafing at the bit, since she was not allowed to get out of bed.

"How come you look so good right after delivering that twelve-pound moose baby?" she asked Tegan when they were alone. All of the kids were down with Alexander, admiring the baby, who was having his vitals checked in the nursery.

Tegan laughed and reached for another cookie. "I'm still not feeling any pain, since the continuous epidural takes care of that. I didn't do any delivering anyway...I just lay there, while the doctors filleted me like a fish and pulled him out. Just wait until later tonight, when they want me to cough...I'll be afraid my intestines will pop out, so I'll try one of those ahe-ahem kind of things, and they won't let me get away with that. Then I won't be so smiley." She blew a kiss to her partner. "These cookies are great, Patti. And the milk smuggled in from the vending machines downstairs is a nice touch. Thanks a whole bunch."

Patti reached over and hugged her as best she could, what with tubes still sticking into her arms and "vitals" monitors still attached. "No problem, girl. There's a whole lot more being baked by J.T. as we speak."

Tegan smiled. "Did you see how Alex looks?"

Patti smiled back at her. "You mean that silly, loopy, *I'm totally in love with my new son and the woman who made it all possible, so life is good,* look?"

When Tegan nodded, Patti laughed. "Yeah, it was kind of noticeable. It's a new look for him, but I think it suits him."

Juanita and Edgar walked into the room carrying a balloon and flowers and more congratulations were in order. Edgar went out to find his brother and Juanita told the women her in-laws were on their way to the hospital to meet their new grandbaby. Patti told Tegan she would take her own kids back home once the grandparents arrived with Alexander's sister. There would be too many people in the room at once and the nurses would start to get too bossy if they thought the baby was being exposed to too much noise.

"Call me if your kids need a ride home if Alex decides to stay the night here in the room with you and the baby, okay?" Tegan nodded.

Alexander returned, followed by the nurse pushing the baby, squalling and obviously hungry, into the room, followed by Edgar and the older kids. Mass pandemonium was the rule for the next few hours, as relatives piled into the room and everyone admired the new family member and congratulated the proud parents.

Eighteen
Comfort Food

It was dark by the time Juanita and Edgar left the hospital. They had just gotten into the car when Edgar burst into gales of laughter. He laughed until there were tears in his eyes and said, in gasping breaths, things like, "Did you see his face?"

"He's acting like no one ever had a baby before!"

"When he said he had no idea it was so hard to have a baby, I thought I was gonna have to leave the room so I didn't laugh right in his face!"

Juanita let him laugh, then she patted his shoulder. "Let it go, Edgar. It's not really that funny." She eyed him thoughtfully. "I'm just glad you kept a straight face while he raved on and on about how wonderful his son is."

Edgar turned to look at her. "After all of these years, after all of the abuse he has heaped on me, saying things like: *Don't you two have any other hobbies?* and calling us *breeders*, I'm not supposed to be able to enjoy seeing him acting like such an idiot?"

Juanita shook her head. "He's not acting like an idiot. He's in love…with his first son and with his wife. Leave him alone and let him enjoy it."

Edgar started the car, turned the heat on, then started to drive. "You mean, you forgive him for all of these years while we were having babies and he never thought it was any big deal? That never bothered you?"

Juanita nodded. "Yes, I forgive him." She shook her head. "He didn't know what he was missing, or how empty his life was. He was the one missing out on one of the best experiences of life. How could I get upset with his snarky comments when he didn't know any better?"

Edgar chuckled. "Well, he knows better now. Did you see the look on his face when he got to change his first diaper? You'd have thought he was being given the most precious gift in the world instead of a diaper full of baby poop. Honestly, he looks like a love-sick puppy dog. And not anything like my always-in-control oldest brother. I guess he may be the oldest, but he's always been a slow learner about what's really important in life, huh?"

Juanita nodded. "I'm just glad he finally found someone to love, someone who loves him back. They belong together, and now they have a baby to keep them tied together. I'm happy for all of them."

Edgar pulled into the driveway in front of his brother's empty house and Juanita turned to him questioningly. He turned off the car, unhooked his seatbelt and hers, then pulled her roughly over to him for a long kiss, involving dueling tongues and groping hands. His urgency surprised her. He moved his mouth over her ear and whispered into it. "Let's make another baby, *cariña*. I want you more than ever, my love...*mi querida*."

Juanita smiled at her impetuous husband, who was in the process of trying to undo the buttons on her shirt. "Here? In the car? Now? Are you crazy?"

Edgar nodded. "Crazy for you, *mi bonita 'Nita*. The only woman I have ever loved."

Juanita touched his hand. "Edgar, my love, we agreed, no more babies. Seven was the last, you said."

"No," he said softly, while he continued to undo her clothing, "That was what *you* said. I only went along with it to keep you happy."

His tongue traced a path from her mouth to her ear, then down her neck to the breasts he had freed from their bra and now held in his hands; he licked, then sucked at each one in turn, and smiled up at the soft sighs Juanita was making as she still tried to hold out against him.

"*Uno mas*...one more baby, 'Nita. Then I promise, I'll get myself fixed."

She shook her head, looking dazed. "You said that the last time, then you didn't."

He smiled at her, kissing her eyelids. "I had my fingers crossed that time. Seven is such an odd number, my love. Let's make it an even eight; then we'll stop, I promise."

His hands were busy now, sliding up under her skirt, pulling her pantyhose down to give him access to the moist area that was growing wetter every minute.

Juanita opened her eyes. "You had your fingers crossed the last time?"

He nodded, then put both hands where she could see them in front of her. "See, no fingers crossed this time. One more baby, then I'll get snipped, I promise."

She looked into his eyes and smiled. "Take off your shoes and show me your toes, lover."

He raised his eyebrows, as his fingers resumed their assault on her senses, "Ah, my love, you know me so well." He kept on rubbing her while he spoke into her neck and ear, "I love to feel you respond to me, my wife. I love to let God use us to create new life. I love to feel my child move in your body and to know you are mine. One more baby, Juanita. Just one more."

With a sigh, she raised herself up off of the seat so he could slip her pantyhose off, then she reached over and began to undo his belt buckle. "I have never been able to say no to you, Edgar. Not since the first time you touched me when I was sixteen and you changed my world."

He was panting now, his breaths coming in gasps, as they moved themselves around in the car so she was sitting facing him on his lap, his engorged organ now out of his pants and eager to give them both pleasure. He leaned his head forward and sucked one of her nipples into his mouth as he pushed himself forward and into the wetness that he sought.

"*¡Dios mio*! All of these years making love to you, and each time is better than the last." He groaned, as they moved themselves together, in a rhythm both familiar, and yet new. Experienced as they were with each other's bodies, it wasn't long before the moment of maximum pleasure.

Juanita screamed as she came, her swollen walls clenched on him and he fought himself to maintain control, then failed. The car rocked, as they rode the waves of pleasure. Edgar felt as if he was pumping his life's blood into her and Juanita felt as if she should be able to taste him with the force of his orgasm. For a long time afterwards, they remained still, her legs still wrapped around him, his face buried in her breasts, as they held each other.

Juanita began to giggle, "I'll bet we are the only ones we know who get so horny seeing a new baby!"

Edgar smiled at her as she lifted herself up and off him, then sat demurely next to him, smoothing her skirt down, as if she hadn't just been riding him like a cowboy on a bucking bronco.

He slowly zipped his pants over his still enlarged organ. "Let's play some more, after we get all the kids to bed, my sweet."

She shook her head at him. "Edgar, you are an incorrigible bad boy. I don't know what I see in you. You never know how to behave and you forced me to have wild sex with you in your car in your brother's driveway! What will the neighbors think?"

He smirked at her, "The men will think '*lucky bastard,*' and the women will think '*Here comes another Reyes baby.*' And they will all be right! I am the luckiest man in the world and I intend to work at it until you have another of my babies in you. That way the whole world knows you belong to me."

She patted his face gently. "Edgar, I have belonged to you since the first time you touched me. I have never even been interested in any other man. That's why my daddy finally let me marry you, even though he thought I was too young and he wanted me to finish more than two years of college. He believed me when I told him you were the only one for me...especially once I was pregnant."

He kissed her palm and smiled at her. "I'm glad he believed you. I would have eloped with you if he hadn't allowed us to get married. I have never wanted any other woman since the first time I saw you."

She smiled at him. "Not even when Alejandro would come over and tell you all about his wild single life? Or invite you to go to see strip shows with him?"

He made a face at her, "You would never have allowed me to go and he knew it. He was just being mean."

She shook her head. "I'd have let you go."

He looked at her in surprise. "Really?"

She nodded. "Yes. But you would have had to sleep the night on the sofa since any hard-on another woman gave to you, is not one I would want to deal with!"

He gave her a mischievous look. "Then you would have allowed me to have the woman who gave me a hard-on take care of it?"

She nodded again. "Of course. But then you would have had to find somewhere else to sleep, because I would have changed all of the locks on the doors."

He grabbed her and pulled her close for another long kiss and fondle.

"There is only you for me, my love. And only me for you. We belong together, forever."

She put her head on his shoulder and sighed with contentment. He draped an arm around her. "And what will you say when some boy comes to you and asks for Rosa's hand?"

He looked at her in surprise. "You don't think they are that serious, do you?"

She patted his hand and smiled, "No…at least *she* isn't. Not about this one. But what will you do, when some 'Edgar' comes to ask for *your* daughter?"

He smiled at her. "I will say no and wait to see what happens. If they both agree to abide by my decision, I will know it was the right thing to say. If they spend every waking moment figuring out ways to be together, as you and I did, I will have to bow to the inevitable, as your father did, and allow them to ensure their babies are born to a married couple."

The tinny sound of mariachi music playing on a cell phone interrupted their discussion, and Juanita had to grope around in the car for her purse.

"Hello," she said, and told Rosa they had indeed left the hospital and would be home very soon. She nodded and hung up the phone, turning to her husband. "She says she ordered a bunch of pizzas, since they are all starving to death. They will be ready in about ten minutes. She wants us to go pick them up."

Edgar shook his head ruefully. "And just incidentally, pay for them too, I suppose."

She patted the side of his face. "Eight mouths will be even more expensive to feed pizza to than seven. Counting us, that will make ten."

He grabbed her hand, kissed her palm, then licked it trailing his tongue up to her fingertips; he flicked his tongue delicately over the tips of her fingers before he pulled her close for another long, serious kiss and grope.

"What can I say? I'm crazy about you, *mi bonita* 'Nita."

She raised an eyebrow. "*Uno mas.* Then no more."

He nodded gravely at her. "Anything you say, my love."

She slapped his arm, and he laughed as he drove them to pick up the pizzas.

Nineteen

The next few weeks were a blur to everyone. School was out for the holidays and the trees had to be put up and decorated, the presents wrapped and the rest of the cookies baked. Once Tegan and the baby got home, Alexander took a week off work so he could adapt to being a father. The following week he had to be back, but it was the holiday week, so he only had to be at work for Monday and Tuesday.

"It's like he was always meant to be a dad!" Tegan told Patti on the phone Monday morning, while they took a break from chatting about the parties being booked for January.

"He changes the diapers, gets up in the middle of the night to bring Carlos to me, then he snuggles us both while I nurse the baby. He takes him back to his bassinette and puts him down, so I can stay in bed and rest. Then he snuggles me until we both fall asleep." She sighed. "The only thing I'm not happy about is having to wait to have sex with him again."

Patti observed, "After vaginal births, you are *never* in the mood, for weeks."

Tegan giggled. "But after my c-sections, I'm raring to go. Even the nursing hormones are not stopping me this time."

"Well, you *are* married to the man of your dreams." Patti reminded her. "How does he feel about having to wait?"

Tegan giggled. "He's worse than I am. Honestly, it's like we are teenagers and I have to hit his hands away all of the time. I have a feeling we are not going to be able to hold off the whole six weeks, like the doctor said."

"Tsk, tsk," said Patti.

"So, how are things going with you and J.T.?" Tegan asked. "I'm slowly getting back into the swing of things and I don't want to miss out on any news. Are you still happy he moved in?"

Patti sighed happily. "Wonderful, and yes. We haven't even used up all of the positions we both like yet, so we are still having wild monkey sex as often as we can get the house to ourselves or we wait until late at night. The kids are thrilled he and I are taking turns cooking, and we both like to try out new recipes, so we've probably *all* put on ten pounds and the holidays are not even here yet! I'm thinking I'll have to put a treadmill in the house somewhere, maybe hook it up to the TV so the kids will use it. We are going to need to do something to work off the gourmet food we've been enjoying."

"Good, then you can start going to Jazzercise with me every morning, once I get the okay from the doctor to go back. That way we can still see each other daily, get some exercise and trade stories about our wild men."

"You've got a deal, girlfriend," Patti said. "Is that baby Carlos I hear?"

"Yeah, I've been wearing him all of the time in that front pack you gave me. He likes to be with me and it leaves my hands free. Plus whenever he wakes up hungry, I just shove a boob at him and he's happy. Then we go lie down and nap together. I'm a whole lot more tired than I remember being with Katie and Kevin, but then I wasn't so old back then."

"At least you don't have a house full of young ones to take care of, eh?" Patti pointed out. "You have two older ones, who both like to help you take care of their baby brother. And I hear Kevin is actually spending time holding the baby…without a computer game in the room. Is this some kind of withdrawal therapy for him?"

Tegan laughed along with Patti. "Yes, I think it is. He's gradually deciding there are other interesting things in the world that don't involve his computer. Can girls be far behind?"

"Bite your tongue!" said Patti. "We already have the girls starting to talk about dating…I don't want to even think about the boys yet." She continued, "Hey, I've been meaning to ask you, why did you name the baby Carlos? I've got a bet with J.T. on that. He says it must be a family name from Alex's side of the family. I say it's to honor Santana, whose music wrote the story of your love affair from the start. Who's right?"

Tegan giggled. "Actually, you both are. Edgar already named his first boy after their dad…but their mother's dad's name was Carlos. I was really happy about the name because of Santana. And my dad was pleased we used his name, Anthony, as the middle name. Kevin was the one who pointed out his initials will be 'C-A-R...kind of cool, huh?"

"Yup," Patti said. "Oops, I've got to run. This new recipe for cookies requires me to start fussing with them the instant they come out of the oven. The timer is just about to ring. We'll see you for Christmas Eve dinner, okay?"

"You do remember it will just be Alex and me with the baby, right? John has the kids for Christmas this year," Tegan said. "When did you say you wanted us there? I've got baby-brain, you know. I'll write it on the calendar now."

"Dinner will be about six, so plan on getting here about three and we can have some time to chat and have appetizers. J.T. is planning on trying some new recipes... and having read them, I can't wait to try them. My kids are already arguing over who gets to hold Carlos first. See you later."

"Okay, see you then, you gourmet goddess!" Tegan smiled as she hung up the phone and wrote the time on her calendar. She went into her room to sit in the rocking chair Alexander had gotten for her and she nursed their son until they both fell asleep.

~ * ~

On the way home from his first day back at work, Alexander stopped his car in front of his brother's house when he saw Edgar shoveling snow in the driveway.

"*Hola!*" he said, as he walked up the driveway.

Edgar, who had been too busy shoveling to notice him drive up, smiled when he saw his brother. "So, how was the first day back at work for the new dad?" he asked.

Alexander frowned as he moved closer to Edgar. "Just fine. Edgar, there's something I've been meaning to say to you, but I'm not sure how to do it."

Edgar raised his eyebrows. "*You* are at a loss for words? The great super-salesman, who has such a gift with words he can sell Ice cubes to Eskimos?"

Alexander nodded, then took a deep breath. "How can I apologize to you, for years of making stupid and hurtful remarks about the size of your family? I was jealous of your happiness with Juanita, at the same time I thought it was something I would never want for myself." He shook his head. "I just didn't understand, Edgar. Now I do. I'm humbled by my own feelings and ashamed of all of those things I used to say to you. Can you ever forgive me?"

Edgar smiled at his brother, clasping both of his arms with his hands. "Forgive you? Of course I can, *mi hermano!*" They hugged each other, then drew apart, both clearing their throats.

"Besides, I was always jealous of your stories about your exciting single life. Now you and I are in the same boat and I've been really enjoying feeling like the older brother. I've looked up to you for so long, I'm really liking this feeling I'm the one who knows what I'm doing, not you."

Alexander nodded. "Good. I'm hoping you will say yes, when I ask you to be the godfather of my son."

Edgar looked into the eyes of his brother. "It will be an honor."

Alexander smiled. "We are not sure yet just when we will be doing this...probably not until after the holidays are over, since it's just too hectic right now. But we are hoping for the first weekend in January. Would that be all right with you?"

Edgar nodded. "Anytime you choose will be fine."

Alexander smiled again. "Good. Now that's settled, I feel much better. I was going to ask you on Christmas day, but since it's going to be at your house, I thought you would be much too busy for me to get a chance to talk to you alone. When do you want us to come over on Thursday?"

Edgar shrugged, "I'm not sure. I'll call you after I talk to 'Nita and find out what her plans are. It would probably be fine if you come over anytime after about noon, so we have time to clean up the mess after the kids tear into their presents from Santa. Then we will have some time for Carlos to be passed around the family, so we all get a chance to hold him before everyone else comes over."

Alexander nodded. "What do you want me to bring?"

Edgar shrugged. "Probably just something to drink. When I call you about the time, later tonight, I'll tell you what to pick up, okay?"

"Okay," Alexander said. "I'd better be getting home, since I'll have to shovel myself when I get there."

"*Adios!*" Edgar watched his brother head down the driveway. He was still watching Alexander's car drive around the corner when Juanita appeared beside him with a mug of hot chocolate. He kissed her and took the mug.

"You'll never guess what just happened," he began, but she shook her head and smiled.

"Yes I will, since I heard it all from the garage. I didn't want to intrude on you two, so I stayed out of sight, but I could hear what you were both saying."

He took a drink, then looked at her as he licked the chocolate off his lips.

"Let me do that." She stood on tiptoes to lick the rest of the chocolate from his lips.

He pulled her close with one arm for an extended kiss.

Juanita pulled back and said with a smile, "I told you he would apologize, didn't I?"

Edgar nodded. "I have learned to trust your instincts over the years, *mi bonita* 'Nita. You are as wise as you are beautiful." He wiggled his eyebrows at her. "Maybe we will have some news to share with the family when we are all together for Carlos' christening, yes?"

Juanita blushed, then laughed. "If we don't, it won't be for lack of trying, you animal, you. Honestly, for as long as we have been married, and as many children as we already have, you are acting like a hormonal teenager having his first crush!"

Edgar's eyes burned into her. "That's how I feel about you, my woman. How I have always felt about you." He tried to grab her again, but she deftly eluded him and took the empty mug from his hands.

"No, Edgar, not now. You need to finish the driveway and I need to get back to dinner."

He gave her another smoldering look. "Later?"

She laughed. "When have I ever been able to say no to you, my husband?"

He smiled back at her. "I hope you never learn to."

204

A well-aimed snowball hit him in the back and he turned to see his younger children getting ready for a major attack on their father. He laughed, stooping to gather up some snow to throw back at them and Juanita beat a hasty retreat back into the garage.

Twenty

The fifth of January was the Monday school started again, and everyone else returned to their normal routines. It was also the day Patti's Place was to open. So bright and early, Patti was in her kitchen in the back organizing the food she was going to offer her first day in business. Since she wasn't going to open until eleven, the front door was locked at nine-thirty when Tegan came around the back and walked in, Carlos' cries alerting Patti to the fact they were there.

Tegan hugged her partner as best they could, with the baby in the front pack, between them. She sat down and shifted the baby so he could nurse.

"Hey, partner. I had to come to wish you luck on your first day. I intend to stay and have lunch here, too. I want to be your first paying customer…for luck." She looked around. "So where's J.T.?"

Patti smiled, looking up from the food she was preparing. "He's at the store. He decided he was in the mood to whip up a big pot of flan, so he's off getting more milk."

Tegan smiled conspiratorially. "So, we can talk?"

Patti smiled back. "Sure, girl. What's on your mind? As if I didn't know?"

Tegan laughed. "Well, since I can't do it yet, I'm spending all of my time thinking about it. And talking about it."

"So, you are still following the doctor's orders?" Patti asked.

Tegan made a face, "Yeah. Alex is too afraid he will hurt me. He's hard to convince we don't really need to wait any longer." She sighed. "We didn't have the kids with us last week, and we did manage to skirt the rules a bit, if you know what I mean."

Patti laughed. "A-B-P?"

They both laughed. "Yep. Anything but penetration. Let me tell you, after weeks with nothing, anything was sure better than nothing."

Patti smiled. "You don't have that much longer to wait, do you?"

Tegan nodded ruefully. "I'm hoping to get the okay at my one-month check up next week. Even if I don't, I'm thinking of lying to Alex and saying I got it."

Patti shook her head. "Tsk, tsk. You bad girl. You'd better hope those nursing hormones protect you, or you're gonna find yourself knocked up and popping out Irish twins!"

Tegan nodded. "Alex will probably use a condom, at least for a few months. He's so concerned about me. But after all, I *am* Irish! Since we are going to have one more, I like your idea of getting pregnant again before Carlos is a year old; then we can be done with this whole baby-making thing and get back to hours of nightly wild monkey sex."

She gave Patti a sideways look. "Speaking of that, how did things go with you and J.T. for New Year's Eve? Did you get to ring in the new year with a bang?"

Patti nodded and laughed. "Yes. The kids stayed up until midnight and did the countdown with us. Then they both went upstairs to their own rooms. I think Chelsea got on the phone, since I heard her talking up there. Jake was playing that new computer game Kevin gave him for Christmas. So we had lots of time to celebrate."

"Did their dad even call?" Tegan asked.

"Yes, he did," Patti made a face. "He told them he's got such a small place, there isn't any room for them both to come and visit him. Chelsea doesn't care if she never sees him again, but Jake wants to go visit him sometime soon. So I guess we'll set that up. But it won't be monthly visitation, like you have."

She sighed. "Just as well. I sure don't want to see him that often; and besides, I'm afraid J.T. might try to make good on his offer to teach him a lesson about hitting women. I don't want to have to separate them."

Tegan nodded sympathetically as she burped her son, then switched him to the other side to continue feeding him.

"So, did you tell him J.T. is now moved into your house?"

Patti nodded. "Yes, right before I hung up. He was hinting around he'd like to come over for dinner sometime and I told him that wasn't such a good idea. I could have him over on one of the nights J.T. is working at The Party House, but I'd want him gone before J.T. got home."

Tegan asked. "And how did he take that news?"

Patti rolled her eyes. "Not well. You'd think we were still married, the way he was carrying on; then he started on about how it wasn't good for the children to be exposed to *that kind of lifestyle*, and I almost barfed. So, he thinks having them see their dad hitting their mom, or belittling her, or staying out all night getting drunk and chasing other women, is a good way to bring them up?"

Tegan nodded sympathetically. "What a jerk!"

Patti continued thoughtfully. "Though I guess it's not entirely his fault. He was brought up that way, so that's what he thinks is normal. But I wasn't brought up like that, and I don't want my kids to be like him!"

Tegan pointed out, "But you *are* a middle child, so you always like to make nice when people are being unpleasant. I guess that's why you put up with his crap as long as you did, huh?"

Patti sighed. "I guess so. Not to change the subject too much, but speaking of exes, how was your dinner Sunday when you and Alex drove into the city to have dinner with John and Bill and the kids?"

Tegan smiled. "It went well. John was always good with babies...the only problem was Alex watched him like a hawk every time he held Carlos. It was like he expected him to drop him or something. When Bill held him, it was *me* who was worried, because I didn't realize he used to babysit when he was in high school. But they had made home-made pizza and served it with a salad and ice cream for dessert. We all had a good time. We drove the kids back home in the new mini-van we picked up last week. They hadn't seen it yet, so they were excited about that."

Patti asked. "You traded in your old car, right?"

Tegan nodded. "Uh-huh. Katie won't be driving for at least another three years and it was an old beater anyway. When she goes away to college, she won't really need a car, since most college towns have mass transit."

"I remember. He's asleep again, isn't he?" she asked, looking at the baby.

"Yes," Tegan said. They both looked up to see J.T. walk in the door.

"I wondered whose mini-van was in my spot," he said smiling at Tegan. "I figured it must be yours."

Tegan made a face. "Excuse me while I extricate my nipple from the baby's mouth and attempt to re-dress myself discreetly."

J.T. smiled at her, "Don't worry on my account. It's nice to see a baby nursing. It's what nature designed them for, after all." He leered at Patti. "Though I'm more in favor of their secondary uses myself."

Patti blushed. "Stop it, you bad boy! Did you get what you needed?" she said, nodding at the bag he was carrying.

"Uh-huh. The guy who rang me out said he's looking forward to coming here for lunch, if not today, then tomorrow. Then a couple of other people asked where, and I got to do a little bit of advertising, talking up your grand opening week."

He smiled. "If half the people who say they are coming, show up, we should have a pretty respectable first week's sales."

Tegan nodded. "And the first kid's birthday party we are doing is next week Friday. Lots of moms are excited about your idea of a taco bar, so the kids can make their own tacos using only the stuff they like. I think they are even more thrilled they won't have to have the party at their houses anymore when we do them. I think we should consider a sundae bar also, so the kids can make their own ice cream creations to go along with the cake, which they almost never eat."

Patti nodded. "Okay. Let's talk about that idea before next Friday. I think I'm going to stick with my original plan and after this week, I'll be closed on Monday and Tuesday."

J.T. ageed. "That's a good idea, since I usually have Sunday and Monday nights off from The Party House. That way I can start taking you camping once the weather gets warmer."

Tegan asked. "Camping, huh? Will you let the kids stay home alone, then, or will you want them over at my house?"

Patti shrugged. "I guess I'll ask them and we'll decide when the time comes."

She looked at J.T. "Honey, could you go out and be sure the coffee is going and the place is ready to open? Then I'll be able to clear off enough room for you to get the flan going."

Once J.T. was out of the room, Patti leaned closer to Tegan. "Speaking of the kids staying over at your place, there is a small favor I want to ask from you."

Tegan smiled at her best friend. "That's what best buds are for, isn't it? Does it concern that big, burly biker in the next room?"

When Patti smiled and nodded, Tegan smiled back at her. "Then how about I just say yes now, and you can tell me some other time, when he's not around, just when you will need this favor, all right?"

"Deal."

J.T. returned to the kitchen. "Everything's ready to go, Patti. Let me get the flan going, and we'll be all set to open."

If he noticed the two women smiling at each other conspiratorially, he didn't say anything about it. After all the excitement and commotion of the opening day, he forgot about it entirely. They were still in the kitchen, cleaning up, when Chelsea and Jake stopped in after school. They gave the kids some of the left-over food and everyone enjoyed the opportunity to chat about their day. Later that night, after the kids were in their rooms, presumably asleep, they soaked together in a hot bubble bath and J.T. and Patti toasted each other, the parts each had played in their successes of the day, and the continued success of Patti's Place.

Twenty-one
Brunch

Almost two weeks later, J.T. was still asleep on Sunday morning, when Patti climbed back into bed behind him. At first, he thought he was dreaming when he felt her naked body press itself against his back. Then, as he gradually realized she was really there and not a dream, he lay very still and enjoyed the feel of her breasts rubbing against his back and her hands that traveled lightly over his skin. Since she was on her side, the hand under her was only able to reach his lower back, but she used it to massage him gently. The other hand reached around to the front, lightly fondled his chest hair and tweaked at his nipples. She then moved her hand down his abdomen to his thighs, seemingly ignoring the rampant erection he woke with every morning. It reared itself in extreme excitement at having a woman's touch so early in the day. Her hand worked its way up to his abdomen again and was lightly bumped by the insistent organ that jumped when her lips brushed along his shoulder to his neck, as she whispered in his ear, "Are you awake yet, my love?"

"Umm-hmm," he managed. He moaned when her hand finally grasped his manhood and proceeded to gently stroke it, up, then down; she explored his balls, her fingers tickling him, then she grasped him again. His breathing sped up as his pulse began to race and he was torn between the desire to keep lying there, being stroked and rolling over to pull her on top of him, so he could bury himself in her warmth.

He felt her warm breath tickling his neck again and her lips brushed his ear.

"Happy birthday, Jules. The kids are already at Tegan's house and won't be back again until tomorrow after lunch. I'm taking the day off and so are you. We have the house to ourselves, and I, for one, don't intend to put on any clothes for the next twenty-four hours...unless you want to see me in some of that lingerie you gave me for Christmas. That's part of my gift to you."

Excited by her words, and unable to resist her touch anymore, he rolled onto his back and pulled her on top of him, then used one leg to gently spread hers apart. He reached down for her and found her wet and ready for him, so he rubbed himself against her and pushed forward. He sucked in a breath, as her muscles tightened in response to his movements. She moaned in ecstasy, as her eyes closed and she drew herself backwards while keeping him deep within her body.

Smiling, he asked her, "How did you know...this is just what I wanted for my birthday?"

She opened her eyes to smile down at him, "I just knew. I want to make your every dream come true, today, to let you know just how much you mean to me."

She reared up backwards again, as his tiny movements made her scream and shudder in orgasm. He leaned forward and caught one of her nipples in his mouth and then realized he couldn't hold out any longer. He grabbed both of her hips in his hands and held her still while he pumped himself into her body, no longer trying to be gentle, intent only on his own pleasure. With a mighty roar, he pushed one final time. He felt himself trapped deeply within her body as her muscles clenched reflexively around him, and he felt the hot coil of sperm burn upwards to spray into her marking her as his woman. They howled together as they shared their pleasure, intensified for each by the knowledge the other was just as incoherent.

They both collapsed and it was quite some time before either of them could breathe evenly enough to speak.

Patti recovered first. "Happy birthday, Jules," she said as she raised her head to kiss his lips.

He reached one hand up to wrap in her hair and pulled her head down. He kissed her; long, hard and passionately. "You always make my every dream come true," he told her. Then he made a face at her. "But you have to let me get up. I need to go to the bathroom. It may take me some time to be able to do anything in there, but I really need to go."

She smiled. "Okay. I'll go get us some coffee and meet you back here."

A few minutes later, he moved back into bed and smiled when she walked in holding two cups of coffee. She handed one to him, then crawled onto the bed. She sat herself next to him, leaning against the headboard.

"What smells so good?" he asked after he sipped some coffee.

"Probably the bacon. I've got Quiche Lorraine in the oven and I already made some biscuits. There's a fruit salad, too, along with the makings for mimosas."

He leaned over to kiss her. "You are going to spoil me, treating me like this, Patricia."

She responded to his kiss and for a few minutes, they didn't speak as they concentrated on the feelings they could share with just their mouths.

With a sigh, she leaned back, sipping her coffee. "That's the plan for today, mister. If I didn't have kids, this is how I would envision every day for us. But since I do, it has to be for special occasions only."

He gave her a sideways glance. "They will both move out of the house eventually, won't they?"

She looked at him in surprise. "Why yes, I assume so." She gave him a shy smile. "I guess if you were willing to stick around that long, we could do this sort of thing more often."

She made a face. "Of course, I'll be almost fifty by the time Jake is old enough to go away to college."

He leaned over to kiss her. "That's okay, honey. I'll be in my forties by then, too." He smiled at her conspiratorially. "And I've always liked older women. They know a whole lot more about how to please a man. And this older woman, in particular, seems to be *really* skilled at pleasing this man."

She leaned over and they gave themselves over to lip and tongue pleasure. This time, when they parted, he asked her. "How much longer until the quiche is done?"

She shrugged casually. "Probably only about fifteen minutes or so. I've got the timer set and it's right outside the door."

He set his coffee mug down and began to kiss his way down her body. "If you don't mind, I'm going to have myself a little taste of honey to whet my whistle for breakfast."

She nodded assent. "I don't mind at all. Help yourself."

And he did.

~ * ~

May 20

Dear Mom,

In case you are wondering, I'm writing all of this to you in a letter, because I don't want you to interrupt me, and I know you always like to lecture me about how I'm no good at picking good men. I think I've found a good one.

Remember when I told you I had to advertise for a part-time cook to help me with my restaurant/catering business? And I told you I hired someone with lots of experience in south-of-the-border cooking? Well, the part that I didn't tell you is that the cook is a man and his name is J.T. And I'm in love with him.

J.T. moved into my house back in December and the kids really like having him around and not only for the good food. The kids are happy that I'm happy and I'm glad that Jakey has a good role model for how to be a gentleman. And we all like to do the same things for fun. J.T. gave both of my kids their own tents and sleeping bags for Christmas, telling them he would take us all camping as soon as the weather got warmer. The first time he took me camping, it was early March, and the kids were still in school. It was still really cold, but the snow was all melted. I thought he was nuts when he suggested it! But we rode on his Harley up to southern Wisconsin. (Yes, Mom, I know motorcycles are inherently unsafe...but we use helmets, and J.T. is very careful.)It was one of the coldest rides I have ever been on. But when we got there and had the tent all set up, he made me this gourmet steak dinner that was to die for!

In late March, when the kids were on Spring break, we took my car and went up there again, taking them with us. They loved having their own space in their own tents up there, and we all enjoyed hiking all day, then working together to prepare delicious meals over the campfire. Remember how I always used to like camping when I was in college? I still like it. The kids loved camping, too, and we all can't wait to go on a longer trip together. J.T. and I went again in early April and took the kids along for a long weekend in early May.

So, that's the story of my new man, Jules Tremenczyk. Mostly everyone, calls him J.T. I call him Jules, mostly when we are alone. He likes to call me Patricia, and for some strange reason, I let him get away with it. I wasn't looking for anyone to love, and all of a sudden, there he was. He treats me like a queen and I treat him like a king. I have no idea how long this will last. I've stopped thinking in terms of forever, since my "happily ever after" blew up in my face when I realized what my ex was up to. J.T. may stay around for years, or he may leave tomorrow. I'm working very hard on being strong enough to take it, whichever way it turns out. But as you well know, there are no guarantees in life and even less when it comes to men. You always told us that you and Dad being so happy together was a whole lot of hard work. I hope that since my new relationship feels easy and natural, that doesn't mean it won't last.

Lots of love to Dad and you,
Patti

~ * ~

When Memorial Day loomed close, Patti and her kids were all disappointed to find out from J.T. they would *not* be camping that weekend. As he patiently explained to them, "Everyone who is *not* a camper will be up 'posing' for Memorial Day, the fourth of July and for Labor Day. So those are the three holidays it is *not* a good idea to plan to go camping."

Bowing to his superior experience, they instead planned to head up in mid-June after school got out and there would not be much of a crowd yet. He even suggested if the kids wanted to, they could each choose one friend to bring and to share their tents with them.

The first week of June was the last half-week of school for the kids. Since Patti's Place was still not open on Monday or Tuesday, Patti was home on Tuesday morning sitting at the kitchen table working on the plans for the two birthday parties planned for next week. She had made the grocery list for this week's Friday and Saturday parties, but she wanted to buy ahead as much she could to get shelf-stable items on sale, whenever possible. Since she was deep in thought planning consumption levels for parties for four different ages of kids, she distractedly got up to answer when there was a loud knocking at her kitchen door. Few people ever knocked at the back door, but she was so deep in thought, the oddity of it didn't occur to her until she opened the door. "Yes? Can I help you?"

All she got was a quick look at two men standing outside of her door smiling at her. She was pushed back into her kitchen and hit very hard on the side of her head. Disoriented by the blow, she felt herself being dragged to her kitchen chair. Her arms felt as if they were being torn out of their sockets and she was vaguely aware she was being tied up, the men talking to each other as if she wasn't even there.

"Tie her arms up good and tight. It makes her tits stick out more! Jesus, she's got big 'uns, don't she?"

"Yeah, her old man said she had the biggest knockers he'd ever been able to wrap his lips around. No wonder old J.T. likes living here."

"Wonder where that big, bald prick is right now?"

"Who cares? We get her tied up… he's bound to show up, sooner or later. If it's sooner, we can make him watch while we have fun with her. If it's later, if there's any of her left, we can let him watch us finish her off. Either way, we get to have some fun and get to make that son-of-a-bitch suffer before we kill him."

There was some nasty laughter. Patti heard her fridge door being opened as the two men argued over whether or not they wanted anything to eat along with the beer they found. She looked around, trying not to draw any attention from them and was horrified to see her son Jake looking in the open window at her. Suddenly she remembered this was the last day of school, so he was coming home for good to start the summer, after a half-day of school. She fleetingly wondered where Chelsea was and remembered Chelsea was going home with Katie, so they could go to the mall with some other girlfriends. She met Jake's eye and shook her head when he held up his cell phone. She did want him to call for help, but not where these men could hear him.

She mouthed at him, "J-T! Get J-T!"

Jake nodded at her. His head disappeared from her view a split second before the men slammed the fridge door shut. One stalked over to her, while the other one went over to the window her son had just been at.

"I'll keep a look-out for that gypsy bastard; you go ahead and feel up his bitch if you want to."

"Ah, she's not awake yet. It's no fun if she's not awake and scared."

"So, wake her, then!"

"How?"

"Slap the shit out of her! Remember, her ex said she really likes that."

Patti felt the sting as her face was slapped on first one side, then the other. She looked up in time to catch the third slap right across her nose, which promptly started to bleed. As the two men argued over whether or not they should even bother to clean her up, she found herself praying for J.T. to come soon. He would know what to do. These men were looking for him. He had to get here and soon! In the meantime, she bled all over herself while the men drank her beer, smoked in her kitchen and argued over who got to rape her first.

Twenty-two

There were only three places J.T. could be found with any regularity. One was Patti's house, where he lived. Another was The Party House, where he worked, but only at nights. The other was Patti's Place, so that was where Jake took off for, riding his bike as if his life depended on it. What he was truly afraid of, was that his mother's life depended on it, so he rode faster than he ever had. He saw the Harley parked out back long before he got close enough to yell for J.T. Once he got to the parking space, he jumped off of his bike while it was still moving, then he tripped over it and sprawled on the pavement. He skinned his knee and both of his hands, but he didn't care.

He got up quickly and ran into the back door into the kitchen, yelling, "J.T.! J.T.! Where are you?"

J.T., who had been washing the floor of the restaurant out front, yelled, "I'm out here!"

Jake raced through the door into the front and stopped because he was panting so fast, he was unable to talk. He felt like his heart was going to explode and his lungs were pumping like bellows. There was blood running down his leg into his socks, but he ignored all of that.

"J.T. You have to get home right now! Mom is tied to a chair in the kitchen and some guys are arguing over whether they should kill her before or after you get there!"

J.T. stopped dead and looked closely at Jake. "What do the men look like?"

Jake shook his head, to concentrate. "One of them is tall and blond and the other one is a light brown color, but shorter. They both have tattoos on their arms. The blond one is missing some front teeth. The brown one has curly hair."

J.T.'s face went white. His eyes burned as if they had been turned to fire. He dropped the mop and took off his apron. "You're sure?" he asked, while he was moving towards the back door where his Harley was parked.

Jake nodded, still trying to catch his breath.

J.T. spoke quickly, "Listen to me, Jake. Your mother is in great danger. You need to call nine-one-one and tell them there are two escaped fugitives from the federal penitentiary in Indiana at her house holding her captive in her kitchen. Tell them to call the FBI, because they are after these two men. They are rapists and murderers and they are both armed and dangerous. Then you need to wait here until the police come to get you. Give them your addresses, both of the house and here, and wait for them. I forbid you to come home until the police bring you. Is that clear?"

Jake just stared at him. J.T. moved over and took hold of both of Jake's arms and shook him gently

"*Is that clear? You are not to go home, under any circumstances!*"

Jake nodded slowly and took out his cell phone.

J.T. nodded, "That's right. Call them right now. I'm on my way over to stall the men, so they leave your mom alone.

It's me they want to hurt. It's me they are after. So I'm going to give them a chance at me and hope they leave her alone."

He turned and strode towards the door.

"J.T.!" Jake yelped.

J.T. turned to look at the terrified boy, "WHAT?"

Jake's voice was strained and thin, "Be careful. I love my mom. But…but… I love you, too."

J.T. nodded at him, "I know, kid. I love you and your sister, too. But your mother gives me a reason to keep on living. Now make that call!"

J.T. ran out of the room, fired up his Harley and took off.

Jake fumbled with his phone, then dialed nine-one-one and started to explain.

~ * ~

Patti had never been so angry or so scared in her life. She had no way to express her anger and was tied tightly to a chair, but she tried not to let her fear make her panic. Whenever one of the two creeps holding her captive touched her, revulsion fought with fear and she had to bite back her desire to scream or throw up. She felt like she was trapped in her worst nightmare, with no possibility of waking up. The only thing that had kept her from being raped, so far, was the position she was in, tied in a seated position, in the chair. The two men had argued over how to make her body parts more accessible without having to untie her. While they discussed this, they took turns groping her breasts, which they had made accessible by tearing open her shirt, or rubbing themselves against her face, thankfully, without yet having removed their pants.

They were both in the process of opening another beer when she heard the Harley roar up to the house. The two men stopped arguing and assumed crouching positions; the tall blond one pulled a gun out of his jacket pocket.

The front door slammed open and J.T. called out, "Patti! I'm home, sweetie. Where are you?"

The shorter man grabbed Patti's hair and twisted it, telling her in a low voice, "Tell him where you are or I'll kill you now."

"I'm in here," she yelled, then as he pushed open the kitchen door, she screamed, "Look out!"

J.T. ducked as the man holding her hair slapped her face again, causing a fresh spurting of blood from her nose.

The other man aimed his gun at J.T.'s face and said, "Get over there, asshole. Sit in the chair next to your whore. And don't try anything or I'll shoot both of you. Understand?"

J.T. slowly made his way over to the chair and sat down heavily. Immediately, the other man started to tie J.T. to the chair, using heavier ropes and bigger knots.

J.T. grimaced as the man pulled his arms back, but he looked at Patti. "Are you all right, honey?" Then, as he noticed the blood on her face and her opened shirt, his eyes turned the color of blue flames and he asked, "Which one of you two cowardly cocksuckers hit my woman?"

The tall blond barked a laugh. "We both did. Her ex told us she likes it rough. We figured you can't have all the fun around here. So we've been taking our time, enjoying her. And now you're here, you get to watch."

"Her ex? What are you talking about?" J.T. asked, looking from one to the other. Now he was safely tied up, they both got chatty.

"Yeah, we met him last night in a bar a couple of miles from here."

Nodding, the blond one continued. "Yeah. He was bitching and moaning about some big, fucking ugly bald biker who was poking his ex old lady. He said she threw him out of the house, just so you could move in."

The other man nodded. "And once he said you had tattoos all over, we figured it was time to buy him a drink and see what else he could tell us."

"When he said you were a gypsy, too, we knew it had to be you."

The blond man walked over to J.T. and slapped the pistol across his face, making blood spurt from his nose. "We've been following your trail ever since you left the big house, but lost track of you once you got to Chicago. It's like you just disappeared."

The other man nodded. "But we kept on looking, figuring since this was the biggest city around, you'd have to be working somewhere to make enough money for you to head on back out west to find the rest of your lying, thieving family. Hearing that pitiful puke going on and on about the woman you stole from him was bad enough. We were going to just kill him to get him to shut the fuck up. But once we realized just *who* he was so pissed at, we let him live, since he pointed us in the right direction. And here we are, just one big, happy family!"

Both men now laughed, evilly, and the shorter one, who was closer to Patti, put his hand down in her bra and smirked at J.T., while he pulled at her nipple, twisting it until she wanted to scream with the pain. J.T.'s face was carved from granite…he looked angrier than any man Patti had ever seen, but he seemed to get calmer the angrier he got.

"You'd better stop doing that," J.T. told him in clipped, sharp words.

"Why is that?" he asked, as he stuck his other hand down the other side of Patti's bra and once again she had to bit her lip to keep from screaming.

"Because, when I get out of these ropes, I'm going to tear your heart out of your body, after I pull your head off and feed it to the dogs."

Both men now laughed heartily, as if J.T. had just told them a great joke.

"Hear that?" The blond one was saying, as he moved closer to Patti and twisted her hair to make her look at J.T. "He's going to hurt us? He's all tied up and we have the gun, and he's going to save you by hurting us? This is the man you let move into your house? This pussy?"

The other man now moved in front of J.T. and kicked him in the kneecap, making a bone-crunching sound. J.T. sucked in his breath. "Not so tough, when the feds aren't behind you, are you? Does she know about you? Does she know you were in the pen for murder, just like we were? Does she have any idea what kind of man she's been sharing her bed with? And exposing her kids to?" He slapped Patti again, making fresh blood shoot out of her face.

"Ah, I'm tired of this bullshit. Let's just rape the bitch, then kill both of them."

The blond man now said, "Wait a minute. There's kids too, remember. Maybe we can wait around until they get home. Rape them too, then leave. Sounds like a good day's work, to me."

The other man was just beginning to laugh in agreement, when there was a knock on the back door, and a loud voice

228

announced, "POLICE! OPEN THE DOOR, AND COME OUT WITH YOUR HANDS OVER YOUR HEAD! THE HOUSE IS SURROUNDED!"

Immediately, Patti felt herself being pushed to the floor by J.T., who swept his leg under both of hers, and knocked her chair forward, so they both fell heavily to the floor on their faces. The men didn't even seem to notice, since they both were instantly alarmed by the sudden appearance of the law.

"SHIT! What the fuck do we do now?"

"How the hell did they find us?"

"Who cares? How do we get out of here?"

"Stay calm, dude. There's got to be a way to get out."

"I'm not going back to the big house! They'll never let me out again."

"Listen to me, we're not going back!"

J.T. had freed his hands, and he worked feverishly at untying Patti. The convicts noticed what he was doing and the blond man with the gun, turned to him.

"YOU! YOU BROUGHT THEM HERE! I'LL KILL YOU, YOU SON OF A BITCH! AND YOUR WHORE, TOO!"

He took aim at Patti, and fired. She closed her eyes, expecting to die. Instead, she felt herself being shoved out of the way, and she felt the impact of the bullet as it hit J.T. and he fell heavily on top of her. She screamed and all the doors burst open. The room was suddenly full of SWAT team members, whose bullet-proof armor protected them from the few bullets the blond man was able to shoot, while a bullet in the arm made him drop his gun. The other man was already in custody and fighting with the agents who grabbed, cuffed, then led him out of the room, kicking and screaming that he wasn't going back, no one would take him alive.

The blond man had hit the floor when the bullet hit him and he writhed in pain as blood spurted from his wound where the bone stuck through. Patti screamed hysterically, calling out J.T.'s name, and calling for an ambulance. When the medics walked in, they moved J.T. off her, but she clung to him. They gently pried her fingers open and laid him on the floor to examine where the bullet had struck him.

"It's a shoulder wound. He's losing blood; we need to stabilize him."

"What about the other one?"

Patti looked around to see who they were talking about and realized they were looking at the blond convict, who was still on the floor, whining about his pain. Then she did something she would never be proud of but would remember for the rest of her life. She pushed herself up to her feet, walked over and kicked the man in the face. His head jerked backwards and he was quiet.

Hands were on her, holding her back and keeping her from touching anyone else. She was close to hysteria when they kept her from touching J.T. He was put on a stretcher and carried out the door to an ambulance. She fought to go with him, but was told she needed to stay, to talk to the police. They had to get her statement. She had to tell them what had happened. She felt hands examining her face and soothing lotion was rubbed on her skin. Her nose was bandaged.

There was more commotion at the door and she heard her son's voice, sobbing and yelling. "You have to let me in there! She's my mom! Mom, are you okay? Mom, where are you?"

Patti heard herself answer, as if in a dream. "Here, Jake. Mama's here."

He ran through the door and into her arms. She held him closely, as they both wept. Now that the danger was over, Patti gave herself permission to panic. She shook and trembled, then ran to the sink to throw up. Jake stood next to her and held her hair back while she retched until she was weak. He guided her to a chair and she sank into it, while he kneeled next to her and held on for dear life. And from that position, she answered the questions that were put to her in her house. She and Jake were taken to the police station to give their statements again and again.

During the ordeal of answering the same questions over and over, about what she knew about the convicts, which was nothing, she heard Tegan's voice ringing out over the noise and commotion of the station, "Patti? Where are you? Patti?"

Jake waved to Tegan from the door and she rushed in, followed by Chelsea. They both grabbed Patti and held her as they all sobbed together. Alexander, whose face was set, followed them in. He argued with the detectives who were questioning her and somehow convinced them she wouldn't leave town, but would be available for further questions. Then he got their permission to take her home.

But home was not where Patti wanted to go. Once she was walking out of the station, she demanded to know where J.T. was. When told he was at the nearby hospital having the bullet removed from his shoulder, she insisted on being taken there, not home. Alexander tried to argue with her, but bowed to the inevitable, when his wife told him firmly, "NO! After all she has been through, she gets to choose where she goes! Not you, not them, not any other men! *She* gets to choose!"

They soon found themselves sitting outside of the surgical area, waiting for news about J.T. Patti had managed to hold down a can of coke and some crackers, but she refused to try to eat anything else. Alexander took Chelsea and Jake to the cafeteria for some food. Tegan sat next to Patti and held her hand, as Patti stared straight ahead, not making a sound. When the doctor finally came into the waiting room, he walked over to the waiting women.

"Mrs. Tremenczyk?" he asked.

Patti answered. "That's me."

"You are his wife?"

She shook her head. "No, but I'm the closest he has to a relative, here. He lives with me."

He nodded. "Okay. He came out of the surgery just fine. He's a strong young man, so he should recover completely. But the bullet shattered part of his collarbone. He's going to be in pain for a very long time and will need some rehab afterwards, once he heals, to relearn how to use his arm safely. But he was a very lucky man. A few inches lower and the bullet would have been in his heart."

Patti gave the doctor a stricken look.

He smiled at her. "I have to ask. Are you Patricia?"

She nodded wearily. "Why?"

He smiled warmly at her. "Not only is your name tattooed on his chest, right under where the bullet went in, but he kept on repeating your name. The only way we could keep him quiet was to keep on telling him you were just fine and waiting outside to see him. He's in the recovery room now. Usually only relatives are allowed in there, but I will make an exception for you…but only you."

Tegan nodded to Patti. "Go on. I'll be here waiting for you. I can tell them where you are."

Patti felt as if she was sleepwalking as she was led into the recovery room; then the doctor left her side. She walked over to J.T.'s bedside and looked at him. He was paler than usual and there was blood pooling under the skin of his nose and cheeks where he had been hit with the handgun. He seemed to be unconscious. Patti started to cry looking at him, then gently lifted his hand, held it to her face, and kissed it.

He stirred, murmuring her name, then his eyelids fluttered open.

She held his hand to her face and smiled at him, the tears flowing down her face. "Yes, Jules. I'm here. I love you."

He shook his head, "No…not good for you. Too good… for me."

His eyes closed and he sighed, then he was out. The nurse came to stand beside his bed on the other side. "He's under a lot of sedation, honey. I'm surprised he was able to talk at all. He'll be out for quite some time now. You look like you need some rest. Go on home now, and we'll take good care of him for you tonight."

Patti kissed his hand again, then gently place it by his side. She turned and walked to where Tegan was waiting for her. Then she burst into tears and was still crying when Alexander and the kids got back upstairs. They took her home and Tegan stood outside of the bathroom while she took her shower.

She helped her into her bed. "I'm staying here with you tonight. Alexander has already gone home to take care of Carlos. But I'm staying here, in your bedroom, with you tonight. You're safe now, Patti sweetie. So you can rest now."

Patti lay in her bed, fighting sleep, trying not to think of the events of the day, but replaying them over and over in her head. The door opened and Chelsea crept into the room, followed by Jake.

"Mom? Can we sleep with you tonight?"

Wordlessly, Patti nodded. Her children crawled into bed on either side of her and held her between them, cocooned safely in their love. And while Tegan kept watch over them all from the nearby chair, Patti finally gave up her struggle and fell asleep.

Twenty-three

Over the next couple days, whenever J.T. was fully conscious, he was questioned by authorities. The local police wanted to know what he knew about the two offenders and the FBI wanted to know how he knew they were following him. They all wanted his testimony about what happened, so they could compare his story with Patti's…and Jake's.

In his waking moments when he was *not* being questioned, J.T. agonized over what had happened…over the danger he had unwittingly brought with him into Patti's house. He spent a lot of time trying to convince himself moving out would hurt her more than staying with her. But he felt a crushing load of guilt whenever he saw in his mind her face when she was being beaten. Even though she had not been raped, the sanctity of her house had been violated. He had no idea how he was going to be able to look her in the eye and apologize, let alone guarantee it wouldn't happen again. He was also worried her absence from his side meant she didn't want to see him again…that she had decided he was more trouble than he was worth. The worst part of that thought was he agreed with it.

On his third day in the hospital, no police or detectives appeared after breakfast, so he began to pester the nurses, demanding to know when he would be allowed to leave. They told him they would call the doctor and make his request known. They left his room and he was alone with his own thoughts again. He was considering just how he might sneak out of the hospital without being seen when the door opened and Patti walked in, carrying a dish of her famous oatmeal pecan chocolate chip cookies.

"Jules?" she asked, tentatively. When she saw he was awake, she smiled at him and he felt as if the sun had come out from behind a cloud.

"Patricia!" He held out his arms and she rushed over to the bed to grab onto him. He wrapped her in his arms and held her as if he would never let her go. When she pulled back slightly to look up into his face, there were tears in her eyes and his. They kissed each other and everything was forgotten for that one moment of happiness.

Reluctantly, she pulled back to see him wince in pain from moving his shoulder and arm around to hug her. She was instantly contrite.

"Oh, my God, Jules, your shoulder! I'm so sorry! I should have realized you are supposed to keep it still."

He shook his head. "Nothing will make it feel better. But having you in my arms did wonders for my peace of mind." He grimaced. "I was beginning to think you weren't ever coming to see me. I figured you had written me off as a lost cause."

When she shook her head, he continued. "You probably should, you know. Keep yourself and your kids as far away from me as possible."

"What are you talking about? Are you still being drugged?" She shook her head at him. "I wasn't in to see you before today because the detectives told me I couldn't come to see you until they were through questioning you. There was a police officer outside of your room for the last couple of days and he told me I wasn't allowed to come in to see you...and no amount of cookie bribery was able to change his mind! Believe me, I know...I tried!"

"Why?" he asked her, then sighed. "Wait, I know. They were afraid we would compare notes and give them a story, instead of what really happened, right?"

She nodded. "I've told them what happened hundreds of times, sometimes to the same detective over and over again. They never seemed to believe I had no idea who those guys were. After yesterday, you must have convinced them I wasn't lying, because they stopped asking me to come in to the station to tell them again what happened."

J.T. sighed more heavily. "I owe you the truth, Patti. There's things I should have told you before I endangered you and your kids by moving in with you. But I let my emotions take over, and I did what I wanted to do instead of what I knew I should do."

At her questioning look, he continued. "I should have left town when I realized how I was starting to feel about you. I knew those guys had escaped, because a friend of mine who is still incarcerated, called me when they did. He warned me they would probably be after me. But I figured I could stay one step ahead of them. If I would have kept on moving, I'd have been fine. But then I met you."

Patti looked into his eyes. "Don't bother waiting for me to tell you I wish you had never walked into my place...or my life. I can't say that. It's not true. I love you, Jules. I've barely been able to sleep; I've been so worried about you."

He shook his head now, as he looked away. "My marriage wasn't the only thing I didn't tell you about when I should have, honey. At least that was over a long time ago. But not telling you I'm an ex-con and that's why I had to apply for jobs that don't require background checks, was not fair to you. I'm ashamed of myself. Because I didn't warn you, you didn't realize you needed to be extra careful about who you let into the house. Because of me your house was violated and you were threatened and beaten. You may never feel safe again, and that's my fault, too."

Patti interrupted him. "Hey! It's not like they actually got around to raping me, though they talked about it a lot; and yes, they did hit me. But you are not the only one to blame here. You are forgetting my ex—that asshole, was the one who told them where I live. And he told them I like being beaten. As if! I've already called my lawyer and started proceedings to cut off his visitation rights. I'll probably lose some, if not all, of the alimony; I may even lose the child support...but the kids aren't sure they ever want to see him again."

She gave him an intense look. "In fact, the kids are saying they have no interest in seeing him anytime soon, but they are just waiting for the okay to be able to come to see you."

He shook his head. "I don't want them coming in here. I'm trying to get the doctor to agree to let me go home today. Remember, I don't have any insurance. I've been in here for three days already. They are going to have to take it out of my wages for the rest of my life, for me to be able to pay all of the medical expenses."

Patti was shocked. "But what about the danger of infection? What about the therapy the surgeon said you are going to need to teach you how to use your shoulder safely after it heals?"

J.T. shook his head. "Too bad. I can't afford that. I'll just have to muddle along and heal along the way."

Patti looked away. There were tears in her eyes. J.T. took a deep breath. "But I have to tell you why I was in jail, Patti. You have to know what kind of man I am. Then you can decide if you want to let me back into your house or not."

She gave him a stricken look. "There's no question of where you are going, when you leave here. You are coming home. To my house. To *our* house."

His eyes filled with tears, but he ignored them. "Listen to me first, then decide."

She nodded.

J.T. took another deep breath. "I told you I'm from a big family, right? I have three brothers and six sisters. Most of them have settled in one place or another around the country. I have them all programmed into my cell phone...but we don't talk often. Only a couple still travel around all of the time with their families and my parents.

The whole tribal thing gets kind of old, quickly, if you are trying to live a normal life."

She nodded.

He sighed. "But whenever one of us needs help, all it takes is a phone call and the one who lives the closest will be there to do whatever needs doing. A couple of years ago, I was spending some time with the family out in Wyoming, where they were staying on the land of one of my dad's cousins. We got a phone call in the middle of the night from one of my baby sisters, who was living in Indiana, telling us she was in the hospital and scared she might lose her baby. That's all she told us, but from what my mother and grandmother said, they were convinced Sophia's boyfriend was beating her. They asked me to head out there, to see for myself how she was doing and report back to them. Implied in that was I was to do whatever the situation required to be sure Sophia and her baby would be safe. The next day I left and rode for three days, almost straight through, to get to my sister. Sure enough, when I got there, she was out of the hospital, but she looked like a boxer: bruises on her face, eyes swollen and one of her teeth was missing. She got scared when I was the one who knocked on her door because she knew I would be outraged at any man beating any woman, but all the more so because she is my sister. I asked her to tell me the truth and she cried as she told me how the man she loved had changed and was now making her life a living hell. But since she still loved him, she didn't want me to do anything. Plus, she said he had a gun he had threatened to use on her right after he won it in a poker game. She was afraid he would use it on me. She told me to go back home and tell the family she was fine...in other words, to lie. I refused. We argued, she cried, I hugged her and I took her out to dinner, then took her home."

J.T. stopped to take a drink of water from the glass next to his bed. He continued.

"When we got back to her apartment, I walked her in, because I had to use the bathroom before I rode back to the campsite where I was staying. Her man came in and started yelling at her, asking her where she had been since he had called a few times, and she was not home. Then he heard me flush the toilet and he got nasty with her, calling her a whore and accusing her of being with another man behind his back. When I got out, she told him I was one of her brothers, but he was too out of control by that point to even listen to her. Everything happened so fast after that, I didn't have any time to think about what I was doing."

He stopped and looked at Patti. "Like in your kitchen, remember?"

Patti nodded. "Time races by, things happen and you barely notice, then you have to repeat the story of what happened over and over again so many times, you almost start to believe you are making it up, because that's how it feels."

He nodded. "Yes. Exactly. Her man hit her in front of me and I lost control of my temper. No man should *ever* hit a woman. I charged and tackled him and we hit the floor. I was bigger and stronger, but he was a street fighter from way back. He was sneaky and devious and was causing me some pain...almost as much as I was inflicting on him. Then he started to get tired, and realized he was going to take a serious beating for having hit my sister in front of me. I swear, I have no idea where the gun came from...I didn't even see it. All of a sudden Sophia screamed at me that he had a gun and I felt the barrel in my ribs. I was quick enough to get his hand and turn it away and a bullet got shot into the wall. We struggled with it for a while and he had it pointed back at me and his finger was pulling the trigger when Sophia hit him on the back of the head with a lamp, just like in the movies. That broke his hold on the gun and I didn't realize he was already pulling the trigger, when I turned it away from me, back to him. I heard the shot, but also just like in the movies, I didn't realize he had been shot until his eyes rolled back in his head and he slumped over on top of me. I pushed him off and we saw all the blood. There's a massive amount of blood with most bullet holes. They never show *that* in the movies."

Patti nodded weakly. "I never wanted to know that, but now I do."

Consumed with guilt, J.T. looked at her for a long moment before looking away.

"The neighbors had called the police at the sound of the first shot. They were there right after the second one. I was thrown to the floor and cuffed. Sophia was screaming hysterically that I was innocent, she was to blame, I was her brother and I was just trying to help her, but no one was listening to her. I didn't struggle but this was an inner-city area and I'm sure the cops are rough with suspects because they have learned to be. I was arrested for murder and thrown into jail and Sophia did end up losing the baby."

He sighed heavily. "My parents drove themselves to Indiana and stayed until my trial was over. When they went back, Sophia went with them. I think she's still with them. I don't know…"

He shook his head again. "Anyway, the court-appointed lawyer was able to convince the judge it was manslaughter, not murder, since the gun was not mine and I hadn't been trying to kill him…I just wanted him to stop beating my sister. I was sentenced to two years in the federal penitentiary, since the local jails were all full of convicted drug offenders. By that time, I had already been incarcerated for close to six months, so I was sent away for another year and a half of hard time."

A look of comprehension now dawned on Patti's face. "That's where you were a year before last Thanksgiving! That's why you didn't want to tell me where you had been…you said it was somewhere you didn't want to be."

He nodded. "I was selfish enough to want you so bad that night I was afraid to tell you the truth, to let you decide if you wanted to take a man like me into your bed. I wasn't sure what you would have chosen."

He looked away, and was surprised to feel Patti's hand on his, as she said softly, "I wouldn't have cared. I was already in love with you by that point."

He looked searchingly into her face. She leaned forward and kissed him, but he pushed her gently back.

"I'm not done yet."

She sat back down. "How did you meet those two guys?"

He looked away again. "You meet all kinds in prison. Some okay, some not. But all are damaged, in some way or other. Most repeat offenders had terrible childhoods, so they are not in control of themselves…they are acting out scenes from their forgotten past, over and over again. The beatings, the yelling, even the raping…these are the only things they ever saw, so that's the only way they know how to behave. Then there's guys like me, who just got caught up in something that got out of control. You learn to keep your head down and not to draw any attention to yourself, if you can help it. What worked in my favor, of course, is, like you said, I look like a real bad-ass. I'm not, but that's what most men think I am, so mostly I got left alone. I've never been what you might think of as pretty, in a gay-man kind of way. I'm too rough-looking. But I felt really sorry for the guys who weren't as big or mean-looking as I am. They got raped a lot; some had to take a lot of beatings before they would allow the raping, but most learned you do what you have to in order to survive. You count the days until you get out. Of course, that means nothing to the lifers, who are the ones doing the most amount of damage to others…what have they got to lose?"

A nurse came in to take J.T.'s vitals. She nodded at Patti, then told J.T., "We called the doctor. He's in the hospital, doing rounds. He should be up here soon, then you can talk to him yourself."

Once she had left the room, he resumed his story to Patti.

"One guy I met was constantly putting up with shit, because he was short, thin and kind of metro-sexual looking. I don't know if he was gay or not, but it doesn't really matter. He should not have been forced to have sex if he didn't want it. He was young and had been convicted of dealing drugs while he was in college. Probably trying to pay his way through. Who knows? Anyway, the two thugs who broke into your house had been after him for a long time. They were just waiting for an opportunity and when they finally got it, they took advantage of it. I was on laundry duty, so I was bringing the clean towels into the locker room when I saw them raping the poor kid. Let's just say, he must have put up a really good fight, because he looked really badly beaten and almost dead. Then when they were done, they threw him against the wall of the shower and I heard his head crack when it hit the concrete. Turns out they snapped his neck. I was the only witness. Needless to say, I beat a hasty retreat out of there, but they had seen me for a split second and I'm kind of recognizable."

He sighed, as he continued to look out of the window. "I thought about not saying anything, but they sent word around they knew I had seen something I should not have seen, and they would be coming for me next. I'm big, but not nearly as tough as I look. So I got scared…hey, even I need to sleep sometime. So I went to the warden and asked what might be in it for me if I told him what I had seen. He said the men involved would get life, if convicted, because they had been in the revolving door circuit for years. I would get my sentence reduced by as much as he could talk the judge into. I had already been in there for over a year…I probably had about four months yet to go. So I was transferred to another area and I testified against them. They were in the same room, of course, since even criminals get to see who their accuser is. They both jumped up repeatedly, threatening to kill me, to hunt me down and butcher me and my family, yadda-yadda. Because of their behavior, the judge barred them from the courtroom after that and they were sentenced to life; I was rewarded by having the rest of my time commuted, so I was set free shortly after the trial ended."

He sighed and turned to look at Patti. "The first thing I did, once I was out, was to go to a church and pray for forgiveness for my own sins. Then I prayed for the soul of the poor kid whose death was the key to my freedom. I got a job, worked for long enough to be able to pay to get my Harley back out of storage and afford a physical to be sure I didn't pick up anything while I was in jail. Then I headed up towards Chicago, meaning to chill with some old friends for a while, working to get enough money to head back to the family, so I could see my sister again. I had been up here a couple of weeks and only had the bouncer job, when I got the call from my old cellmate, telling me the two guys I had testified against had escaped and were probably going to be looking for me. I figured since I wasn't even in the same state anymore, I should be relatively safe. But just to be sure, I have mostly stayed out of the city, since that's where it's easier to find people. There are always homeless guys willing to look for you, or identify you to someone for a couple of bucks for drugs. I thought I would be safer in the suburbs, since convicts, especially homeless ones, really stick out like a sore thumb here in suburbia. I thought if they ever appeared, I'd have enough notice to be able to leave town and they'd follow me."

He took Patti's hand in his. "I *never* imagined they would hurt you. I never figured they'd even find you. I never would have endangered you and your kids. I love you all too much for that."

"You seem to be forgetting it was their father who gave away our address, not you. It wasn't your fault we were all endangered."

He shook his head. "Maybe I'm not totally to blame. But I can never forgive myself. I'm afraid since they escaped once, they might be able to do it again; and now they already know where you live. Plus, I can't ever be certain no one else is after me either. I'm not trying to be paranoid, but criminals stick together and no one likes a snitch. That's what they see me as."

Patti shook her head. "I'm not scared. Believe me, Jules, I *was* scared, when it was all happening. But I refuse to live my life in fear of what might happen."

She got up and sat on the bed next to J.T. When he turned his head to look at her, she leaned forward and kissed him. He groaned. His hand rose up and into her hair and they both gave themselves over to expressing their feelings with their lips and tongues. She ran her hands over his chest, but stopped short of touching his injured shoulder.

They jumped guiltily apart, when the door was opened and the doctor strode in.

"Has the detective been in here to talk to you yet?"

Both of them shook their heads, trying not to look as aroused as they were. The doctor said, "Damn," then turned and walked out of the room. They could hear his shoes as he stomped down the hall. They looked at each other and shrugged. The door opened again, and it was one of the detectives who had repeatedly questioned them.

"Oh, good. You are both here. So I won't have to make any phone calls. I have some good news for you two."

They both looked at him. "Neither of those two career criminals will bother either of you again. Tyrone Jones jumped one of the deputies in the back of the police wagon and fought him for the gun. He shot the deputy, who will live, by the way, then he jumped out of the back of the wagon. The next two cars behind the wagon ran him over. There wasn't much of him left to scrape off the pavement. The other man, Jimmy Douglas, tried to escape out of the hospital. He was under armed guard, but he jumped the guard outside of his door and ran for the window at the end of the hallway. I guess because he had been in a room without a window, he had no idea he was on the twenty-fifth floor. He bounced off a couple of cars, then got run over by an ambulance. Not much of him left to scrape up either. Since both of the suspects are dead and we have corroborated the statements made by you two, as well as your son, ma'am, this case is officially closed. End of story. Have a nice day."

The detective shook hands with Patti, then turned to J.T. While he was shaking hands with him, he said, "Oh, and by the way, you need to keep your nose clean from now on. You got let off early once. You had a close call, but will live through this, your second chance. You know what they say about 'the third time is the charm'? Make sure there isn't a third time."

J.T. nodded. "I plan to. Thanks."

The detective left the room.

As soon as he was gone, the doctor strode back in. "So he's gone? He's told you? Good. Now, I understand you, sir, are not enjoying the hospitality in the hospital?" He chuckled at his own wit.

"Actually, no, I'm not. I'm a chef, as is this woman here, who is my boss. The food here sucks, if you don't mind my saying so."

The doctor shook his head, smiling. "Too true. Too bad you don't want to get a job here and show them all how it's done."

J.T. shook his head. "No thanks. I have a couple jobs already. But that's the main reason I don't want to stay. They are both good jobs, but neither offers insurance. So I have to pay the bills myself. I'm sure I can recuperate at home even better than I can here. I know it will cost me less."

The doctor nodded. "I see. Well, alrighty, then. I'll sign the paperwork and you will be free to leave once they process it. I assume you won't be showing up for the follow-up appointment?"

J.T. shook his head. "Probably not. Unless I have a problem, I really can't afford to."

The doctor shook his hand. "Well then, take good care of your shoulder. Don't do any heavy lifting on that side for at least a few months. You need to favor it for as long as you can. If you can ever afford therapy, it would be a worth-while investment to be sure you get full usage of your arm back."

He turned to head out the door, checking the pager on his belt as he walked.

Once he was gone, Patti gave J.T. a big hug. "You're coming home today! The kids will be thrilled."

He gave her an earnest look. "Are you sure it's okay?"

She patted the side of his face. "I'm more than sure. I insist! Your Harley, clothes and toothbrush are at my house. For you, that's proof of residency."

He nodded at her, but still looked thoughtful. The nurse bustled in with the release paperwork he had to sign and it took the next hour or so for everything to be done. Finally, J.T. eased himself out of the hospital-required wheelchair into Patti's car and they headed for home.

Chelsea was the only one home when they pulled into the driveway. She was sitting on the front porch with Katie and another friend. When she saw J.T. was in the car, she jumped off the front stoop with a squeal of delight.

"J.T.! You're back! Oh, my God, you're back!" She started to cry and J.T. gave her a hug, trying not to grimace when he moved his left arm.

"I had to come back, honey," he said. "I live here now, remember?"

She smiled at him through her tears. "Yeah, of course I remember. It was *my* idea, remember?"

Katie, in the meantime, had dialed home and handed the phone to Patti, so Tegan could hear the excitement for herself.

"Oh, Patti! I'm so happy for you that he's back!" Tegan told her. She asked, "Do you want me to watch the kids tonight?"

Patti watched as Chelsea held onto J.T., while he spoke to Katie and their other friend. She saw Jake come pelting around the corner from the direction of Tegan's house on his bike. He barely stopped, jumped off, and ran up to grab J.T. for an extended hug. It was hard to see his face, but with a mother's knowledge, she watched his shoulders shake while he hugged J.T. and she smiled as she answered her friend.

"No, I think we need to spend some time just being together tonight. In fact, we are probably going to need a few days for all of this to sink in for everyone. But thanks for the offer. I'll let you know when that might be a good idea. He's still pretty injured. I have a feeling he's going to need a nap as soon as I get him into the house. I'd like to plan a welcome home party for him, but I'll have to think about when to do it, so I'll talk to you about that later, okay?"

She handed the phone back to Katie, and went into the house to put on a fresh pot of coffee.

~ * ~

For the first week out of the hospital, J.T. slept most of the time. He was too weak to work at The Party House, but was assured by his boss that his job was available to him any time he was feeling up for coming back. Gradually, he lengthened the time he was able to be in the kitchen, and by the end of the second week, he was showing the benefits of two weeks of home-cooking and all of the loving attention that had been lavished on him by Patti and her kids. Patti had resumed her work schedule as soon as he was home, but the kids took special care that one of them was always home to do anything J.T. might need them to do. So it wasn't until the Monday, almost three weeks after the incident, as they had all taken to referring to it, had taken place, that J.T. and Patti were alone in the house during the day. Since Patti's Place was not open on Mondays, Patti had given her kids a ride to the pool and given them both some money to reward them for their nurturing skills which they had honed while they took turns caring for J.T.

It was a hot day, so when she didn't find him in the house, Patti looked out back and saw J.T. talking on his cell phone, sitting on a lawn chair in the shade. As she went out the back door, she stopped to admire the good job he and Edgar had done fixing the frame and the door, which had been badly damaged when the police broke through it during the incident. When he saw her coming out, he finished his call, and watched as she dragged a chair over to sit next to him. She handed him one of the glasses of lemonade she had brought out, and he took a sip as she planted a kiss on top of his head, then sat down in her chair.

"So, Jules, the kids are away and it's a hot day. It's been a couple of weeks since you got out of the hospital...you seem to be feeling a lot better. So, what on earth do you think we can do to pass the time?" She winked at him, and smiled hopefully.

He shook his head slowly. "Patricia, I have something to tell you. You are not going to like it, but you need to hear me out."

She looked at him in alarm. "You're not hurting, are you?"

"No, nothing like that. In fact, I'm feeling much better. So much better, I think it's time for me to pay my family a visit."

She looked at him in shock. "I take it you are *not* referring to *us* as 'your family' here?"

He shook his head. "No. Patricia, remember I told you I was on my way to see them when I ended up here, looking for work to earn the money to get back there. I really need to see them. I need to see that my sister Sophia is all right. I need to see my parents again and let them know I'm out of jail and all right. I told you family is really important to us. I just need to see them all again."

Patti looked away from him. Her eyes filled with tears, "This is it then? This is how it will end? I wondered why you hadn't been making any moves on me, but I figured you were still in too much pain. But now I see the real reason. You are leaving me and are trying not to have it hurt too much, aren't you?"

"No, Patricia, that's not what…"

She gave a quick sob, and interrupted him. "But don't you see? It's going to hurt a whole lot no matter how you do it! It's going to tear me apart. And the kids? Chelsea will cry. And Jake? He's been asking me if it's possible for you to adopt him, so he can let the whole world know *you* are his role model. You are the man he wants to be. My God, Jules, this is going to destroy all of us!"

"Patricia, listen to me!"

"Why? So you can try to tell me it's for my own good?" Her whole body was shaking, as she tried to control her emotions. "So you can tell me you are doing it to protect us? Because you love us?"

She jumped up to yell at him. "Love us a little less, then, and stay with us!"

253

She turned and ran into the house. The door would have slammed if J.T. hadn't been right behind her. As it was, it caught him on his good shoulder as he grabbed for her. She kept on running and threw herself down on her bed to sob as if her heart was breaking, because it was.

J.T. followed her into the room just a heartbeat behind her. He watched her shake for a split second, then he was on the bed. He pulled her up and cradled her in his arms, ignoring the pain from his left shoulder. She pounded her fists on his chest and shook the bed with the force of her grief. She sobbed until she had no more tears to shed... growing quiet in his arms. Still, he held and rocked her, murmuring loving words into her hair that she only gradually became aware of.

"Patricia...my love...my woman...my own. You are the woman of my dreams. You are my other half. You complete me. I have never loved any other woman before you. Not like I love you. I need you. I want you more than I have ever wanted any other woman. Listen to me. I'm not leaving you. Not now, not ever."

She was so quiet and still that he grew afraid. He reached his hand down and turned her face up to his. Her eyes were still closed, wet with tears. He kissed each of her eyes, then he lightly brushed her lips with his.

"Patricia, you hear what I'm saying, right? Tell me you hear me."

She looked up at him, and he felt as if he could drown in the depths of the pain that was in her dark eyes.

In a small voice, she said, "I hear you. But the words mean nothing. You are leaving me. Nothing else matters."

He enfolded her back into his arms and rocked her again. "Patricia, I will come back. I promise."

She pushed herself back and looked him in the eye, "When?"

He shook his head. "I don't know. Soon. It depends on how long it takes me to get out there, where they are now and how long they want me to visit. I was talking to them on the phone, but it wasn't a good signal. My dad said he would head into town and call me soon, to give me directions for where they are camped now."

Patti shifted herself around on his lap, causing both of them to become acutely aware of the hardening erection she was sitting on. She looked up at him and asked, "Is there anything I can do, to ensure you come back quicker? Like, maybe, give you something to remember, that you will want to come back for?" She began to kiss his neck, licking her way along his scratchy chin, with the half-grown beard that had been growing while he didn't have to leave the house to work.

He twitched when her tongue dipped into his ear. She licked her way along his face, up to his lips. For a heartbeat, they looked at each other, then they both moaned, and their lips pressed together, with a passion as strong in its intensity as her grief had been. Once again ignoring the pain in his shoulder, J.T. proceeded to tear off the clothing Patti had on and she tore at his. Fortunately for him, she didn't ignore his injured shoulder, but gently lifted his arm to remove his tee shirt from that side. She tore it off of the other side and they frantically worked together towards a single goal.

Within minutes, they were both naked; J.T. spent another heartbeat admiring her curves, then she pulled him down on top of her and he plunged himself into her welcoming wetness. Their movements were desperate as it had been so long and so much had happened to them since they last touched each other. They climbed the hill together, but when Patti fell off the other side, screaming with the intensity of her orgasm, J.T. tried to hold himself back. He pounded himself into her, pulling out, then pushing back in while she screamed and clawed at his back; trying to pull him deeper into herself, she wrapped her legs around his back and she rode him, as his thrusts grew shallower and quicker. With a mighty roar, he joined her in free-fall and rode the waves of ecstasy with her as she soared up and down on a rollercoaster of pleasure, each new orgasm intensified by the last one.

Long after J.T. had fallen off the ride, Patti continued to quiver from the aftershocks. Eventually, even those ended, and she lay quiet. J.T had rolled off of her and lay with the back of one hand draped over his forehead. Since his arm was up on the side she was on, and it was his good shoulder, Patti pushed herself onto his chest and idly ran her fingers through his chest hair, as she snuggled her face into his skin.

"In case you are wondering, I'm memorizing the smell of you and the feel of you," she told him. "I have no way of knowing how long it will have to last me, so I want it to be fresh in my mind when you go."

He reached his hand down, to caress her face. She leaned over him now, and they kissed, long and luxuriously. She regarded him seriously, "You are planning on leaving tomorrow, aren't you?"

He nodded. "The sooner I go, the sooner I'll be back."

She sighed heavily. "At least that's what you are telling me. And since I want to believe it, that's what I want to hear."

He caressed her face. "Do you have any idea how beautiful you are, Patricia? Or just how much I care about you?"

She shook her head.

He kissed her again. Then his phone rang. They both almost fell out of bed as they jumped up to find his pants. She got to them first and pulled the phone out, then tossed it to him. He caught it with his good arm.

"Hello? Dad! Let me get a piece of paper and something to write with."

Patti handed him a notebook and a pencil. She walked down the hall to the kitchen to get them another couple glasses of lemonade.

Chelsea took the news that J.T. was going on a road-trip back to visit his family much better than Patti had. She nodded at him when he said he had to go see them, but he would be back soon. It was Jake who asked if he could go with him. Patti held her breath, waiting to see what J.T. would say.

"Nah, Jake, not this time. Maybe the next time. This is just something I have to do, you understand."

Jake shook his head. "No, I don't understand. Maybe it's a man thing. I'm not a man yet. I'm still only a boy. I will really miss you." He had thrown his arms around J.T. and held to him like he would never let him go. Patti turned away so neither of them would see the tears in her eyes.

~ * ~

When J.T. pulled his Harley away from their house, Patti couldn't watch. Chelsea and Jake stood outside and waved at him until they couldn't see him anymore. They both walked into the house and sat on either side of their mother, and hugged her. Finally, Chelsea said, "Now what, Mom?"

Patti replied. "Now, we wait."

Jake looked up at her. "For how long?"

She regarded him seriously. "As long as it takes."

Twenty-four

Life went on. There were meals to prepare, since Patti's Place was gaining a reputation for dependable, excellent Mexican food. Patti was still only open for lunch, but now found herself having to make extra food for carry-outs that people would take home to reheat later for dinner. And birthdays happen all year, so the summer was just as busy with children's parties as the rest of the year.

On the second Friday after J.T. left, Patti was setting all the tables for that day's lunch crowd when a petite young woman came in and sat at the table closest to the front window.

Patti smiled at her. "Hello." Then she waved at all of the empty tables. "You can sit anywhere, you know. You're the first customer of the day."

The young woman smiled at her. "But I want to keep my eye on the door. I'm meeting my husband here. He only gets an hour to eat and he's wanted to try the cooking here since you opened."

Patti smiled at her again. "Let me get you something to drink while you wait." She returned a few minutes later with the lemonade requested and caught sight of the playgroup's second choice in the fantasy top five of most attractive men, as her mail carrier walked up to the front door. She turned to grab her outgoing mail from the ledge behind her and almost dropped the lemonade glass that was still in her hand when he walked over to the woman at the table and kissed the top of her head, then her lips when she turned her head up to smile at him.

Patti walked over to the table to deliver the drink and heard him say, "Sorry I'm late, honey. I hope you haven't been here waiting for too long."

The woman shook her head, telling him, "No…see, she's just bringing my drink now." The woman gave Patti a knowing smile and winked at her. For the second time, Patti almost dropped the glass. She couldn't imagine how her surprise must look on her face, so she nodded when the mail-babe ordered a glass of lemonade for himself. She promised to be right back to take their order, so he could get out quickly enough to get back to work. She hustled back into the kitchen and hit redial on her cell phone while she poured the lemonade. When Tegan answered, she spoke quickly and furtively.

"Hello?" Tegan answered, while Carlos could be heard babbling into the phone.

"Tegan! You have *got* to get here as quickly as you can!" Patti whispered loudly. "Fantasy man number two is in here with his wife! I'm just going out to take their order now."

Tegan yelped. "Stall him! I'm on my way."

Patti put her phone down and tried to act casual as she carried the drink out and took the order for the two young lovebirds, who were gazing into each others' eyes.

They were almost done eating their chili *rellenos* with corn and bean salsa, when Patti had to pinch herself to keep from laughing at the sight of the women in her playgroup appearing at the outside tables, sitting where they would be able to watch the inside table, as well as enjoy the view when their favorite eye candy left the restaurant.

They waved and hollered. "Yoo-hoo!"

She went out to inquire if they were planning on being paying customers, or just voyeurs. When she asked them that, Tegan appeared insulted she would think they would sit and *not* order. Patti wrote down what they wanted and headed in to start filling their orders. Chelsea had arrived by then to help her by delivering beverages and clearing off the tables. She sent her out with the drinks. Patti went to her register to take the money from the young woman who had been her first, and most interesting, customer of the day.

As she got up to approach the register, the young woman had first hugged and kissed her husband.

He turned to Patti saying, "Thanks for such a great meal! I've been wanting to try some of your gourmet cooking ever since you started Parties by Pat-Teg years ago. But our kids aren't really old enough for parties yet; also, we live kind of far away, in the city."

Patti smiled and nodded at him, with what she hoped was a relatively calm, nonchalant look on her face.

He kissed his wife again. "See you later, darling."

He grabbed Patti's outgoing mail from the ledge and he handed her the day's mail.

With another smile at them both, he turned and walked out. He nodded, smiled, and said, "Hello, ladies," to all of the women sitting outside, and didn't seem to notice his departure made all of them fall reverently silent as he walked by.

Patti was just handing the woman her change, when she was surprised to hear a stifled giggle. She looked up to see the woman was watching the playgroup ladies' reaction to her husband walking past them.

She leaned closer to Patti, so the other customers in the restaurant would not hear her.

"If they keep drooling like that, they'll soak their shirts!" Then she winked at Patti.

Patti studied her a moment. "How long has he known?"

The woman shrugged. "What? That he's so gorgeous grown women melt when they see him? Or that you ladies push each other out of the way to get the best view of his butt when he walks by?" She leaned closer to Patti. "Why do you think he wears his shorts so early in the season?"

Patti smiled at her. "But does he know he's only number two in our fantasy top five now?"

The woman looked at her in consternation. "There's someone else who's better-looking? Do you have a picture of him?"

Patti winked at her. "Well, let's just say he's *as* good-looking...but we have heard personal testimonials about his abilities, so that moved him up in the ranks. He's married to my partner; she's the one holding the baby out there. The baby looks just like his daddy."

The woman looked out the window, and nodded. "Hmm. Cute kid. We've been looking for a house out closer this way, so Chris could have a shorter commute. If we were to move out here, do you think I might be able to join your playgroup?"

Patti smiled at her. "We're not a closed group. You just have to live in the neighborhood and have children."

The woman smiled. "My name is Clair. I'm a nurse, part-time, but I'm home during the day when Chris works, so one of us is always with the kids."

"We have lots of teenagers who do baby-sitting in our neighborhood, too," Patti observed.

Clair smiled at her again. "I'm sure I'll be seeing you again soon, Patti."

"I sure hope so."

The woman turned and walked out, past all of the women who pretended not to notice her and she waved at Patti standing in the doorway as she pulled her car into the street, then drove away.

Patti barely made it to the outside tables before she burst into gales of laughter. Fortunately Chelsea was there to help, because it was quite some time before the other women allowed Patti to get back to her job. They insisted on hearing all about the unexpected turn of events that had just unfolded on this hot afternoon. And Debbie, who was a realtor part-time, announced if it was the last thing she ever did, she'd find them an affordable house in the neighborhood. The entire table high-fived her.

~ * ~

Chelsea's fourteenth birthday party was at Patti's Place, the second week of July. Patti allowed Chelsea to set up a boombox in the restaurant and the girls and boys at the party danced between binges of eating and drinking.

Patti had tried to allow for the increased appetite of teenagers in her calculations of how much food to buy. Still, even she was amazed at how much food could be consumed in such a short amount of time by only a handful of kids.

Juanita and Edgar's son Enrique laughed when she complained about his third trip up to the taco bar.

"You should have to cook for *my* family," he teased her. "Why do you think my mom can't get a job? She doesn't have the time. She spends the whole day cooking and we eat everything in a few hours, so she has to wake up and do it all again the next day."

To fill the days, Tegan brought Carlos over every day so Patti could admire his chubby legs and smile, which he liked to show off to all his favorite people. When he smiled, he showed off his mother's dimples, which seemed to be the only part of him that looked like her.

"Honestly," Tegan complained. "I got the stretch marks and the knife and he looks so much like his daddy, you can't even tell he's mine!"

Patti, who was holding the offending baby at the time, smiled as he pulled at her blouse button.

"But that means he's going to be just as gorgeous as his daddy! And that's nothing to be upset about. Think of how the future women of America will thank you for that."

Tegan smiled, a dreamy look coming over her face, "Yeah. Gorgeous. Hot. Mine. Ummm!"

Patti laughed at her. "Having lots of wild monkey sex again, are you? You lucky gal."

Tegan laughed. "Well, if we are going to have *Irish twins*, we have to get a move on, don't we? I've got to be pregnant by the time Carlos is nine months old. That only gives me another couple months. Why do you think my kids keep wanting to spend the night at other people's houses? Like *yours*? It's a whole lot quieter than where I'm screaming all night long. Thank God Carlos is a sound sleeper."

Patti made a face at Carlos. "Does the poor baby have any other choice? No, he doesn't! His mama and daddy are a couple of sex maniacs. Probably scarring you for life, you poor little thing."

Carlos grabbed for his mother and she took him on her lap and opened her blouse to nurse him.

"And how can you call this moose a little thing? The doctor keeps asking me what I'm feeding him, because he started off the weight charts and he's staying off them. He's almost big enough for size two clothes, and he's only seven months old."

Patti clucked in sympathy, took a drink of her lemonade and got a far-away look in her eyes. Tegan smiled at her.

"How long has it been?" she asked.

"Two weeks tomorrow," Patti answered. "But who's counting?"

Tegan reached over and patted her hand. "He'll come back. He said he would."

Patti sighed. "If I didn't believe that, I'd have stuck my head in the oven already."

"Even if all you got was dirty hair, since your new oven doesn't have a pilot to blow out?" Tegan teased her.

Patti stuck her tongue out, "You know what I mean."

Tegan nodded.

"It's like, I only feel partly alive when he's not here…" Patti began. "And I don't even want to think about what I'm going to do if he doesn't come back."

Tegan nodded. "Believe me; I *know* what that feels like. But you were here for me and I'm here for you."

Patti gave her a helpless look and Tegan patted her hand again.

They sat in companionable silence in Patti's backyard as they each enjoyed what little breeze there was on a hot Monday afternoon. Carlos nursed himself to sleep.

Twenty-five

Patti was going through the mail at home later that afternoon and was surprised to find an official-looking certified letter addressed to Jake Johnson, Jr. Since Jake was not home and not yet of legal adult age anyway, she knew it would be all right for her to open it, so she did. She read it over a half-dozen times to be sure she was not misunderstanding it. She called her lawyer, and left a message for him to get back to her. Then she called Tegan.

"Hello?" Tegan answered, sounding harried, with the sound of baby Carlos crying in the background.

"It's me," Patti answered, "I can wait until you get him latched on, if you want. I have to talk to you about something."

"Okay, hold on a minute," Tegan said, then there was quiet, broken only by the small sounds of humming satisfaction coming from the baby.

"So, what's up?" Tegan asked.

"You'll never guess what I got in the mail today!" Patti said, then corrected herself, "I mean, what Jake got in the mail today."

"Your ex?" asked Tegan.

"No, my son," Patti answered. "It's an official-looking letter from the FBI, stating he has earned the reward for information that led to the successful recapturing of two criminals from the Most Wanted list. It says there was a five-thousand dollar reward for each of them, so he's now earned ten thousand dollars and he has to respond to this letter officially to let them know if they are to cut him a check or to auto-deposit it into a bank account of some kind."

"Wow! That's really weird," Tegan observed. "Are they aware he's only ten years old?"

"There's no indication in the letter, but there is a spot for a parent or guardian's signature if the recipient is a minor, so I think it's just some standardized form. I had no idea there was any money out there for something like this. Do you think it's a hoax?"

"I don't know, girl. Did you call your lawyer?"

"Yeah, but he's not there, so I left a message on his voice-mail. I don't want to tell Jake about it until we know if it's legit or not. But if it is, this would really help a lot, with college bills for him, wouldn't it?"

"Yup! And maybe get him a car when he gets old enough? Depends on how you invest it, but that's a nice chunk of unexpected change! "

"Ooops, got to run. Late for Jazzercise! Talk to you later, okay?"

"Sure. I went to the early class today…good thing, since Carlos is having a crabby afternoon. Talk to you soon. Bye."

Patti put the letter on the fridge and rushed off to class.

When the lawyer got back to her later in the afternoon, he took some information from her and hung up to do some checking. He called her back again to report as far as he could tell, it was a legitimate offering and Jake should be able to get the money. He suggested having it directly deposited into Jake's savings account for now. She could always get advice later, as to how to invest it to maximize the benefit to Jake.

Later, during dinner, Patti told Jake and Chelsea about the money and let them both read the letter. Jake looked thoughtful, when he read it.

When Patti was saying good night to him, he mentioned it again.

"Hey, Mom, "he said. "You know the money you said I'm going to get, for telling the police about those guys who were hurting you?"

"Yes, honey, what about it?" she asked, while she pulled his covers over him and smoothed back the hair that always got in his eyes.

"I was thinking about it, and I won't be needing it for a car, or for college for about eight years, yet, right?" Jake looked thoughtful again.

"Yes, that's right. We'll invest it and get you more money off the interest."

He took a deep breath. "Can we give some of it to J.T. to pay for some of the medical bills that are being delivered every day? He said he checked himself out of the hospital extra-early, since he doesn't have insurance and he will have to pay the whole bill himself."

Patti was sitting on his bed now, regarding him with surprise.

Jake continued. "Well, I wouldn't have known what to even say, if he hadn't told me to tell them where the guys had escaped from. If I hadn't told them that, they might not have had their bullet-proof stuff on and some policemen could have been killed. So actually, we *both* were the ones who warned them, right?"

He looked earnestly at his mom and she took a deep breath before answering him.

"Jake, that's most generous of you, but you don't have to do anything like that. The money is going to be made out in your name only."

Jake nodded. "But I want to share it with J.T. I won't need it for a while and if I invest it right, it will grow to more by the time I need it. But J.T. needs it for bills now. And maybe that way, he will realize just how important he is to me." He looked at his mom and patted her hand, "to all of us."

Patti leaned forward and hugged her son with tears in her eyes. "If that's what you want to do, Jakey, then it's okay. But we have to wait until J.T. is back here before you can offer it to him."

Jake nodded. "Yup. Once he's back here, back *home* where he belongs, then I want to be the one to tell him about it, okay? Since it's made out to me?"

Patti now leaned back, and smiled at Jake. "Okay. It's your gift to make. Now I think you need to get some sleep, young man. It's getting late and you've been staying up too long playing computer games the past couple of nights. Lights out."

He smiled at her and gave a huge yawn. "Okay, Mom. But soon I'm going to have Kevin overnight again and we are going to play all night."

She smiled at him and kissed the top of his head. "Okay, honey. Good night."

She turned out the light and walked slowly out of the room. When she stood in the hall, she leaned against the wall and hugged herself. "J.T. where are you?" she asked herself aloud, sighed, and walked back down the stairs to try to get some sleep in her empty bed.

~ * ~

Patti was driving home from Jazzercise class the next morning when on a whim, she turned down one street earlier than her usual route home and admired the front of her restaurant. She had added some flowers to the outside tables, so now there were extra splashes of color on the outside as well as inside. She was admiring the view and thinking what a good eye for color and design Chelsea had, when she realized she saw movement in the kitchen. Instantly alert, and wary from her recent experience, she wondered if she should call the police. She decided to pull around the back, look in the window and make her decision after she saw if there really was anyone in her closed business.

When she turned the corner to get to the parking spaces out back, she felt her heart begin to race as she recognized the Harley parked in its customary spot. Forgetting she still had on her spandex, forgetting her kids would be expecting her home soon, forgetting everything but her need to see if it was really him, she parked the car. She jumped out and hurried to the back door. She pushed it open and almost ran into J.T. who was standing in front of the oven, adjusting the temperature.

"Hi, Patricia," he said, conversationally while he moved back around the counter top to where he was assembling some kind of meat and rice concoction that he was rolling up using what appeared to be cooked cabbage.

Standing there, her heart racing as if she had run a mile, Patti stared at him.

"You're back!" she gasped out, stating the obvious.

"Uh-huh," he agreed while he continued to work.

"How long?" she demanded.

He looked up but kept on working.

"How long have I been back, or how long am I going to stay?"

She looked at him with alarm. "Both."

He continued to work, occasionally looking up at her.

"Well, I got back early this morning, but figured you were either still asleep, as I would have been, or at Jazzercise. Judging by the spandex, which by the way is so very hot on you, I'm guessing it was the latter."

She nodded, her breathing still not back to normal.

He continued, "So, I headed over to the grocery store, where, incidentally, everyone told me about how they are all being sneaky now. They order your food at lunchtime, then take it home to reheat later for dinner. You know, sooner or later, we will have to be open for dinner, too. At least during part of the year. Maybe during the colder months, when we won't be planning to go camping quite so much."

She stared at him.

He started to put the assembled cabbage rolls into a big pot.

"So, I picked up what I needed to make you my grandmother's secret *golabki* recipe, which is an old family recipe for Polish cabbage rolls. I already made a pot of chocolate pudding for dessert. And these are almost ready to go into the oven, so we can have them for lunch. Of course, you'll need to go get the kids, too. I missed all of you. I can't wait to see them again."

She continued to stare at him. He smiled at her as he finished getting everything into the pot.

"As for how long I'm going to be back, that's entirely dependent on you."

He walked over to the oven and put the pot into it, then closed the door and set the timer. He walked back to the counter and sat on one of the bar stool chairs and poured two cups of coffee, pushing one towards her.

"Sit, Patricia. I need to tell you about my trip home."

In a daze, she walked over to the chair he indicated and sat down. When she put out her hand to grasp the coffee cup, her hand was shaking. He smiled at her and took her other hand in his and kissed the palm.

"So," he began, "I got kind of a late start out of town on the day I left. I took a small, unannounced detour and paid your ex-husband a quick visit."

She continued to stare at him, as if he had rendered her speechless; her eyes widened.

"I felt the need to explain to him how unacceptable it was for him to share your address with strangers in bars and just how unhappy it made me that he put so little value on your safety. I caught him while he was just heading out the door to work. We had a pleasant little chat outside of his apartment door. Well, that is, until I threw him through his door. Then it wasn't so pleasant anymore. But I think I impressed on him the need for greater discretion in the future. Basically, I told him if he does anything ever again to endanger you or your children, I will take him apart and feed all of the pieces to the rats in the alley behind his apartment. Then I told him, '*have a nice day, asshole*,' and I left for my road trip."

He smiled at her. "Are you with me so far?"

She nodded, taking a drink of her coffee.

"Has he bothered you in any way since I've been gone?"

She shook her head.

He nodded. "Good. I headed out onto the highway. But after just a few hours, what used to be a special pleasure became very painful. My shoulder ached and I had to stop early for lunch. And my knee had locked up also. That's when I realized it was going to take me a lot longer than the three days I had planned to get out there. I guess I never realized just how much your body gets jarred on a motorcycle. I used to be able to ride a good ten, maybe twelve hours, on a good day. This time around, I couldn't do much more than five or six hours before the pain got so unbearable I had to stop. And very few campgrounds have Jacuzzis, so I was basically stuck with rubbing ointment on my shoulder and knee, then trying to move them around so they didn't get frozen in any one position. Anyway, that's why it took me so long to get back. It took me almost six days to get out to South Dakota, where my family is staying for the summer with a local Indian tribe.

One of my older sisters is married to one of the tribal elders, so it's okay for non-American Indians to be there, since one of us is related and the tribal council has okayed it."

He stopped to take a long drink from his coffee, then resumed his story.

"The family was thrilled to see me. Sophia has a new boyfriend, one of the tribe members, and she's pregnant again. I swear, that girl needs to learn what birth control is! Or what a marriage license is. But anyway, she's happy and he's a nice guy who already knew what happened to the last guy who hit my sister. When he realized just who I was, I thought he was going to faint. But we got along just fine after he got to know me a little bit. My parents are looking a little the worse for aging, but they were so glad to see me my mother promptly cooked up a bunch of *golabki*, just like we are going to eat today. When I told them about you, my mother was shocked I had never made you any of my old family recipes. She cuffed me upside the head then yelled at me to cook traditional for you, so you become part of the family. I promised her I would. That was the first night I was back. We had a party, with everyone over to eat and drink until all hours of the night. Then we all slept until almost noon, when it got too hot to stay in tents or mobile homes without air conditioning anymore. I laughed to myself, wondering what on earth you and the kids would have been doing with yourselves all of that time while you were awake and there were sleeping Romani and Indians all over the landscape. But we'll find out, soon enough, I hope."

She stared at him, and he poured them both more coffee.

"The second day I was there, word came to me Grandmother wanted to talk to me. She's eighty-five, so she's our family elder. Whatever she wants, she gets. She says that's the benefit of outliving everyone else. You finally get your way. Also, you get to tell everyone else how to live. Anyway, she told me she had heard from my mother I was involved with a woman. She wanted to know all about you. I told her everything. I didn't even leave out the bad parts. I told her about the incident, and how injured I got trying to save you. I told her how I feel about you. I told her how I feel about Chelsea and Jake. Then she waved at me to be quiet. She thought for a long time. Did I mention I was sitting on a stool at her feet? She's only about four-foot, maybe ten-inches tall. So she likes to sit on her rocker and have everyone sit on a stool at her feet so she can feel tall. Actually, when I'm sitting on the stool, I'm about as tall as she is, but I learned a long time ago to slouch to make her feel better. When she was done thinking and smoking her pipe, she asked me to lean closer. She kissed me on one cheek. Then she slapped me on the other."

J.T. now stopped and laughed.

"You could have knocked me over with a feather! She hasn't hit me since my divorce. She hit me then, to tell me to stop being depressed over a marriage that was over and a woman who didn't love me enough to want to stay with me; and to leave to find my fortune elsewhere. Let me tell you, that old woman still packs a wallop! Anyway, I asked her what that was for. She told me the kiss was because she has always loved me more than she should, and she was so happy to see me again, out of jail and happy with my life, finally. She said the slap was for being so stupid as to come out to see her as only half a man. Since I'm now in love with a woman who completes me, I should have known I should bring you along with me. She told me she wouldn't allow me to come back to see the family again unless I bring you with me, for her to give her approval. Then she leaned closer, and whined to me, saying, *Grandma's feet need to dance at another wedding. Who knows how much longer I have left? I need to dance again!* She told me to go away and not to bother her again until you were with me."

J.T. stopped talking, walked over to the oven, opened the door to check on the food, closed it and walked over to stand in front of Patti.

He smiled at the dazed look on her face. "So, you see, I'm an outcast now. I'm not allowed to go back without you. I left the next day and it took me another six days to get back here. Patricia, I want you to come with me to see my family. I want you to bring Chelsea and Jake, because once you marry me they will be part of my family, too. If they still want me to adopt them, then that's what I want, too. I can't make the ride again on my bike, but if all of us go, we'll need the car anyway. Maybe I'll be able to ride longer again some day, or maybe I'll have to learn to make only shorter trips on my hog. Since we live fairly close to Wisconsin, I should still be able to make it up there with you. But I have a family now, and so I guess I better get used to riding in a car."

He studied her face. "You're even more beautiful than I remembered. And I missed you so much, it hurt."

He tilted her face up to him, with one finger under her chin and he kissed her lips once, twice, then with a whimper, she stood up on the rung of the chair and wrapped herself around him, as his arms enfolded her. They clung to each other, and with one mind, both of them started to undo each other's clothing. Patti only had on spandex bike shorts and a loose tee shirt. The shirt was gone, then with a groan, J.T. popped open the back of her bra and buried his face in her breasts. She was busy pulling his shirt off. They moved to each other's lower clothing. Her spandex was pulled roughly off, but he had to help her with the belt buckle on his jeans. Then his jeans were down and she moaned as she grasped him in her hand and guided him into her naked body.

They both moaned as they moved in harmony with each other, as if they were indeed one person in two bodies, split in half, but now joined together again. Their rhythm was so familiar it made her heart ache and Patti was surprised to find she was crying while she held her man and they rocked against each other. She wrapped her legs up and around his waist and he leaned heavily against her, with her butt supported by the chair. Deeper he drove into her, then deeper. She fell off the other side of her building pleasure and screamed on the way down. J.T. made no attempt to hold himself back. He drove into her with the force of two weeks of waiting to back him up and force him on. He drove into her until he roared out his own pleasure as he filled her completely with himself; still he pumped into her, slowing down, then stopping completely, trying to be able to breathe again.

He leaned weakly against her.

"Can we move back to the couch? I think my legs are going to go!"

She giggled and he staggered backwards, still holding onto her body, which was connected to his. He fell onto the couch, her weight driving him deeper into her and her giggle was swallowed in a surprised shriek when she came again. He collapsed completely, his head thrown back against the wall, his breathing coming in gasps.

She wriggled herself on him and kissed his lips.

"Welcome home, Jules."

He opened his eyes and smiled at her, wrapped his hands in her hair and held her head close to his, so he could kiss her again and again.

Then he stopped and gave her an enquiring look. "Well?"

She looked puzzled at him. "Well, what?"

His brows knit as he studied her face. "Will you come back there with me, and marry me? Will you join your family with mine?"

She looked at him seriously.

"You really *are* asking me, aren't you?"

He raised his eyebrows and gave her a mischievous look.

"Did you think I was kidding? You've never met Grandmother. Believe me, *she* wasn't kidding. I'm really not allowed back to see my own family until I bring you with me."

She shook her head.

"So you are really asking me to drop everything, round up the kids and drive half-way across the country with you, to marry you in some kind of tribal-type ceremony that may or may not be legal?"

He frowned at her.

"I didn't think of that. I guess we can always detour back through Vegas, where you don't have to be a state resident to get married. Or we can see if there's anyone in the tribe who knows state law well enough to give us legal advice. But basically, yes, that's what I'm asking you to do."

She smiled, opening her mouth to answer him, when all of a sudden her eyes grew big.

"Oh shit! I forgot! I ran out of pills and since you weren't in town, I didn't think there was any hurry to get more. Crap! I don't want to be pregnant ever again! What was I thinking?"

She pulled herself up and off of him and started to get up, when J.T. pulled her back onto his lap.

"Honey, there's one more thing I have to tell you, then I promise you will know all of my secrets."

She was still angry at herself, but now she was intrigued as well.

"All of them?"

He smiled again.

"Well, almost all...the important ones, anyway."

He cleared his throat.

"Umm, it's kind of embarrassing to talk about, which is why you are the only person I have told, in fifteen years, since I got divorced."

"What? And please tell me it's not that you have some kind of life-threatening disease, so you really want to have just one kid. God, I'm such an idiot! Tegan told me you'd probably want kids with me! But I don't want anymore! Is that really so hard to accept?"

"Patricia, please be quiet and let me finish."

She looked at him mutinously, but quietly.

He cleared his throat again.

"I...um...I told you my marriage only lasted a couple of years, and we got divorced because we were too young. But that's not the real reason. Actually, she divorced me because I'm...um...I'm sterile."

Patti's eyes grew wide. "What?"

He nodded sadly.

"I told you, it's really embarrassing. We men like to think of ourselves as loaded guns. Well...my gun fires blanks. You see, we didn't get vaccines when we were younger and I got mumps when I was seventeen. Swelled both of my testicles up to the size of cantaloupes. I was sicker than a dog for weeks. We didn't go to doctors much either. Maybe if I had gone to one early on, I might have been able to stop the damage. But when the swelling finally went down, the doctor that my mother had finally insisted I go to, warned us I might be sterile, and encouraged me to get tested. I never followed through on it, and forgot all about it. I got married when I was eighteen to a girl I had grown up with, since she was a distant cousin whose mother traveled with my parents on and off for years. Having children is really important in our culture, so we really worked at it for months. But by the end of the first year, when she wasn't pregnant, she started to get worried that something was wrong with us. Her mother even consulted a couple of fortune tellers to see if we were cursed. No one had any answers, so she broke down finally, and went to a doctor. He ran some tests on her and told her everything looked fine on her end. He told her to have me go to one of his colleague's office and provide a sample for testing. And that's when I got the news. Nothing. Nada. *No viable sperm visible.* Shortly after that, she divorced me and got the marriage annulled in the church, so she could get married again, to another one of our cousins. Last time I saw her, they had about a dozen kids. She complained to me about how exhausted she was from chasing all of those kids around, and I said, '*Aww, what a drag for you.*' Then I left and laughed all the way home."

He looked directly into her eyes, "So, you see, Patricia, I can't get you pregnant. Not even if you begged me to. So…um…I guess if you don't want to marry me now that you know, I'll understand."

She lightly tapped his face with her hand.

"You idiot! Didn't you listen when I was talking? No wonder your grandmother and your mother hit you. You never listen. I don't want to have any more babies. Not now. Not ever. I was on the freaking pill to avoid just that. And *now* you tell me, when I could have been saving my money all those months, and not messing up my hormones. When did you plan on telling me? When I went through menopause? Ever?"

He laughed in relief, and pushed her so she was lying on the couch. He held her arms above her head and he kissed her lips, neck, breasts, and then he stopped at all of the places in between, and started all over again. She was writhing and giggling and finally twisted out of his grasp.

"So?" he asked her again when she was pulling her panties back on and reaching for her spandex.

"So, what?" she asked, enjoying toying with him and trying to make it last.

"So, are you going to agree to become Mrs. Tremenczyk or not?"

She raised an eyebrow. "Can't you take my name?"

He vehemently shook his head.

"No way am I taking the name of that putz you were married to."

She shrugged. "Well, my maiden name was Valentini. How about that?"

He had only pulled on his jeans, and he now advanced threateningly on her.

"What's wrong with Tremenczyk?"

She smiled at him, asking, "Besides the fact I can never remember how to spell it?"

He smiled back at her.

"Well, good thing your handwriting is so sloppy and hard to read, then. No one will be able to read what the hell you wrote, so as long as they know it's you, it should be fine."

She looked at him in mock anger.

"So, that's how it's going to be, huh? Insults all of the time? And I have to be the little woman and take your name, like I'm a piece of property you are laying claim to?"

He advanced all the way up to her, grabbed her wrists and held them up against the wall,as he pressed himself into her lower body.

"Your handwriting is sloppy and you know it," he growled at her. "You *are* a little woman and I have *already* laid claim to you. You belong to me, remember?"

With that, he lowered his head and kissed her, long and hard, until they were both panting again.

"Okay, okay!" she gasped. "I give up!"

He looked quizzically at her, "What?"

"Yes."

"YES?"

"Yes."

He let her arms go then and picked her up to twirl around the room with her. He stopped and kissed her again and again.

"You won't ever regret this, Patricia. I'm going to spend the rest of my life making you happy!"

She smiled at him. They both looked at the oven as the timer rang.

"Damn!" He said. "I thought we had more time!"

She smiled at him.

"You wanted me to get the kids here to eat. You are going to have to let go of me, so I can call them. I'll go get them and bring them back here. Then you will need to ask them if they want to go along on this little trip you have planned. And if they want to be a part of your family."

He gave her a serious look.

"What do you think they will say?"

She smiled, and stroked the side of his face.

"Probably the same thing that I did. They will want to know if *they* have to learn to spell Tremenczyk also."

He chuckled, "Well, if I adopt them legally, they'll have to."

He gave her another, more serious look while she finished pulling her tee shirt back on, and called her kids. He listened to her telling them he was back and telling them to get ready for her to pick them up for lunch.

"You know," he began to muse aloud, "I never figured I'd ever be able to call any children mine. No son to carry on my name. No daughter to walk down the aisle, while I glare at the man who isn't nearly good enough for her. Do you really think Chelsea and Jake will want that from me?"

Patti smiled at him. She had put her phone into speaker mode so her kids could hear what he was saying. He heard both of her children yell, "YES!"

She started for the door. "I'll be right back and you can ask them in person. Then we can all eat Tremenczyk family food. And pudding. And we can celebrate that you are back home, where you belong."

J.T. smiled after her, as she left. He took out of his pocket the ring that Grandmother had given him from off her own finger, for luck. He grinned at that memory, which he had not shared with Patti.

"Yes, Grandmother. She is going to wear your ring. I will put it on her finger when I marry her, then your feet can dance, one more time, at a wedding."

J.T. started to hum a traditional tune and he bustled around the kitchen, getting ready to feed his family.

Epilogue

When Tegan heard Patti was getting married, she was ecstatic. When she heard the wedding was going to take place in South Dakota, she was determined not to miss it. So when Alexander got home that night, he found candles lit, cha cha music playing softly and his wife in the teal negligee he had given to her when they were dating. Baby Carlos cooperated and they enjoyed a few incredibly pleasurable hours working on giving Carlos another sibling.

Only afterwards did Tegan mention the upcoming nuptials to take place in South Dakota. Since he couldn't really be angry at his wife, who was everything he had ever wanted, Alexander bowed to the inevitable and immediately re-scheduled his two-week vacation, from August to the last two weeks in July. They decided not to drive, since they had to bring the baby along and Alexander had never been camping in his life, nor did he have any desire to start learning how, at this late stage. They flew out to the area, rented a mini-van and drove to their motel.

Katie and Kevin flew out with their parents, but when they saw how cool it was to sleep in a tent on an Indian reservation and Chelsea pointed out to Katie just how good-looking the boys of the tribes were, both the Romani and the Indian tribes, it was decided all four kids would camp out near Patti and J.T.'s tent. Near was, of course, a relative term, since this was, after all, to be their honeymoon.

As luck would have it, one of the tribal elders had a son who was a lawyer. Mostly he worked at trying to get the U.S. government to honor the treaties they had made with his tribe over a hundred years ago. But he did some checking and found as long as the wedding took place on the sacred ground of the tribe, with their full permission, residency rules wouldn't apply and the wedding would be legal, in every sense of the term. A priest, who headed the local Catholic church and ministered to J.T.'s family, did the honors and the wedding was short and sweet.

When J.T. put Grandmother's ring on Patti's finger, there was a murmur around the area, since Grandmother had never taken that ring off since she had married Grandfather, years ago. Everyone realized Grandmother must feel her time was near, so they made a point of toadying to her more than usual. This, of course, was her plan all along, as she later confided to Patti. Grandmother had drunk a couple of glasses of wine before she invited Patti to sit on the stool at her feet, so she could welcome her properly to the family.

Patti finally got to tell J.T.'s mother what she thought of how she had raised her boy. What she said was, "Thank you so much for raising such a gentle man for me to love.

I only hope my own son can learn from him how to be such a wonderful person, so some woman some day, will be as grateful to me as I am to you."

They hugged each other and J.T.'s mother told her, "Welcome to the family. You have made him happier than I have ever seen him. You and your family are now his family."

J.T., who had come over to claim his bride for a dance, heard what they were saying and smiled at his wife, telling the two women he loved the most, "Take one strong woman, one gentle man, one beautiful young girl and one brave young boy and add love. That's my recipe for a family...for *my* family."

He took his wife's hand, and they danced into the crowd of people who were celebrating their love.

Meet

Fiona McGier

I have been an avid reader my whole life. And I have always "written" stories in my head, when bored, or occupied with some other task like baking or cooking. I used to think that everyone had characters "talking" to them all of the time. My 4 kids learned early on that when Mom had "that look" on her face, to not interrupt what I was doing. A couple of years ago, I finally decided that my head was getting too "crowded", and that some of these people and their stories had to be written down. I feel like they are telling me their secrets, and then once the book is done, they are happy to have been heard, and they are quiet. I have always enjoyed romances, and hope that you find my characters to be as interesting as I do.